A Knight Errant

By Barry Irwin

ISBN: 979-8-234-09301-1
Cover design: JBook Designs
Publisher: Team Valor Publishing

CHAPTER 1

Unbeknownst to regular racegoers in attendance that winter afternoon in 1977 at Santa Anita Park, this was not a regular day at the track by any stretch of the imagination; nor was it for my peers in the press box perched high above the grandstand overlooking a racing landscape dubbed by General Manager Alan Balch as "The Great Race Place."

It was just a Thursday, so no stakes race was carded. The feature was a classified allowance designed for horses that had already run through their condition eligibility by having won a maiden, followed by non-winners of 1, 2, 3 and 4 races. Generally, these animals were not up to successfully competing at stakes level, or they were prepping for a feature race.

I had just left the walking ring; you know, the one that has the statue of the great warrior Seabiscuit, the horse that had brought fame to the track's iconic Santa Anita Handicap just before World War II when racing dominated newspaper headlines, regularly was shown in movie theatre newsreels and annually led all sports in attendance.

The horses going through their paces around the ring in advance of the eighth race that afternoon were an ordinary bunch. Perhaps the most common of the lot was an English import named Swallow's Tail. He was not named after the migratory birds that venture annually about 65 miles south of Santa Anita to the historic mission at San Juan Capistrano. The name was derived from the gelding's sire, My Swallow, a former top-class sprinter-miler in the British Isles.

On paper and physical appearance the 4-year-old had no business impacting the feature race because he had not even won a non-winners of 2 allowance race and he had never raced beyond a sprint distance in England.

I was in the paddock because, as a side gig, I was consulting for an independent American film producer and noted anglophile that had bought an historic stud farm just outside Newmarket in England. Prompting him to buy the property was a desire to have a base to prove his young stallion My Swallow.

My Swallow's owner had sought me out because he reckoned from reading my columns in *Daily Racing Form* that I could help him promote My Swallow, given my interest in foreign racing. He had an idea of importing a son of his young stallion to race in Southern California. He thought if an offspring performed well locally, he could transfer the stallion to stand at a farm in California, which appealed to him since the snobby breeders in England were not supporting his young stallion by sending many mares to him.

Importing a My Swallow son would accomplish two things. First, the fellow could have a "bit of fun" with him as he lived in the Hollywood Hills, half an hour's drive to the track. Secondly, he would have a chance to spread the word about his beloved stallion My Swallow.

Being a *Daily Racing Form* columnist brought more eyes on me than I wanted. Because the so-called "Bible of the Turf" included a snapshot of my face adjacent to my by-line William Richards with every column, most racegoers recognized me. Too many for my liking shadowed too many of my moves at the track and watched my behavior and interactions in the paddock and walking ring, searching for clues about what information I might be picking up to aid my quest of picking and betting winners.

I couldn't even take a leak in the men's room urinal in the underground level of the grandstand without somebody trying to engage me in conversation. Sometimes it became hard to focus on pissing straight and talking at the same time, let alone chewing gum.

On this afternoon, few if anybody—not the degenerate gamblers, not my press box peers—followed my movements, as the horse I had come downstairs to see in the walking ring was a rank outsider.

I was careful never to glance upward at the elevated display of odds on the grandstand wall, because sure as shit if I did, somebody would have made something of it. A look at the odds could very well signal gambling intent on my part and I wanted to be as inconspicuous as possible on this particular afternoon.

When the gelding's trainer came into the paddock, I approached him. He did not attempt to make eye contact. Anybody familiar with Irish-born ex-jockey Kieran O'Boyle knew him to wear a taciturn expression. He always seemed irritated at some underling or owner or reporter or racing official. He wore the tight-lipped face of a guy that lived on antacids.

Kieren managed to make a single nod as we awaited the

arrival of Gordon Pierce, whom trainer O'Boyle had named to ride. The gelding's owner was abroad on film business, so it was just me, Kieren and Gordon.

Gordon had ridden the gelding in the import's first and only race at Santa Anita, when he had beaten just a couple home in a grass sprint on the Arcadia racetrack's uniquely configured downhill infield turf course, which began at the top of a rise bordering a lightly traveled street behind the track. After a couple of twists and turns, then crossing over a dirt strip, the course reached the flat stretch run to the wire.

When I had bumped into O'Boyle the morning after that first race, he grabbed me by the arm and pulled me into his tack room that doubled as a backstretch office. He motioned for me to close the door.

I had known O'Boyle for half a dozen years. We'd had our ups and downs, as he had his own views on everything and hardly anybody else shared them, apparently least of all me. He was always bitching, complaining, telling me old stories to illustrate his points and trying to "wise me up."

I had been to his small ranch property in Bradbury Estates about 12 minutes east of Santa Anita, I had been to his home and I knew his wife quite well, as she worked part time for the local breeders' association, which had employed me to edit its monthly magazine.

Never had I ever seen Kieren smile. Unlike most Irish folk I have known, who are as friendly and warm as people anywhere in the world, Kieren was dark, both in his skin tone, his black slicked-down hair, his sunglasses and his complete and total lack of anything approaching humor.

After shutting the door, I turned to find out what Kieren

was up to and I was greeted by a visage and level of sheer excitement I had never witnessed from him. He was downright giddy, slapping his thighs and almost doing a jig. I wondered if he had seen one too many Hollywood leprechaun flicks.

As his tale unfolded, I quickly learned that what had animated the hitherto poster child for misanthropy had been a conversation he just had with Gordon Pierce.

"Did you watch the replay of the race," Kieren asked me. "Did you watch our horse carefully?"

I answered in the affirmative.

"Did you notice anything. Something important in the running?" he emphasized.

I said he seemed in mid-stretch to steady a bit.

"The ting of it is," he began, his voice lilting in that singsong pitch Irish folks slip into when they are telling a particularly exciting tale, "Gordon told me that he clipped heels at that point and Gordon told me just this morning that he thought for all the world he was going down. He said he felt like he was skiing downhill for several strides, completely upended with no way to put on the brakes.

"He simply marveled at the horse's athletic ability in maintaining his upright posture and the horse's composure. Gordon said he had a ton of horse underneath him and was positive he was sitting on a winner.

"Now, here's the upshot of all this…Gordon says the race took so little out of the horse we can run him back right away. I mean *right* away.

"And I've a notion the little fella might be just as effective, if not more so, going two turns. He galloped out after the race like a tiger.

"My young friend, we can run this horse back in an easier spot going a mile and a furlong and we can cash the bet of our lives!"

Now if this chatter had come from any other horseman on the Santa Anita backstretch, it would have been business as usual. I hear and have heard stuff like this from the day I first set foot on a racetrack as a kid.

But coming out of the pie hole of Mr. Kieran O'Boyle, this was revelatory at a bare minimum. It was completely out of character for him.

This is the same Kieran O'Boyle who had lectured me at every opportunity about not focusing on pecuniary matters, whether in gambling or commissions for selling horses. "The Game" always comes first. Your client, your customer always comes first. Never forget this is their horse, not yours.

One such tale Kieran never tired of telling was when he was a stable lad for the great English trainer Sam Armstrong. To hear him tell it, working at Armstrong's Beech Hurst Stable on Warren Hill was like being in boot camp.

Lads were not allowed to gamble or impart information about the horses to any outside sources. Letters dropped in the office mail basket were all opened and read by staff, with any inside information redacted. Many times these revelations about a horse's training prowess led to the direct dismissal of the lad in Armstrong's employ.

So, to witness this complete turnaround in O'Boyle attitude and demeanor was shocking.

"Now we've both got to be quiet, totally closed mouth about this," he said. "I know Gordon won't breathe a word. I will bet for him. I am not even going to tell my wife. I've got a little stash of cash in a secret place in my house she knows nothing about.

"As for you, please for the sake of all that is holy do not whisper a word to any of those cronies of yours in the press box. This is a gift from heaven for you and me. So, to ensure we get the best possible odds, I am going to wheel the horse right back in 4 days, as there is a race for him on Sunday."

My mind was racing a mile a minute, first to understand how a sprinter was going to step up successfully to 9 furlongs. Then the quick turnaround. I had trouble getting the words out as my brain struggled to process the last revelation—back in 4 days? Was this guy going mad before my very eyes?

I said "Excuse me, *this* Sunday? Everybody will say you've lost the plot."

O'Boyle retorted "Well most of them tink that already. In their eyes this will make a good performance all the more improbable. Now, one word of caution. You are a clever young fellow but just tink about how and when you will make your bet and be smart about it. Now get the hell out of here so I can get back to work and try to keep my feet on the ground until Sunday!"

Like his sire, Swallow's Tail was not a big horse and looking at him in the paddock Sunday he had the conformation of a sprinter, being short coupled, quite compact, with round quarters and a loaded shoulder. How in the hell this sucker was going to see out this much longer trip was beyond me.

O'Boyle never said a word to the jockey. He gave him a leg up, nodded at him and walked off, leaving me standing in the paddock alone.

I quickly made my way to the grandstand elevator that would take me to the sixth floor, where the cream-colored wooden catwalk led to the press box. Fortunately for me nobody else rode the elevator except the operator, Jake Janikowski.

"So, what about this horse, hee hee?" he said in his patented goofy manner. "You told us all he couldn't lose last time. So, what about today? Is it a go, or what? Can I bet my money? Or do you want to bet a little for me out of guilt, hee hee?"

Jake was, as the saying goes, not playing with a full deck, so one could not get upset with his silliness. He was harmless and perfectly suited to the demands of going up and down all day and trading jabs with those traveling to and from the press box and stewards' stand. And he was not above working his customers to promote a small bet for himself. Jake had become quite handy for stashing scribes' girlfriends at various locales along his route, so being slipped the occasional mutuel ticket was not out of the ordinary for the elevator jockey.

Without responding verbally to Jake, I gave him a fish-eyed glance and exited the elevator. When I reached the two betting windows situated just outside the press box proper, I made eye contact with Pat Smith, who occupied his regular spot at the first window.

As had been the plan hatched a day earlier in the parking lot after the races, I winked at Pat. He nodded back at me. We both understood the bet was ok to be placed.

Then, instead of having to face a series of smart-ass remarks, locker-room style kidding and askew glances from the press box wise asses, I did an about face, turning back towards the elevator. Instead of continuing to Jake Janikowski's domain, I hung a right turn and continued to traverse the entire length of the catwalk until I reached another right-hand turning point that led to the Cupola.

Rather than being engaged in any fraternity-style nonsense with the other writers, handicappers, publicists, Hollywood hangers-on, long-since-famous ex-athletes and other low life-forms seeking tips and a literal free lunch, I decided to hang out by myself in the Cupola.

Originally constructed and named by Doc Strub, the Cupola was perched at the same level as the press box but was decidedly smaller and situated closer to the furlong pole than on the finish line like the press box.

Co-founder with famed movie producer Hal Roach of "The Little Rascals" fame, Charles H. (Doc) Strub established the Los Angeles Turf Club when pari-mutuel wagering was legalized in California in the early 1930s.

The Cupola served as a command post for Strub, where he was in direct communication with track employees to signal when horses that had been circling behind the starting gate would be allowed to enter the "Iron Monster" for a start.

So common had the practice of horses being led away from the back of the gate down the backstretch become that onlookers dubbed it the march to Caliente, the Tijuana, Mexico track. Doc watched the tote board and when he reckoned enough money had been bet, he deigned to let the race commence.

I had worked up there for a few years for a handicapper that had talked Strub's son into giving him $50,000 and an office in the Cupola to produce a daily publication that provided racing information to horse players that was not available in *Daily Racing Form*. It was a lucrative side gig that provided me with funds to supplement my meager salary as a columnist and indulge myself in gambling on horse racing.

The publication was still in existence, but the handicapper was told he had to give up use of the Cupola.

So, there I was all alone. No wise guys, no Jake Janikowski.

My bet was down. A day before I told Pat Smith I was going to make a wager on Swallow's Tail. I wanted him to cash a personal check for $1,000 that I had arranged with publicity director Sally Goldfarb to authorize. Pat was to wait until the very last minute or two before post time to punch out the tickets. He was not to talk to anybody before or after the race.

If the horse won, Pat was to cash the tickets, put the winnings in a brown paper bag and meet me the following morning at 11 in the lot where we all parked. I told Pat he would share in the winnings and he did not need to bet his own money. I trusted Pat implicitly. How and why he ever became a mutuel clerk I never learned, but it was obvious to me that he was working well below his pay grade. I imagined him in the role of a bank manager at some point and figured he had decided to leave for work in a racetrack position that would be far less demanding and stressful.

I could just imagine Pat sitting behind his mutuel machine as the race began, sweating right through that shirt he wore every day that looked like he had swiped it from a dentist's closet. His face would be completely flushed, with sweat dripping from his forehead into his stinging eyes that he would use a handkerchief to wipe dry. He was one very stressed-out cat.

Thank goodness the Cupola had a restroom, because I used it a few times in the moments before the race. I heard track announcer Dave Johnson call the start. I was trying to stay calm, but it was not working. By the time I left the small bathroom, the horses were heading into the first turn on the infield turf course.

Swallow's Tail, unsurprisingly, was in front on a clear lead. As a sprinter coming out of a downhill dash just 4 days earlier, he figured to be hard for Gordon to hold in the initial stages.

Gordon, a thinking man's rider, was no ordinary jockey. He was a university graduate, he had a pilot's license, he looked and acted normal, and he had a secure and fruitful homelife.

Riding with extreme patience, Pierce was able to gather his mount once settled for the run down the backstretch. He kept a light hold on the reins but never allowed the horse to reach his full stride, to save something for the stretch run.

Doling out the speed as his mount rounded the far turn, the eagle had taken flight. The gelding opened up his stride and he was every bit of 6 lengths on top. He had managed to get the quarter in :25 2/5, the half in :51 3/5 and the three-quarters in 1:15 2/5. The pedestrian pace suited him perfectly, as he retained all of his energy.

Pierce never had to uncock his stick as the horse held on to a 5-length advantage passing me in the Cupola after a mile in 1:39 3/5. Swallow's Tail cruised past the wire, stopping the electronic teletimer in 1:51 4/5 to win straight by about 2 ½ lengths.

So keyed up had I been over the entire episode I startlingly had forgotten to look at the gelding's final odds on the tote board. He went off at more than 60 to 1.

I was so jazzed that I never once thought about joining Kieran O'Boyle or Gordon Pierce in the winners' circle.

The adventure had been so sanitized by me that it was almost as though the entire episode had taken place in a vacuum.

It was the biggest bet I had ever cashed in my life and, yes,

I missed cheering for him in the press box, accepting congratulations from my peers, strolling to the window with my winning tickets fanned out on display in my hand, watching the clerk count out the hundreds, fingering all that money in my hands and walking out of the track accompanied by an armed security guard.

But I remained in the Cupola until everybody in the press box had left. I chose to walk down the stairs instead of taking the elevator. I walked to my car and drove home. Mission accomplished.

There were bigger fish to fry, I said to myself.

Chapter 2

Fridays were always busy for me at *DRF,* as columns and advances for the weekend's features were both due for publication. But I carved out some time to pick up my loot in the parking lot. Of the $66,000 in the bag, I doled out $6,000 to Pat Smith while we were both seated in the front seat of my BMW 2002, then drove down Colorado Boulevard—the very same route that Rose Parade floats travel—to the Bank of America on the corner of Lake Boulevard.

I needed to make sure the funds were deposited before that hot check I wrote for a grand showed up in my bank account for collection.

Instead of depositing the money with a teller, I waited to deal directly with the branch manager Brian Dougherty, a racetracker in his off hours who had been introduced to me by a trainer.

He winked at me, never asked a question, took my deposit slip and brown paper bag and brought it to a teller. When he returned with my receipt he said "Next time you know something this good, can you remember your old neighborhood banker?"

I promised that I would, but doing so was always a double-edged sword. If a tip loses, the recipient holds it against you. And if it wins, then the recipient complains about not having bet enough, as he invariably blames *you* for not telling him how much confidence you had in the horse, and then he hounds you until the end of your life for more winners just like this one. Tipping or touting people, except a close friend or family member, generally is a losing proposition for the provider of the information. It's a no-win situation for sure.

It was 11:45 a.m. and I had just enough time to meet Dr. James Church for a quick lunch at his 6-acre ranch in the Bradbury Estates right down the street from the O'Boyles.

When the guard at the gated community raised the barrier, I turned right and drove down the lane where Doc Church lived with his famous wife Anita. I had met Doc Church in the Santa Anita stable area a few years earlier when he was doing work for trainers such as James Maloney, Tom Pratt and Evan Shipman Jackson.

Anita was a trainer and ex-rider of jumping stock at a world class level. She came from money, dealt with high-brow people of considerable means and provided the wherewithal to allow Doc Church to operate a boutique practice comprised of just a few trainers that were well connected to socialites, the fox-hunting crowd, dressage dilettantes and the "right folks" in Virginia, the Carolinas and Kentucky. He and Anita were well known at posh Hunt Balls from coast to coast and the ladies all looked forward to dancing with the handsome vet.

A month earlier in the days before Christmas when morning temperatures flirted with freezing, I had stopped by Doc Church's small ranch. I accepted an invitation from the noted veterinarian to discuss what I knew about trainers that cheated with performance enhancing drugs.

Although nobody looking at him then could picture him as a successful half-miler at Stanford University due to the poundage he had packed on indulging in a rich man's diet, Dr. Church was quite the college athlete.

Like me—an ex-runner and jumper—he continued to follow the sport. And like me, he was all too aware of the shenanigans that went on with world-class tracksters. So we often found ourselves on the Santa Anita backstretch talking longer than was prudent for either of our schedules about the downfall of Track and Field, how the game had been infiltrated by cheaters using drugs they learned about from members of the competitive cycling community and how these drugs were now finding their way into our game.

After his live-in housekeeper/cook had prepared a belated breakfast of eggs cooked in bacon grease in an iron skillet that tasted just as good as its sinful aroma, Doc and I went outside for a brief walk before getting down to the business at hand.

While looking at a few horses in a 2-acre paddock, an athletically built dark bay that was kicking out his hind legs and obviously enjoying being out in the crisp climate caught my eye. Horses love the cold as it energizes them.

"Hey, I know that colt," I said to Doc. "Small star, right-hind sock. He trained very early in the year after James Maloney brought him West from New York with his string for the winter. Unraced as far as I know. Freaky, phenomenal works, then disappeared."

Jim gave me a quizzical look. "Now how in the hell do you know all that? Have you been clocking my action, spying on me?" he said in not a particularly friendly manner.

"Hey, no…settle down Doc," I said, with a bit of a laugh. "Not at all. Remember earlier this year when I was dating that exercise rider of Charlie Whittingham? Well, we moved in together for a few months and, because she got up so early, I wound up getting out to the track before dawn myself.

"So out of boredom I went upstairs where the clockers work and began timing a few horses. One of them loaned me an old stopwatch and taught me how to identify and clock horses. That's where I saw this guy. Knight Errant is his name, right?"

Dr. Church calmed down, a smile returning to his more relaxed face. "Aha…now I see. Sorry."

I told Doc Church that the clockers could not wait to unload on Knight Errant when he made his first start. "He moved like a Cadillac. What happened to him?" I asked.

"Puzzling story to put it mildly," he said looking down at the ground, where he kicked a clod of dirt in what looked like disgust. "As you say, moved like a goddamned Cadillac. Very sound then, and as you might be able to tell, very sound right now.

"But systemically he fell apart on us. His blood work was a complete mess and was all out of whack. He had deficits in some key values, serious upticks in others.

"So, we took him out of training and brought him up here. I've checked his blood every month. Each blood test has shown significant improvement, but I've been reluctant to recommend that he be put back in training because I am convinced the moment he starts getting stressed again he's going to fall apart like he did last time."

I asked Doc what the connections would wind up doing with a horse like Knight Errant.

"I love the guy," he said. "He is classy, he is kind, he is well mannered and, for such a fast sucker, he has been quite adaptable for me here. I've been putting a stock saddle on him and riding him on the trails around here. So, I am going to ask Mr. Harwood if he'll let me have him as a riding horse."

Wow, I thought to myself. Not try a horse of this one's looks, parentage and already proven speed? Not give him one more chance? Just so you can have a high-quality riding mount. Crazy, crazy, crazy I thought.

"And you're not tempted to try him once more?" I asked Doc with all of the incredulity I could muster. "Seriously?"

Doc lowered his head once more, kicked some more dirt on the ground and said "Well, to tell you the truth, I had thought about it. I've actually given the matter a great deal of thought.

"There are things that he might be treated with, courses of action using new scientific discoveries in human medicine that could course correct his abnormal metabolism. But they are costly, possibly dangerous or debilitating. In theory, though, they might just work."

I pressed him further and he said "How costly? I could see the treatments and constant labs running up a tab of three or four thousand dollars a month. That plus the training could reach nearly 6 or 7 grand a month.

"And by the way, you called him a colt. Well, we gelded him once he got to the ranch for management purposes. Mr. Harwood approved it. So being a gelding, it wouldn't make a lot of sense to plow that sort of dough into a horse with no end game as a stallion."

Remembering the goosebumps Knight Errant had given me in a couple of his morning moves, my mind raced a mile a minute in trying to come up with a way to capitalize on the horse's incredible level of talent.

Then I asked the obvious question: Do you think Mr. Harwood would sell him?

Doc Church said "Well, Ellerslie Stud does sell rejects and I guess one would classify this sucker as being of that ilk."

"Yes, I know all about that," I said. "I remember visiting Ellerslie once to look at a horse they advertised for sale in one of those little classifieds at the back of *The Blood-Horse.* When I went out to inspect it for a price of $10,000, I was stunned at how dwarfed the animal was. The size of a child's pony. That ten grand price tag should have been a red flag, but what did I know, right?"

After a while I said "Say…why don't *you* try to buy him and put him back in training?"

Doc explained two reasons why this was not going to be feasible for him. "First, if the horse did turn out well, it most likely would not sit right with the Harwood Family. Secondly, I don't earn enough to fund much of our lifestyle, as you can well imagine, and if I were to blow a sizeable wad every month on an unsuitable racing prospect, it would go over very badly with the Mrs."

"OK…I get it…you are not well positioned to take on an experiment like this," I said. "What if I want to try it?"

Dr. Church launched a lengthy narrative that went something like this: first I would have to convince a difficult hardboot like Mr. Harwood to let go of the horse. Then I would have to convince him that I would put the horse with people he approved of. Then there would be the matter of price. And where are you going to get the dough to pay for the horse *and* pay his monthly expenses to a trainer and me? You don't strike me as having any such funding and I doubt if your parents are going to provide you with dough for a nutty venture like this. Am I missing anything?

"Well, just thinking out loud and brainstorming off the top of my head," I began. "I have interviewed Mr. Harwood a few times, so if I contacted him he would recognize me and he should not be averse to talking to me.

"Once in contact, I would try my best to charm him by telling him that anything Knight Errant did on the track would inure to his benefit, as new stakes credentials would flesh out the pedigree of the horse's immediate family members.

"Look, Mr. Harwood and his great rival Leslie Combs seek out stakes wins and placings at some of the most rinky-dink tracks in America. Getting some black-type on a high-class circuit in Southern California would be a great boost to the pedigree. He surely would understand this.

"And then I could tell him I would put the horse with a trainer he had a relationship with. That would elevate his comfort level. I would like to approach him.

"As for money, yes, that is the biggest problem for me. I make $250 a week at the *Form.* Frigging elevator man belongs to a union and makes twice what I earn. So that's not going to get me very far. But I know a lot of people in the game, I could approach them one by one until I found the right angel.

"So how about this…let me work on this on a mum's-the-word basis, see how far I get and, when and if I make some significant progress, we will reconvene."

So now with my ducks in a row, I returned to Bradbury, where I was met in the driveway of Dr. Church, a devilishly handsome 60-something veterinarian with movie star looks and distinctive, straight grey hair combed straight back with what looked like brilliantine. He met me as I drove up and I lowered my window.

"What's up?" he asked.

After exiting the car, I stood in the bright noon sunlight in front of the vet and blurted out "I've got the funding…I've got the dough for Knight Errant!"

Looking nonplussed, he wore the skeptical expression of a parent dealing with an over-exuberant teenager, which was not too far off the mark, as I was only 26 years old.

"Explain please," he said.

So, I relayed the entire story to Doc Church, trusting him implicitly not to ever spill the beans. The upshot of the entire episode, I told him, was that I had sixty grand in my checking account and I was fully prepared to use all of it to buy the horse and pay his training and vet expenses long enough for the horse to be given the chance he deserved.

Doc said "You are my hero young man. I have no earthly idea exactly where on God's green Earth you sprung from, but that you have landed right on my doorstep is nothing short of a dream come true for a fellow like me that never had a son."

I told Doc Church that I had to rush back to the press box and churn out my stories for the weekend editions, so I begged off. But we agreed to meet up again on Monday, my day off from work, and design a plan that hopefully would land Knight Errant in our collective laps.

Before I had reached the security gate to exit Bradbury Estates, I ran into Kieran O'Boyle, as he was walking one of his outsized Irish Wolfhounds. I asked how the horse had come out of the race.

This was the Kieran O'Boyle I knew and was leery of. "Horse came back all right, he is ok," he said curtly. "The owner is happy, but I told him as I am about to tell you, this horse is never going to win another race.

"Blind luck fell right into our lap and I do not expect Swallow's Tail to ever duplicate the feat. In point of actual fact, he is not a router. He did route on the day, but we cannot expect him to repeat it.

"I've been at this a long time. You can never plan a ting like this. But when it happens you have to make the best of it, as we all did, but not tink lightning is ever going to strike twice.

"He bled badly. My groom caught it instantly, dabbed some drips off a nostril and mopped up some more back at the test barn before anybody caught sight of it. On scope he bled as badly as one can bleed.

"Look: we all got the money, we pulled off a stroke, but we must move on and not expect another miracle from this horse. I hope you cashed well enough. Lord knows whatever you bet did not suppress the odds. So, what're you doing up here in my neck of the woods?"

I explained that I had visited Dr. Church and we might buy a horse to race together. He asked if the subject of a trainer had come up and I said "no, not yet."

O'Boyle quickly came back with this remark: "So you didn't tell him that I am your trainer?"

Realizing that O'Boyle had reverted to type and was about to launch onto the war path, I said "Well, I am sure that will come up in due course."

To which O'Boyle said "Well, given all that I have done for you, the fact that you would not immediately tell him you wanted me to train the horse is more than somewhat disconcerting. It is a slap right in the kisser young man."

O'Boyle, as was his selfish bent in life, never acknowledged that he only got Swallow's Tail to train and a new client because of my recommendation.

I was dumbfounded and without adequate words.

O'Boyle looked at me for what seemed an eternity, then said "I bet I know what it is. It's that snooty wife of his, Anita. She has always looked down on me and my wife, as we are nothing more than working people and she is a coupon-clipping society matron. And Doc Church thinks that by virtue of his marriage to Anita, this in some way elevates him from having to deal with the likes of me. OK. I get it."

Kieran O'Boyle then turned around and walked off.

I have never spoken to Kieran O'Boyle again.

And, truth be told, I was happy not to have his negativity in my life as I needed to stay positive approaching the delicate maneuvering that was in the offing in my quest to become the owner of the mighty Knight Errant.

CHAPTER 3

Monday morning when I answered the telephone in my studio apartment in Arcadia I heard Doc Church say "I've got the answer to your Bear Harwood problem. When can you come up here?"

Being my day off I was still in bed in my pajamas at 8:30 a.m. As excited as I was to get up to Bradbury, I took the time to shower, get dressed and drive down Huntington Avenue to Rod's Diner, where I had breakfast. It being a dark day with no racing at the track, the racetracker hangout was quiet, with few customers.

However, being who and what I was, there would always be one horseplayer to deal with. I had seen the fellow around town and at the track, maybe spoken with him once or twice, but did not know his name.

From my seat at the counter I had to look up to see his head that stood atop a strapping 6-foot plus frame. Through his tidy blonde mustache came the comment that I had dreaded might surface.

"Heard you made quite the little bundle on that O'Boyle nag last week," said the 40-something with the hair and ruddy complexion of an aged surfer. A lot of Dust Bowl evacuees had settled in and around Arcadia and he fit the mold. "Yessiree Bob, quite the bundle."

Motherfucker, I thought to myself—wonder where this know-it-all gossiper had heard about it. "How did you happen to hear about it?" I asked.

Quick as a cat came his response. "Pal o' mine knows a mutuel clerk in the press box. I know him, too."

I refused to believe it was Pat, so I asked "Pat…Pat Smith?"

Again, he shot back in a millisecond "Hell no, not Pat. That choir boy wouldn't out the most sex-craven padre. No, it was the other clown. He told Mickey—you know the ex-jock who runs Charlie Whittingham's bets. Mickey prefers to place his bets out of the sight of prying eyes in the press box."

"Yeah, well, it just happened to work out this time," I said, turning back to my over-easy eggs and hashbrowns.

The blotchy-faced wise guy, with a tilt of his head, offered "You gotta hand it to that prick Kieran O'Boyle. For an ex-pinhead he can pull a stroke every now and then. You know what they say about jocks—size 1 shoe, size 1 brain. But not the Irishman, no sirree Bob."

Driving on the way up to Bradbury, I wondered how long it would take to make the rounds, to get back to my peers in the press box. How long would it be before Bernie Bokun slagged me for not sharing the information "after all he had done for me" And that was just the tip of the iceberg.

There would be my *DRF* co-workers: Ray Leeward, who called the chart margins and wrote the footnotes; Steve Klein, who took down RayBird's margins; Jasper Ward, who operated the teletype machine; Jimmy Nedlan, who dished up lunches and poured drinks; Dave Bottle, the ex-MLB player who answered the phone in the press box and of course Jake Janikowski. Knowing Jake, he would likely tell anyone that would listen that I let him in on the play and actually bet $20 for him. Well, fuck, I thought—let the circus begin.

I had nothing to fear. I had done nothing wrong. I played by the rules. I had, after all, accomplished my goal and played my part. I was coy, I was quiet and I placed my bet with all the sensitivity the enterprise required.

Anything that came out afterwards was nothing but jealous A-holes venting because they were mad about being left out of the play. The entire scenario was certainly more above board than what the clockers do every week of the racing season.

They are paid by racetracks to provide accurate information to the public, yet these guys are in business for themselves, with their own private clients they pass along information to in exchange for the client making bets for them. They can only win, they can never lose. And they always clam up.

Every once in a while word will get out that the clockers "were all over" a winner, which invariably prompted morning-line maker Bernie Bokun to cry like a baby because his paranoid mind had reliably informed him that "everybody in the press box" but him had been in the know. The unscrupulous and unethical nature of these machinations was not part his calculation, only the fact that he missed cashing on a winner.

I sat on a stuffed chair across from Doc Church who was in a leather chair behind his desk. "Tad Smithwick," he whispered. "Tad Smithwick. That's the answer. Tad is the key guy in your little operation."

"Tad Smithwick…Tad Fucking Smithwick? Are you kidding me?" I blurted out.

Doc, still speaking softly and leaning forward across the expensive-looking red leather desktop, said "Yes, I know… Tad Smithwick at first might seem a lame choice. And I realize that if anyone knows Tad Smithwick it is you. I know you two have a history but hear me out."

Over the next few minutes, Dr. Church explained why Tad Smithwick was the right man for the job. First, Tad was the son of a highly respected horseman that ran the Middleburg Training Center in Virginia. His dad is tight with Bear, the two of them going hunting for grouse in Scotland every year in the off season.

"Tad himself has been thrown a few bones by Bear, you know fillies that might need to break their maidens before being sent to the breeding shed. Tad has Bear's trust.

"Now I have known Tad since he was a teenager. He is a true horseman. And he can train. His main problem is that he would rather get up early for a tee time instead of breezing one, unless of course he was laying the groundwork for a gamble, in which case he would sleep in his car at the barn and get one out before dawn.

"Your first hurdle, my young friend, is to find a way to get possession of the animal. Tad is key because the Bear will trust him. From there I feel that Tad can get the job done for both of us because, as I say, he is a horseman that can flat out train. Your job will be to keep him on the straight and narrow. To keep him away from the bar and to get him into bed on time at night."

Doc was right about one thing— Tad Smithwick and I had a history.

Standing every bit of 6 feet 2 inches, Tad had the kind of good looks that first attracted his wife but later became her liability as they attracted other women. Tad had an easy-going manner. He said "goff" instead of golf and "coats" instead of colts in the manner of horsemen from the show ring to hunt country. He took little seriously other than his swing, which he honed every afternoon at the driving range; putting, which he practiced every morning before his tee time, and occasionally selling a reject for Bear Harwood's Ellerslie Stud.

Tad had been kept alive by Bear letting him sell highly-bred but slow fillies from families long developed by the master of Ellerslie Stud. If breeders wanted access to these families, they were forced to deal with Tad Smithwick, because Ellerslie never offered them at public auction.

Tad Smithwick first came on my radar 5 years ago when I was working at my first job in racing in Lexington, Kentucky. He was training at Latonia just south of Cincinnati, Ohio. It was in the early winter of the year, after Keeneland and Churchill Downs had finished their fall meetings. He had a handful of fillies and mares for breeders looking for maidens to become winners before the breeding season commenced on February 15.

One of those in his small string had shown uncommon ability, which mystified Smithwick. In half a dozen starts she had shown absolutely no form, even though her owner had moved her from the big leagues to the minors. Yet, for reasons that were beyond his understanding, one morning before dawn she breezed five-eighths of a mile in a stunning :58 2/5. Nobody but the security guard who opened the track early for Smithwick and the Mexican kid that was on her back knew about the high-octane early-morning rocket ship test.

Smithwick marshalled his financial resources, entered the surprising filly in a maiden special weight going 6 furlongs at Latonia and tried to keep his feet on the ground until race day. He stayed in his room at night, away from any local bars, and kept to himself, as he daydreamed about first cashing a big bet and secondly winning a filly-and-mare stake at the meeting.

In the paddock before the race on a frosty winter-time evening at Latonia where the temperatures flirted with the freezing mark and snowflakes could be seen wafting through the bright lights from atop the grandstand, Tad was approached by the paddock judge. He was told his filly's lip tattoo did not match the name of his filly. She had a different identity.

Smithwick, before the filly was scratched by the stewards, noted that his instrument to future riches and career advancement was sitting on the board at 35 to 1.

Turned out that the vanning company in charge of moving some fillies from Keeneland to Latonia had mixed up two of them, bringing one to Smithwick at Latonia and the other to a trainer in New Orleans.

Smithwick wound up with Miss Patootie Pie, a multiple stakes-winning daughter of the superior stallion Sir Gaylord and owned by the Danada Farm on Frankfort Pike of Dan and Ada Rice.

Although Tad had never met the Rices, he did know their farm manager, whom he contacted to see if he might be allowed to race the filly in the upcoming sprint stakes at Latonia, a race Smithwick assured the Rice's employee the filly absolutely could not lose.

Miss Patootie Pie duly cat-hopped by 6 ½ lengths to put a button on the tale.

Tad took a liking to me because, unlike most Southern California racetrackers, I had lived in the Bluegrass, knew many of the players from my days as a staff writer at the *Thoroughbred Record,* I had been to Middleburg, Camden and Aiken and I could swing a golf club.

One summer we decided to share a suite at the notorious Winners Circle Lodge directly across the street from the backstretch of Del Mar racetrack on Villa de la Valle.

Although we stayed in the same room, except for putting, driving balls and playing golf on dark days at Torrey Pines Golf Course, I never saw much of Tad that summer until one notable incident. He had, after all, just one horse in training, one given to him by a friend of his father's.

Tad would "close" the bar at a place a couple of miles up the road. He would always caution me not to use the chain lock on the door as he would be coming back to the room late.

Well, one night I forgot to do that and when he came in drunk at around 2:30 in the morning, he caught his arm between the door and its frame, fell down and the impact of the crash to the floor resulted in a broken arm.

Naturally, I felt like shit, even though I figured that I never should have been put in the position of a caretaker for a drunk in the first place. I drove Tad to an emergency room in Encinitas, where his arm was put in a cast. Because of Jewish guilt over my failure to heed instructions, I volunteered to drive Tad to his stable every morning for more than a month and help him tend to his horse.

In retrospect it was, as racetrackers say, "a blessing in duh skies," as I learned more about how to take care of the needs of a racehorse in those weeks than I had ever known before, so it turned out to be a valuable schooling session. And I discovered firsthand that Tad was a thoughtful horseman, paying considerable attention to all aspects of care and feeding of the Thoroughbred racehorse.

Aiken for a Win, the horse comprising Tad Smithwick's one-horse stable, had come around nicely for his trainer, who seemed to be doing an excellent job in keeping a chronically sore left front suspensory ligament from blowing up a third and likely final time in his career. The horse lived in an ice bucket and when he had had enough of that he was hosed by his groom who sat on an upside-down metal bucket with the animal's shank in one hand and the hose in the other.

They say Ruffian's taciturn trainer Frank Whiteley used to love nothing better than hosing a horse's leg, as he found it relaxing and gave him a legitimate opportunity every day to contemplate race plans for his horses. So, I did not feel too badly for the groom. If it was good enough for Whiteley it sure as heck was good enough for the groom.

Tad was pointing Aiken for a Win for a Starter Handicap, for which he was eligible to compete because he had raced for a $16,000 claiming price. Tad had raced the horse twice at Hollywood Park, making sure his jockey Johnny (John Boy) Fox did not allow him to run too hard as the trainer was pointing him for a race at Del Mar that would provide a big betting opportunity.

As usual, for the 6-year-old gelding's final major work 2 weeks out from the Starter Handicap, Tad Smithwick found a way to work the horse in the dark. I went upstairs in the press box, which at Del Mar always remained wide open, so I was able to clock Aiken for a Win from the quarter pole to the wire, even though it was awfully dark and I would not be as accurate as I had been taught.

When I met Tad on the track's apron near the wire I whispered "he came the last 2 furlongs in :23 2/5 as near as I can tell. Do you believe it?"

Tad said let's see what John Boy says.

Back at the stable Fox was breathing hard but he managed to tell us that the horse felt great, he was moving fluently, he was not breathing hard and he galloped out strongly past the wire. He said the horse was ready and that Tad could "bet his money."

Two weeks later Aiken for a Win went off at odds of 33 to 1 in a full field of 12 runners for a 1 1/16-mile Starter Handicap on the main track at Del Mar with Johnny Fox in the saddle.

Tad was dressed in a sharp cream-colored summer tweed sports coat over a pair of rust-colored golf slacks. I don't know how much he bet, but I figured it was close to everything he could get his hands on.

Johnny was in the waning days of his career and his weathered visage winced in pain as Tad gave him a leg up and his knee buckled and dropped momentarily. It was a scene that did not inspire confidence.

Leaving the walking ring at Del Mar I turned to Tad and remarked that the demeanor of the jockey caught me by surprise, to which Tad said "John Boy's been like this for the last dozen years. Don't worry about him, he can still get the job done, especially if the money is down. He's a good boy." John Boy had at least a dozen years on Tad, but the trainer still called him a "boy."

We watched the race from ground level. Turning for home a

12 to 1 shot ridden by Cajun jockey Jean (Boom Boom) Duplantis was slightly in front of Aiken for a Win, but Tad's steed was gathering momentum just past the quarter pole.

Aiken for a Win looked to have the best energy inside the sixteenth pole, but suddenly the Duplantis horse found another gear and drove off to score by at least 2 ½ lengths. Aiken for a Win slackened in the final yards, then did not gallop out with the remainder of the field, as John Boy pulled him up, dismounted and held the horse until help arrived.

Tad and I both rushed out to the track to assess the condition of his horse. His left front limb was raised off the ground. The gelding did not want to put weight on it.

Johnny said "He tried boss, he really did. The horse wanted to win so badly that he ran right through the pain. I didn't hear anything crack, so maybe he can make it. I just don't know. What a game rascal. You have to admire him." Tad patted John Boy on the shoulder and told me that he had ridden well.

The horse ambulance brought the horse back to his stall on the backstretch. Tad rode with him. By the time I had arrived the horse was walking around the ring outside. He had a very large white bandage on the injured left foreleg. X-rays revealed that there were no broken bones, but his suspensory ligament was identified as the issue. In his heart Tad knew the gelding's racing career had been short lived, but he thought he could eke out one more win from him.

Tad shoved something hard in my pants' pocket and told me he would see me back in the room.

Around dinner time Tad returned and asked me what I thought the implement was that he had put in my pocket.

"I'm guessing an illegal joint…a battery, right?" I responded.

Tad said "Exactly. But not just any buzzer…this is the most sophisticated one I've ever seen. I picked it up on the track while waiting for the ambulance. There's no question we got beat today by a horse that had been plugged in by that little tramp Duplantis.

"I knew my boy was ready for a big effort and he ran his race. But we got beat by a horse that was introduced to Benjamin Franklin's discovery. Really pisses me off. I don't mind getting beat, but I hate it when a cheater beats me. That's not part of the game I grew up with or was taught to play."

I asked if we should report the jockey to the stewards.

"No, I don't want to do that," Tad said. "First of all, that little prick wears those black gloves, so likely there would be no fingerprints on the buzzer. His agent probably paid cash for it, so the sale won't be traceable.

"And as silly as it may sound, if I complain *I* will look like the bad guy as everyone will say that I am just a sore loser. It's a no-win situation. Must take my lumps and move on. Do what you want with the battery."

Tad then left to find a bar where he could drown his misery.

Shortly after he had departed the hotel phone rang. "I understand you have something that belongs to my jock," the low, gruff voice on the other end of the call intoned. "I am in the bar at your hotel. My name is Sam. Meet me now. I know what you look like, so I will come and sit with you at a table."

Short in stature and built like the bodies of two shortstops had been slapped together, Sam approached my table and sat down. "So, you got it, right?" he said. "Now let me tell you something…my boy gave a pretty penny for it. He had it made special for him by an engineer from Denver that works for the telephone company. My boy wants it back...he wants me to bring it back to him now, do you get my drift?"

I was a bit unnerved by this guy's tone and look, but I tried to act calm, although under the table my legs were quivering.

"How much you want for it? Name your price pal," he said.

I told the enforcer that it was not for sale, as I would not take money for the implement. However, I was reluctant to give it back to the fellow because I was loathe to see the jockey continue to use it on his mounts at Del Mar.

The guy offered his hand, which turned out to be a double-thick paw with a meaty mass below the thumb. "I got it and I understand," he said, striking a most amiable tone. "My boy is leaving this burg. He is named on mounts for the next two days, then he is going back to Cajun country. So, you just hang on to that sucker and I will meet you here at the same time in two days for the handover. That suit you, pal?"

I shook his hand, he got up, turned his back toward me and walked off.

So even though Tad Smithwick came with deficiencies, he had the right assets to train a good runner—horsemanship and integrity. And he gave me a fighting chance to land the horse I wanted.

CHAPTER 4

I told Dr. James Church that I wanted a day or two to mull over my options and he let me go without lobbying any further to name Tad Smithwick as an ally, confidant, procurer or trainer of the horse.

The next day I arranged to meet Dr. Church in the public park across the street from Rod's Diner. Seated on wooden picnic benches conveniently provided by the Recreation Department of the City of Arcadia, we worked out the short strokes of our proposed arrangement after I had agreed to bring Tad Smithwick into the fold.

Dr. Church laid out his game plan: first, the vet would invite Tad Smithwick to join us for lunch at his ranch. We would explain that we wanted him to work out a deal with Bear Harwood to secure the horse.

"Then I will tell him that our general plan was to have him train the horse for 4 to 6 months to see if the horse could stand training while receiving my medicinal protocol," said Dr. Church.

"I will inform him that you have agreed to turn over $50,000 to me to be used for acquisition, training and veterinary expenses, so that he knows he is going to get paid. I think you should retain the additional ten grand in your own account for your own use and try not to blow it on bad bets."

My first question was about stalls. Smithwick currently was not training a horse on the grounds of Santa Anita. How, I asked, was Smithwick going to get himself a stall, especially for an unraced 4-year-old gelding?

Dr. Church told me in a matter-of-fact tone that he had already done and would continue to do more than his part, so now it was up to me to use my ingenuity to move the ball forward down the field. My next job, so to speak, was to visit the Los Angeles Turf Club Director of Racing W. R. (Buddy) Hillenbrand's office to squeeze one stall for the horse.

Buddy Hillenbrand was the most respected individual in all of racing, from coast to coast recognized as having the best mind, the best grasp of which elements needed to mesh for the sport to thrive. He knew the horses, knew the players intimately, he was supremely well educated and mannered and he had graduated from Columbia University with an idea of becoming a writer of fiction. Such was his gravitas that *Sports Illustrated* tapped him to write an article detailing what he thought horse racing might look like in the future. He was my absolute idol. He had a patrician's bearing, but he could be a man of the people when a situation called for it.

I remember seeing him chatting with a down-and-out English trainer shopping in a supermarket near my apartment in Arcadia one afternoon, after which the fragile horseman asked the butcher behind the meat counter if he could please have 25 cents worth of chicken necks. Chicken necks for fuck's sake! What was a person supposed to do with a chicken neck

I wondered? What kind of sustenance could that possibly provide?

I relayed the anecdote to my boss at the *Form* and wondered how a guy like this was given stall at Santa Anita. He only trained one horse at a time and it usually ran 4 times during the entire year at best. He told me Mr. Hillenbrand considered it his sacred duty to make sure as long as fellows like this Englishman still wanted to train horses at the advanced age of nearly 90 years that Buddy would accommodate him.

So why not Mr. Tad Smithwick? What about Tad Smithwick indeed, I thought? If the chicken-neck guy got a stall, surely Tad could get one, right?

No matter the day of the week nor the hour of the day, Mr. Hillenbrand always found time to talk with me. When his secretary ushered me into to his office in the executive wing of the administration offices at Santa Anita, Buddy came out from behind his desk to shake my hand.

Mr. Hillenbrand had a congenital spinal disorder that caused him to stoop, both in walking and sitting at his desk. But this weakness in no way detracted from his commanding presence.

Buddy always had his window cracked open a bit, as his office was adjacent to the part of the bakery which made the donuts that were sold at Clockers' Corner. Buddy enjoyed the pleasant aroma of those sinkers.

"What can I do for you son, what's on your mind this fine day?" he said.

I was purposely circumspect because I did not want to disclose the identity of the horse I wanted to buy, so I focused instead on Tad Smithwick and Dr. Church, both of whom he was intimately familiar, socially as well as at the track.

Mr. Hillenbrand listened intently. When I mentioned Dr. Church his eyes widened in approval, but when I uttered the name Tad Smithwick he tried not to reveal his opinion, but I could tell he was not overjoyed in hearing it.

"Bill, as you can well imagine, I get people coming in here all day long with one initiative after another," Hillenbrand began. "Most of them involve asking me for some sort of favor or consideration. Sadly, I am only able to accommodate the occasional request.

"This being the first time you have ever approached me with a personal request, I am going to take it very seriously, because since the day you first came to my attention I have been impressed with your understanding of the game. And if there is anything I can do to encourage your continued participation, I am going to go out of my way to help you.

"But let me ask you a question," he said. "I know from your writings that you have taken a strong stance on integrity when it comes to the use of medication, especially those involving performance enhancing and masking of pain.

"So, in this regard, are you certain in Tad Smithwick that you have selected the absolute right individual to further your profile in horse racing as an owner? I am not saying Tad is, has been, or will be a cheater. But you and I both know he has some questionable contacts and associates."

So rather than relate the tale about the joint at Del Mar, I instead relied hard on the opinion of Tad Smithwick held by Dr. James Church and that won the day.

Then he questioned me about my finances, I told him that I had saved up enough money to fund the project and turned them over to Jim Church, who would manage them for me.

Mr. Hillenbrand seemed satisfied. He told me in parting that when I was in need of the stall to give him at least 4 or 5 days to arrange one.

When I called Dr. Church to give him the good news, he told me that he was in possession of even better news and to meet me for lunch again at his ranch the next day around noon.

During lunch of a terrific open-faced smoked salmon sandwich served on dense Scandinavian pumpernickel bread prepared by Doc Church's housekeeper, the vet updated me on his progress. A deal had been struck for Knight Errant to be transferred to the name of William Richards upon receipt by Bear Harwood's Ellerslie Stud of my check in the amount of one dollar. Yes: you read that right—a single U. S. greenback!

There was, he noted and stressed firmly, a one-time bonus as part of this transaction that called for this same Ellerslie Stud to receive one hundred percent of the net purse exclusive of trainer and jockey commissions and fees from the first Graded stakes won by Knight Errant should that event come to pass.

"So basically Tad Smithwick, bloodstock agent extraordinaire, has laid the horse right in your lap gratis. No money, nada dinero, nothing, zilch, unless of course you consider a dollar bill to constitute money," Doc said.

Conditions of the sale were comprised of these following: Tad Smithwick would always train horse unless Mr. Harwood agreed to a switch, Dr. James Church would always be the vet, the horse could never be sold, retirement of the horse was at the sole discretion of Dr. Church and upon the end of the horse's racing career he was to be returned to Dr. Church and signed over to him for $1. Details of the transaction were to remain confidential.

Dr. Church said "I don't want to blow smoke up your skirt or anything remotely like that, but I must tell you that the deal turned not on what me or Tad said to Bear. It was your writing about medication and drugs that tipped the scale in your favor.

"He also mentioned that he was mighty impressed to learn that you showed up at Spendthrift Farm late one evening in the snow and ice to greet Majestic Prince when he was vanned from California to begin stud duties. You were the only writer there and Leslie Combs relayed the story to Bear. He never forgot that.

"So not having to deplete your funds to pay for the horse gives us a big edge in having enough financing to provide this gelding with his best shot to become a racehorse.

"Let's just hope my science works out and your opinion of his talent is correct. We are off the races in style young man. Let the games begin!"

CHAPTER 5

The following Monday I asked Brian Dougherty if he wanted to catch a quick lunch at Beadles, an old-fashioned cafeteria on Colorado Boulevard, just a few doors down from the Bank of America.

We met in the foyer of the vast family-owned cafeteria, a particular favorite among racetrackers because of its simple food, low prices and casual atmosphere.

I felt comfortable meeting in public in a venue in which a racetracker might overhear my conversation, because now that the horse was in tow, there was no longer a need to be quiet about it.

I brought Brian up to speed, from when I clocked Knight Errant, to seeing him at the lay-up farm, to placing and cashing the bet that funded his acquisition and training, to the bargain I had made with Mr. Harwood and the challenges ahead with the medication protocol and dealing with Smithwick, who I described as a juvenile delinquent using an adult's body as a host.

Brian enjoyed the hell out of the tale, his thick black eyebrows dancing up and down at each twist of the tale. Brian was a sophisticated businessman with a quick, fertile mind, the ability to advise high-earning horsemen how to invest and manage their income, yet still able to deal with rank-and-file racetrack workers. He had been born in Ireland and his family had emigrated to Pasadena when he was less than 10 years old.

"Well done Bill," he said. "Well done indeed. Let's hope you've got a bit of the Tinker in you when it comes to selecting the right horse." Tinkers dotted the Irish countryside after traveling in caravans with their gypsy families. Romany in heritage, these rascals lived off their wits and scams. The Irish farmer feared and admired them; feared them because they always had to watch their pockets from being picked in one manner or another and admired them for their horsemanship. Having the eye of a Tinker in matters of picking out horseflesh was a high complement indeed and I hoped that I might have a bit of it in me.

Back at the bank I had Brian wire transfer $50,000 from my account to Dr. James Church's. I then stopped by the post office in downtown Pasadena to mail my check for a dollar to Mr. Harwood to complete the deal.

Tuesday morning I stopped by the executive offices to let Buddy Hillenbrand know that Tad Smithwick would indeed need a stall. I revealed the name of the horse, then enlightened the Turf Club's chief executive about my deal with both Mr. Harwood and Dr. Church.

"I'm delighted for you," a smiling Buddy Hillenbrand said to me. "And I am happy to learn that your check for that thousand dollars was honored by your bank. Oh, yes, I knew about the check, as Sally Goldfarb called me to ask if Santa Anita was all right with cashing it, since we'd had a few minor hiccups in the past.

"Do I presume correctly that you used those funds diligently enough to put yourself in the horse owning business?" He busted me big time and was grinning like he was showing off his teeth to his wife after a recent dental cleaning.

We both had a robust laugh.

"We'd appreciate the stall as soon as possible," I explained, "because there is no need for a slow reintroduction to the game or relative fitness for Knight Errant, as Doc has been trail riding him for the past few months."

Tad Smithwick fortunately did not require any money to buy equipment as he kept all his tack in the Arcadia garage of a friend. When Mr. Hillenbrand left him a phone message with details of the barn and stall number of the new home for Knight Errant, Tad wasted no time in driving to the spot, assessing the layout and striking an arrangement with veteran trainer Timmy (The Limey) Broadhurst to share part of his tack room for his stuff. Timmy, whose nickname derived from the flat English tweed cap he wore, was an old friend of Tad's father and welcomed his son into the barn on the Santa Anita backstretch.

Delivery of Knight Errant did not occur for 3 days. Each morning I would stop by the barn first thing upon my arrival at Santa Anita to check on him. I started to worry that maybe Doc Church had changed his mind and was reluctant to give up control of the horse. Then one morning when I checked in on his stall, there he was.

Tad greeted me and asked if I would like him to take the horse out and show him to me. Of course, I said yes, as I was not really able to get a good enough look at him when he was up in Bradbury Estates.

It was the dead of winter. Yes, we have winters in Southern California. Every year on the evening before the Tournament of Roses Parade up Orange Grove and then down Colorado Boulevard, I would drive downtown to mingle with those folks that lined the streets in anticipation of getting the best position possible to watch the floats, celebrities and marching bands go by.

And every year, wood fires in large metal trash cans were used to provide warmth to keep semi-frozen hands from frostbite despite the use of warming gloves. Each New Year's Eve the temperatures in the early morning hours were at or below freezing.

So I was not surprised to see that Knight Errant had a winter coat. Tad told me immediately that later that afternoon he planned to give the gelding a Hunter Clip to avoid a build-up of unwanted moisture from sweating caused by a long winter coat.

Not all trainers choose to clip their stock when they are racing during the winter. I learned this lesson the hard way after a long-haired horse trained by Charlie Whittingham pissed up by a dozen or so lengths one afternoon at Santa Anita.

When I ran into "The Bald Eagle" the next day in the stable area I remarked that I was surprised the horse had won, let alone by such a wide margin, because he looked so scraggly in the paddock.

Whittingham smirked at me and said "That's because I don't clip my horses in winter." He did not have to add "you dumb shit" because he delivered his line with such contempt that the "you dumb shit" was vividly implied.

Charlie could be like that on occasion. Once, when I asked why a particular filly had not been entered for a race in quite a while, he launched into a tirade about the lack of opportunities for certain of his horses as provided by the Racing Office. His face turned red. I felt like a moron for even asking the question and I timidly slipped out his office.

About half a minute later, Charlie had jogged up to catch me, put his arm around my shoulder, turned me around, started returning to the barn while apologizing along the way for going off on me, as he explained he had unkindly taken out his frustration with the racing officials on me.

I have been an incredibly lucky young man, because most of what I know about horse racing and how to analyze horses and horse racing came from my ability as a Turf Writer to pick the brains of legendary horsemen like Charlie.

As I took in the size and breadth of Knight Errant, the one thing that struck me immediately was how athletic and fit he looked for a horse not in training. In Track and Field, I learned at the college level that there were basically two types of runners.

One type—the vast majority—were like me. Not particularly physically gifted, but hard triers who worked long hours to improve themselves.

The other type—the decided minority—were born with a superior physique and without even working out all that much somehow were gifted enough to maintain an athletic physique.

You see this in horses as well, although it is much more difficult to tell the difference in equines, as they are all bred to be athletes. Their selection is based on producing the fastest horse in a race.

Humans have not been selectively bred for athletic performance, with the exception in modern times in the United States when slavery practices likely focused on matings designed to produce strength.

Knight Errant, standing there as a horse on the verge of re-entering training at a racetrack, looked like he had never left the grounds and had stayed in training.

Horsemen for years have referenced this trait among superior athletes by saying that a horse "keeps himself well."

I walked up to his side, gauged his withers for height, and reckoned that he stood just a tad under 16 hands. As the boy had never contested a race, nobody knew what distance category would fit him best.

Looking at him, it was hard to discern. He was not over-muscled in either his shoulder or his hind quarters. He was not short-coupled, and he was not particularly lengthy either.

So, I did not think that I had become involved either in a sprinter or a distance horse. He fit right in the middle. A Miler—that is what I reckoned I was looking at that cold winter morning.

From the side it was at once apparent that he was beautifully balanced. He also was slightly over at the knee. This bothers some trainers and breeders, but I have always looked at it as an advantage, as it affords the joint a headstart in rolling over a bit, thereby taking the pressure off the bones of the knee. I did not consider it to be a fault, although some certainly did.

Looking at him from the front, both standing and walking, the gelding had a solid if not overly wide or thickly muscled chest. He was more workmanlike in the chest area, with enough room for his legs not to get in each other's way during racing.

His knees were correct. There was little to no deviation. The cannon bones dropped straight down from the middle of the knee to ankles that were not rounded or pooching out from too much use. Best of all his pasterns in front were short and, when viewed from the side, at the preferred 45-degree angle that horsemen and vets agree offer a racehorse the best chance to stay sound.

When he walked toward me, he moved effortlessly and straight as an arrow. When seen walking from behind, once again, everything was in the proper alignment.

When one looks to buy an unraced youngster at public auction, especially at a select sale, prospective buyers have their best chance of coming upon a well-constructed animal; even though they still have to sift through plenty of stock to find the right ones for their budgets.

But breeding a horse that is well conformed is exceedingly difficult, no matter the parentage of the horse. So, for me to glom onto such a perfectly made horse that basically is a homebred is very, very difficult to do.

Looking at him from behind as he stood there, I was happy with the appearance of his hind quarters. They were beautifully molded in their shape, not the bulky or boxy type one notices with a sprinter, nor did they remind one of the lighter hind-end of a long-distance runner.

His head was masculine with that convex forehead one often associates with that of his sire Bold Ruler. Think of his great Champion mare Gamely or, if unfamiliar with her, the face of a Bull Terrier. Knight Errant's eye was expressive, kind and generous.

In short, I would categorize him as a Goldilocks type of individual. He avoided the extremes in conformation and was, to use an expression, "just right."

What made Knight Errant so special and allowed his superior talent to be on display for all to marvel at was his movement. The ease of stride and swing of his legs even at the walk was very much in evidence. But when he was allowed to stretch out on a racetrack, he was able to slip into a movement that can only be described as electric. At full speed he moved with an elasticity that was unlike a machine built by man, but a marvel concocted by the Creator.

"Thank you Tad, thank you very much, for showing him to me this morning and for assisting me in being able to see what we can do with this animal," I said. "I know you haven't seen him in action yet, but I cannot tell you what kind of feeling he gave me and the clockers every time he broke off down the backstretch, floated around the turn and flew down the lane with a stride that is as effortless as anything I've ever seen.

"Yes, I know that I am only 26 years old," I said, "and I know there has been horseracing for decades upon decades before I was born, but in writing scripts for Eric Mannheim I have been able to watch film after film of many of the great horses dating back to before Man o' War.

"Big Red himself, his son War Admiral, Citation, Native Dancer, Swaps, Nashua, Bold Ruler, Kelso—all of them. They all had that special something. I believe in Knight Errant and I think if Doc can cure his metabolic deficiencies he can rise to the top."

Tad looked at me as though I had lost my marbles.

"Whoa, whoa, whoa there young tyke," he said, raising his arms like horsemen do when a loose horse is headed right toward them and they want them to stop. "That's quite a reverie there pally.

"Let's just take this a step at a time. Let's get him to the track, put an old-fashioned foundation in him, work our way up to a breeze, open the package and learn a bit more about this sucker. You are putting a lot of pressure on the old Tadster here buddy boy. Let's dial it down a notch or two."

I realized, of course, that Tad was 100 percent correct. But that spiel came from deep inside of me, having lain dormant for several months after Knight Errant disappeared just as fast as he had appeared. I guess I was so hot-damned excited to have him back in my life that I just got a bit carried away.

Chapter 6

Despite my normal workload of writing a column 5 days a week for the *Form,* writing the weekly West Coast stakes wrap-up for the *Thoroughbred Record* and contributing reports and articles on a freelance basis to various racing and breeding publications internationally, time dragged on for me because the Doc was facing challenging times getting his protocol down pat.

It was two steps forward and one step backward with Knight Errant.

Tad Smithwick had done what appeared to be a proper job in getting a solid foundation into the horse, but both he and Doc were reluctant to step up his work until they were convinced he was handling it well enough.

Additionally, coming from back East, Tad wanted to employ a more deliberate training regimen in bringing the gelding up to his first race. In Southern California we race on what Easterners refer to as "pasteboard" tracks. Because of the make-up of the surface mix, which is mostly dirt with some clay and sandy loam tossed in for good measure, the main tracks in Southern California are designed for speed. Because the tracks are lighter, horses need to do more work on them to become and remain fit.

Back East, where the track composition contains more sand and the cushion is deeper than out West, horses train differently. At Belmont, for example, most horses breeze a half mile and sometimes five-eighths of a mile, but rarely three-quarters of a mile or farther.

In Southern California most horses breeze five-eighths, plenty go three-quarters, some go seven-eighths and miles are not uncommon.

When Knight Errant was ready for serious work, he would start his morning routine by walking for about half an hour, first under the shedrow with a blanket on, then with a rider on his back outside in the ring.

Once walked to the racetrack, the horse would jog a full mile in the opposite direction of how races are run, then turn around and break off into a gallop for another mile and a half. The local horses sometimes did not walk before heading to the track. If it were a gallop day they would break into a gallop almost immediately after arriving at the gap to the track.

Some cowboy types are seen jogging their horses from their barn and breaking them off into a faster clip right after clearing the gap. One notorious fellow, who no doubt would consider himself to be an enterprising horseman, would lurk until he spotted a likely breezer, lay in wait behind him around the first turn and down the backstretch, then jump into the work as an unwanted or unplanned mate. It is not called the "Wild West" for nothing.

Finally by early summer Doc told us he was ready to move to the next step in the process. He advised Tad that he could start to plan a breeze. "I pretty much think I've got his metabolism handling his present workload quite satisfactorily," he said.

Tad decided to remain at Santa Anita instead of moving to Hollywood Park because he knew the horse would not be able to make a race before the circuit moved in late July to Del Mar. That is where Tad hoped to debut the 4-year-old gelding.

The last two weeks of May Tad had the exercise rider let the gelding open gallop the last quarter mile a couple of days a week. The last week of May he let the rider do a 2-minute lick. On June 1 Knight Errant turned in his first timed work since late December of his 2-year-old season.

After warming up Eastern style with the jog and the gallop, Knight Errant was eased into his three-eighths of a mile work a full furlong and a half before the pole at the end of the backstretch.

The move took place close to 10 o'clock, just before the main oval was to be closed. The track of course was pretty chewed up at that point. Knight Errant had been back in training for so long, he really was not sure what his human connections wanted from him, so he did not actually increase his tempo until the middle of the turn, at which point he was well into his work.

The rider was reluctant to chirp to him, but he moved his hands forward once. That was all it took. Like a bird in a tree startled by a street noise, the dark bay went from a sedate pace to full-on running.

"He knocked me in the backseat," the rider would tell us upon dismounting. "The force of his lurch totally caught me by surprise. Once he exploded it took me a while to get him back. But to his credit at the eighth pole he came back to me. I only let him gallop out about a hundred yards before I started pulling him up, as I reckoned he's done enough for the first move. What'd he go in, like 37?"

Neither of us answered Danny Jones. Neither of us wanted to.

Tad railroaded me aside. "Phone the clockers at the gap and tell them if that work makes the tab my name will be mud with too many people," he said. "Get them to tone it down. It's for all our benefit, believe me."

When I got off the phone Tad was waiting for me. He showed me his watch.

"Holy she-it" slowly came out of my mouth in low tones nobody could hear.

"You think you got it right? That's awfully hard to believe, don't you think" I said, shaking a bit with excitement. "He only really broke off at the 2 ½ and was being eased inside the last sixteenth. Something's not right. No way he goes in :32 2/5. No fucking way."

Tad was shaken by what he had witnessed and what his stopwatch read. "Most of the private clockers surely have gone home by now," he said. "It is late enough. Probably only that creepy Rabbi-looking dude might still be high up there in the corner of the grandstand. He's one of your Tribe pally, so you go check it out, let me know."

Sure enough, barely visible in the highest point of the grandstand where it joins the clubhouse right under the press elevator was none other than Fishel Friedman. As he was wearing all black, with a large black hat, he was difficult to spot.

It was a dark day. No racing. So I took the elevator to the

sixth floor, then walked down the green painted circular metal stairway to where Friedman was sitting. A studious individual, he was transcribing notes from his small hand-held tape recorder into a voluminous notebook. He was detailing today's works.

After half a minute or so he raised his head, saw me and said "Vos tut zich?" which in Yiddish means "what's going on?"

"Vos machstu?" I replied, which means "How are you?"

Then he started speaking English with his Brooklyn accent.

"When are you going to help me out landsman?" his familiar, tedious, boring screed began. Like those from the "old country" he pronounced landsman as lonts-mun. "When are you going to interview me and give me a boost in your column for goodness sakes? I'm old and forgotten now at this point in time. I need for you to make me current again so I can attract some owners to send me horses so I can get back in the game instead of sitting here on my tuchus morning after morning timing horses for a bunch of degenerates who need information so they can claim horses. But do you see these Yiddles sending any of these claimed horses to me to train? Gornisht. Nothing. Not a single one.

"Listen, landsman," he said, "it's bad enough you drive a car manufactured by Nazis. God forgive you on that score. But please..give this Yiddle a lifeline already."

"Fishel: I am going to toss the ball right back to you," I countered. "When are you going to give me a horse I can cash a bet on to put me a positive frame of mind to feel so much Jewish guilt that I will be forced psychologically to write something about you! Put me on a winner. Put me on the lead."

Fishel shook his head, his greying payis bouncing back and

forth underneath his large black Chabad fedora that was part of his Hasidic garb. Like some members of his sect, he curls the payis that hang down adjacent to his sideburns.

Fishel was not a rabbi, but after training horses in New York he moved to further his religious studies in Israel, returning only a couple of years ago. I do not profess to know very much about him or how deep his faith was, but at one time he was winning races on a regular basis, especially over the winter at Aqueduct.

"So, listen my friend, have you seen anything lately that you want to tell me about?" I said, cutting directly to the chase.

He screwed up his face into an expression I had seen all too often on the visages of my mother and especially my grandmother. Loosely translated the face—if it could speak—would say "I don't know. Maybe. Could be. A definite maybe. But who knows, you know." Then he started sounding like an actual real life rabbinical student. "Who really ever knows anything for sure? This is one of the major dilemmas of the modern age." All of a sudden I thought I was listening to Woody Allen doing stand-up!

I waited until he was finished with his monolog and said "So tell me about it already before I die of hunger as I have not eaten breakfast yet. Tell me boychik."

He opened his ledger, ran his finger down the page, stopped and said "Well…and I stress once again that I don't know for sure…this Night Errands…he had his first work back this morning in nearly a year and a half.

"And I wasn't really able to fully clock him, because I was unsure whether or not he was actually breezing until the middle of the turn. And then the boy starts taking a hold of him nearly a furlong from the wire.

"So, all in all, he works what? He works maybe 2 furlongs, giving him the benefit of the doubt. So I don't know, you know? I just don't know. Night Errands. I don't even know who trains him at this point, as I didn't recognize the saddle towel. And I doubt he will appear on the work tab because the work was so iffy. But I caught him going a quarter mile in :21 and change. That certainly cannot be correct, can it? Keep an eye on that one."

Back at the barn I relayed to Tad what I had gleaned from my chat with Fishel. "Tad, look, I don't think we should be too focused on trying to cash a bet with this one. I know your modus operandi, I've seen you in action, but how in the hell are you going to hide this one. He's a frigging rocket ship for fuck's sake. But if you like I can try.

"With Hollywood Park in action, all the notable clockers with major clients will be working on the young horses across town. If Fishel is our only worry, I have a way to keep him under control and on our side, so consider The Rabbi to officially be iced."

I stayed around the frontside for a while until the mimeographed worktab was made available by one of the clockers at the Racing Office. As I figured, the work showed up as 3 furlongs in :36 3/5, which as it was written still was the fastest three-eighths move of the morning among 8 going the minimum trip on the tab.

Back at the barn the horse had already cooled out and was back in his stall, with his head buried in his feed tub. His sides were motionless, he was banging the tub around, indicating that he was enjoying the heck out of his meal.

Tad and I skipped Rod's and headed over to Coco's. Instead of waiting to be seated in the main dining room where too many horsemen gathered most mornings, Tad steered me aside once again and motioned me to follow him to the left into the adjacent Rueben's restaurant.

It was only 11:30 in the morning, but Tad was friendly with a waitress who seated us in the far back and within seconds had brought Tad some sort of alcoholic libation. He knocked it off in nothing flat.

"Don't worry about the Tadster," he said to me. "I needed just this one toddy, cuz as we both know, that first work back can be a bit dicey sometimes."

There was about 2 minutes of silence, as the restaurant had few customers, this not being a racing day, and both Tad and I were mired in our own individual thoughts, as we both replayed the workout in our minds.

"Bill…Bill…Billy…Billy boy, hot damn you were right about this sucker" he said, being unable to contain his excitement and enthusiasm. "What in the hell have we got our hands on here Billy Boy. He is the Second Coming, but the second coming of what? Who's your favorite horse? Mine's Forego. But Forego never showed this kind of speed. He was a different type."

I said "Swaps is my favorite, because of his action. His feet looked like they never touched the ground. He ran like the hoverboard of racehorses. As for this horse, the only thing I've seen remotely like what I witnessed today was when Never Bend was a youngster. I never saw him in person as a young horse, but film of him was damn exciting. He was a black blur.

"I can't tell you how relieved I am that he showed you enough today to make you a believer. We could be in for the ride of a lifetime with this one. And we've barely opened the package.

"This is likely going to completely complicate and change my life. I don't know if I'm ready for it. But this is so exciting I can barely stand it!

"You know, I used to run track. The excitement of winning a race is like nothing else on Earth. But I've got a strong hunch that level of excitement is going to have to take a back seat to watching Knight Errant race. Oh boy!"

Over the next month Knight Errant breezed either before dawn when no one could see or clock him, or as close to the end of training hours as possible. I was able to convince The Rabbi to be circumspect in his info delivery to his clients. He was a loner that talked to nobody, so I felt safe he would be quiet.

Because Tad had layered such a deep foundation under Knight Errant and because of how much time the gelding spent on the track each day, Tad told me the horse would not require as many breezes as a normal California horse to be race fit.

He wanted Knight Errant to be ready for his career unveiling in the first condition book at Del Mar. So he hatched yet another one of his ingenious yet totally unnecessary plans that he said not only would render the horse dead fit and ready but also allow us to cash a bet.

Tad was incorrigible when it came to both booze and betting, but I had to admit he had done what appeared to be a splendid job so far.

So 10 days before the Del Mar meeting's opening day, Tad had Knight Errant vanned from Santa Anita down to a private training center half an hour inland from Del Mar owned by a close friend of his in Rancho Santa Fe.

"The track composition is the same as Del Mar," he explained. "Actually, it is better than going right into Del Mar, because the freaking County Fair with all its heavy equipment and the carnie folk hanging about are basically accidents waiting to happen. Every year those guys that get down there early complain about tendons, suspensories and what not. We can keep our boy going, get him acclimated to the seashore climate and salty air and breeze him over a pristine track before noon with no eyes on him but ours."

I could not join Tad and Knight Errant down South owing to my obligations to cover the final weekend of the Hollywood Park meeting, but Tad called me on the last day of the Inglewood meeting to inform me that the gelding had ripped off five-eighths of a mile on the five-eighths bullring training track in :57 2/5 while on the bridle throughout.

"Bill...Billy...Billy Boy," he began. "He has been five-eighths twice, he hasn't taken as much as a deep breath and he is fit and ready for his first start. I plan to run in a maiden special weight going 6 furlongs the first Sunday at Del Mar.

"Are you sitting down my friend," he said. "I am going to ride a bug boy from Caliente. Name of Quintana. Rafael Quintana. I put him on the horse for that :57 2/5 work and he fit him like a glove. He's sits a horse well, he has lovely hands and he is not intimidated by the gelding's talent."

CHAPTER 7

Unbeknownst to me, Dr. James Church had been showing up at various hours in the day and night to continue his practice of taking blood samples from Knight Errant during his months of foundational build up.

Doc had a friend that was a top internal medicine specialist at Huntington Hospital in Pasadena who ran tests on the blood for him at a special rate. In the initial months the tests were conducted and analyzed, one thing jumped off the charts. Knight Errant suffered from a metabolic disorder that crashed a few key levels on his blood panel profile. These deficiencies had caused the horse to be unable to correctly process his food, especially proteins. These deficits piled up and it told on his body's ability to properly allow the horse to gain sufficient nutrients.

To hear Doc Church tell it, the signs were subtle, but very real, manifesting themselves in the form of a skin disease, thickness of the walls of the intestine, drinking a lot of water and peeing a lot, as well as an increase in the length of his hair coat even during the summer months. His color was not right, he was unable to maintain muscle or weight. Basically he was getting too little from his food to thrive or even stay healthy.

When the horse was put under the stress of training, these issues only intensified.

After the main metabolic issue had been identified and a possible medicinal fix was provided by a research scientist, experiments were conducted on Knight Errant. "So it was one step forward, two steps back," explained Doc. "Just when it looked as though we were on the right track, we not only went back to square one, but back to minus two. It was months of trial and error."

Even after the proper dosage of meds had been gauged, Knight Errant required constant monitoring. While I was looking over Knight Errant, Doc emerged from a small lab at the training barn.

"Just checking his levels one more time," he said. "My apprehensiveness has dissipated in direct proportion to the improvement in the horse's blood panel. He has been good for more than 3 weeks now with not much fluctuation at all. I feel really good about him racing on Sunday."

The fix was not just one element but included a series of management issues that could be addressed.

One example he told me about revolved around feed. "Because the hay available to Eastern-based horsemen lacks the quality of the product grown here in California, a horseman like his former trainer James Maloney obsesses about getting the most beautiful hay available for his stock training at Santa Anita while he has access to it.

"The trouble is that producing hay like this involves farm management practices that yield a nicer looking product, but one that results in more sugar and less fiber in the hay. This wreaks havoc with metabolism. Racehorses need sugars, but they require plenty of fiber to slow down the process of delivering sugar to the body, not overloading it.

He said "Another thing about hay is that pesticides are overused to keep bugs away. Invariably in the lab we now see that properties in the pesticides bind to the hay, get into the horse's system and cause a whole set of issues with digestion and absorption of nutrients."

The bottom line, however, was the failure of sufficient protein to be available for utilization by Knight Errant's body. Doc was able to obtain some substances that he gave the horse in the form of powders and injections developed for human beings with the same disorder. This breakthrough treatment was new, but costly to obtain.

Doc Church from time to time gave Tad Smithwick stable management tips to help Knight Errant. Each one by itself may not have amounted to much admitted the vet but taken as a whole they could make a difference.

No more hay nets, only foraging hay on the ground in the corner of a stall. No more straw bedding. Yes it looked beautiful, but the dust and microbes it introduced in the atmosphere of the stable were harmful. The horse had to be walked every afternoon for at least an hour to an hour and a half. No antibiotics, no supplements and as little alfalfa hay as possible should be given to the horse. Alfalfa was way too rich for the system of Knight Errant to handle.

While the blood tests did allow identification of one major deficit and Doc had access to help with that, it was the combination of all the management tools that allowed the horse to be able to continue to train hard, long enough and fast enough to begin to regain 100 percent of his former health.

As his gut's microbiome changed, his telltale symptoms gradually became non-existent. His hair coat began to change for the better. His missing weight over his ribs, back and croup began to normalize. And he began to develop a strong overall physique.

When Doc Church cleared the gelding to begin breezing, Knight Errant looked like a picture of health.

By the time I made my way down to Del Mar and joined Tad at the Winners' Circle Lodge, the maiden race debut was less than 5 days away. So on the Wednesday before the intended race on Sunday I drove over to Rancho Santa Fe, where Knight Errant was still stabled at the private training center.

Tad pulled out the horse from his stall and stood him squarely on all fours so I could take a gander at him. His hair coat, as old-timers might say, was sleek and shiny as that of a wet seal. The winter's Hunter Clip was but a faded memory. In the late morning sunlight, his coat shone magnificently.

Tad beamed with pride. "Look at him. There isn't a pimple on him."

"That's good," I countered. "We'll save a fortune on Clearasil!"

Tad gave me the unapproving wince of an older brother. "Seriously Billy, this horse looks a picture and a horse could not be doing any better than this one is right now. And besides you, me, Doc, his rider Raffy and The Rabbi, nobody knows a thing about him."

Looking him over he was basically the same horse. Now in the second half of his season at 4, he had not grown in height and he had not really filled out all that much, but the quality of what was visible had intensified.

His muscles were not bigger, just more defined, both on the shoulder and in his hind quarters. His gaskins, for example, were not larger in mass, but more ripped. On feeling them, they were still supple. Lots of times with the weightlifters I used to train with in college, the calf muscles had lost their elasticity and were too hard and bunchy.

Entries for Sunday would be taken and drawn Friday morning at the backside Racing Office, in front of which were gathered jockey agents, trainers, owners, writers, pony riders, exercise riders, grooms, hot walkers, supplement hawkers and some fans that had found a way to sneak into the stable area.

Doc and Tad had one final quiver in their bow to foist upon the racing community. As I stood in front of the office waiting for the races to be drawn, Doc Church suddenly appeared to my right side, seated in his stock saddle, wearing a grey felt cowboy hat while astride a dark bay horse that nuzzled at my shirt collar.

"Mornin' Billy," he said. Once some of those gathered at the Racing Office saw Doc making his first backstretch appearance of the meet they greeted him. One woman, a long-time owner and noted Quarter Horse barrel racer, said "You certainly seem to be well mounted there Doc. Who is that, a former racehorse?"

To which Doc said "This ole' horse here? Naaah. He's in on Sunday. It'll be his first start."

"And you're riding him around the stable on that stock saddle like he's some sort of pony? Do the owner and trainer know?" she enquired in hushed tones.

"Sure do Miz Abercrombie," he said, nodding at me. "Why, here's the owner right here. Bill, say hello to Mrs. Abercrombie. And the trainer Tad Smithwick, why he's right up there talking to a jock's agent."

Within a minute everybody assembled in front of the office knew the name of the horse, the owner, the trainer, his impending entry and the fact that the unraced horse was standing there as calm as an old cow pony with a 200-pound veterinarian on his back sitting in a heavy 50-pound stock saddle.

I was as astounded as most that had bothered to listen to the introduction of the horse, his connections and his impending entry. This was the coup de grace as concocted by Doc and Tad and it could not possibly have played out any better.

Anyone that had any notion of Knight Errant being the same horse that had shown such blazing speed in his previous workout cycle at 2 at Santa Anita most assuredly would draw a line through him on Sunday.

Nobody in their right minds would strongly consider betting a horse that was being treated in such a haphazard manner as to be ridden from his stable to attend the draw, with an outsized rider perched atop of big Western saddle like he was a cow pony. Word most certainly would get out and travel fast before post time on Sunday.

I had to hand it to Tad and Doc. They had every bit as much riding on the outcome of the gelding's first ever outing on Sunday that I did, yet they conceived and played out their parts like seasoned stage actors. Their plan was audacious and these fellows enjoyed the hell out of every moment of it.

By the time the draw had been completed for Knight Errant's race, the horse was back in his stall, beside which Tad and Doc stood waiting for me to return with news of the post position and number of runners.

Knight Errant drew stall number 12 in a field of 12. There were four on the also-eligible list. Rafael Quintana would ride the gelding at 122 pounds. All of the runners were aged 3 and older. The race was carded as number 4 on the card with a post time of 3:30 p. m.

I walked directly up to Doc and gave him a square punch to the side of his shoulder. "You have a secretive fraternity boy side you old rascal," I said to him. "You are one funny old bastard Doc. The last time I remember hearing about anything like this was when Mesh Tenny used to ride Swaps around the Hollywood Park stable area to pick up the mail at the office. The publicity department thought it was so unique, they staged an entire photo shoot to send it out over the wires all around the country. Even *Life* magazine ran it."

Doc allowed a smile to creep onto his visage as he kicked at some dirt on the ground, waited about half a minute, then said "Well, where in the heck do you think I came *up* with the idea.

"Do you think I haven't been a regular reader of that tripe you pass off as a column in the *Form* for chrissakes? I got the idea from the one you wrote about Swaps and Mesh Tenny."

Doc, Tad and I broke out into uproarious laughter.

Tad said "Hey, Doc topped me on that one. And it was the icing on the cake. We should be arrested! I just hope I can cash my tickets before the gendarmes show up."

When I arrived in the Del Mar press box it was immediately apparent that something was different. Nobody was saying anything to me. It was my first day of the season at Del Mar and I apparently had become invisible.

When I reached the *DRF* section of the press box, Jasper the teletype operator said "Call The Undertaker."

The Undertaker was the press box nickname for Ron Hemming, my immediate supervisor and managing editor of the West Coast editions of *Daily Racing Form*. I never found out why he was called The Undertaker. Some said it was because he never liked any of his writers and hoped to fire and bury them. But as far as I was concerned it was because he could kill the life in any piece and then he would bury it. Who knows.

"What's with your name on the ownership line of this gelding in the fourth race on Sunday at Del Mar?" he blurted out.

Half a dozen guys were accidentally on purpose hanging out within earshot of the conversation.

I responded as calmly and in as deadpan a manner as I could muster. "Sorry: I don't understand the question."

The Undertaker said "Did you clear this with anybody here?"

I said "Like with whom? Clear it? Is there a policy against it?"

The Undertaker said "You know damn well there is a policy against it."

I said "So if there is a policy against it why does Lief Lindstrom race horses?"

Undertaker "You know damn well that Lief is a pedigree writer and independent contractor."

Me: "An independent contractor with a desk at our office? C'mon! What about Leeward?"

Undertaker: "You also know damn well that Leeward calls the charts and has no input as a writer that covers racing for the *Form*. Unless you remove your name from the ownership line of this horse I am going to have to take this straight up to the top."

Me: "Ron...you are the boss, so you just do what you have to do. I would, however, seriously consider paying for the privilege of being a little birdy on your shoulder when you try to explain to the General what frigging esoteric rule Peck's Bad Boy here has violated this time. You go for it big boy!"

I knew The Undertaker was bluffing. As if anybody among the higher-ups at the *Form* gave a rat's ass about whether I owned a racehorse. The higher-ups knew The Undertaker was always trying to be a hard taskmaster. On one hand they liked that, but on the other hand my column was extremely popular, they enjoyed it themselves and they were not going to rock the boat on the say-so of The Undertaker.

Fifteen or so minutes later when I joined the rest of the press box denizens for lunch on the roof of the press box, word had spread about my chat with The Undertaker and they were all my buddies and peers again.

But it was somewhat of a downer that until my run-in with my boss, which they all enjoyed the shit out of, they had given me the cold shoulder when it became known that I was now a racehorse owner. Jealousy had reared its ugly head for the first time. I was not used to it, as I considered myself to be just one of the regular guys in the press box.

As I would soon find out that turned out to be only the tip of the iceberg.

Chapter 8

When the *Form* came out Knight Errant was listed at odds of 12 to 1. It was noted that he had an unfavorable wide draw. His workouts leading up to the race were half a dozen in number, none of them fast save his first-ever timed workout in his current cycle, that fictitious :36 3/5 three-eighths move. The remainder were all mediocre and slow, especially for fictitious works.

In the newspapers, tout sheets and seminars, comments ranged from the gelding being a non-entity to disparaging remarks about his trainer and visiting Caliente jockey.

Basically, the consensus was that Tad Smithwick was an underachiever, the jockey was an amateur playing in the majors, the works were uninspiring and the gelding was among the rank outsiders.

Del Mar's morning line maker had set his odds at 20 to 1.

Here's how bad the horse's chances looked: not a single denizen of the press box, including the brother of Del Mar co-founder Bing Crosby—a guy that came upstairs every day before helping himself to a free lunch and a look at all six of the tout sheets posted on the wall—asked me what I thought of my horse.

The pressure was completely off me.

Also, I had given Tad $4,000 in bets to make for me so that nobody could see me at the windows.

In deference to Mr. Harwood, I wore a sport coat and a necktie. See, that's another telltale sign of how little anybody thought of Knight Errant, that nary a mention was made by anybody with whom I came in contact as to why I was dressed up. Not a single "Hey, I see someone has dressed up for the winners' circle today." And my press box peers returned to giving me the cold shoulder. I did not even warrant a complementary ribbing about my first-ever racehorse being such a non-entity.

Tad and I both made a nice representative appearance in the paddock with a nod toward Mr. Harwood. The jockey was young, quiet and spoke very few words of English. Tad had already given him riding instructions earlier in the morning.

When the horse moved from his stall to start walking around the ring, he made a striking appearance. He certainly looked much different than the horse under the stock saddle ridden by his vet on entry day in front of the Racing Office.

Leaving the paddock I was approached by one character after another. First up was The Rabbi. Thankfully he was quiet and subdued. I told him that I had bet a grand for him and thanked him for keeping his pisk (loud mouth) shut.

Then came The Indian. I never caught his real name, but he had been around the track for at least 35 years. He had an eye for horseflesh; he told me that he was awestruck by the gelding's appearance and asked if he could bet. I simply shrugged my shoulders and kept on walking.

Then came a woman, a Latina that always gave me the

impression that in her youth she had been quite the looker. Clocking her action over the years I made her some sort of madam specializing in hooking up trainers and riders with nubile young females.

"So what about this cult?" she said in a husky voice damaged by years of heavy smoking. "What...you like him? Tell me. We are friends." Again I resorted to the cold shoulder.

On and on and on and on...they came, they asked, I shrugged my shoulders and just kept on walking.

The last one to approach me was Essie. Her birth name was Esther. She was about 20, tall, shy, bookish, attractive in an odd way and the daughter of parents that ran the gift shop. In assigning a biblical name, her devoutly Christian mother and father hoped she would turn out to be a good girl. She was particularly good in the passenger seat of a parked car, but not as a budding devotee of her faith.

"Hi Essie," I said. "Do you have any money on you?"

She smiled and said "Tapped out again Billy? Oh Billy, Billy, Billy. How much do you need?"

I put a hand on her forearm and led her to the windows at the far end of the grandstand at the top of the stretch.

I said "Come with me. Get your money out and follow me. I want you to bet anything you can spare on the 12 horse. He cannot lose. I am holding onto you until post time because I don't want you to tell anybody."

She could sense this was not the same old Billy Boy she had become accustomed to.

"But I've only got about thirty or thirty-five bucks on me," she said.

So I put a Benjamim Franklin in her hand.

With 2 minutes to post time Esther got in line. I watched her place the bet. Then I moved underneath the grandstand to watch the race from the sixteenth pole on the apron.

Knight Errant, 20 to 1 on the morning line, had drifted to more than 35 to 1 with 2 minutes to go before post time. Then his odds dropped to 24 to 1 with 1 minute remaining. At the off his odds fell to 18 to 1. Somebody had either bet late or word had gotten out to some extent, I mused.

I had to watch the replay a few times to fully appreciate what I had seen in the race, as it became somewhat of a blur and a dream melded together. I could not see the gate but the announcer Harry Henson called Knight Errant first out of the gate. I then saw him outside a couple of others that had as a trio separated themselves from the field by a good half-dozen lengths as the leader reached the end of the opening quarter mile in :22-flat.

Heading into the turn Knight Errant, still quite wide, was cruising in front by what looked like 3 lengths. A tremendous roar erupted from the crowd at the top of the lane where Knight Errant suddenly cleared his rivals by a dozen lengths.

The jockey glanced back, saw his nearest rival some 15 lengths behind him, and eased the gelding across the finishing post. The crowd went berserk. Henson made a big deal of the margin and ease of victory. He enjoyed intoning the name Rafael Quintana with a Spanish flair. With every emphasized "Tonnna" the crowd went apeshit and Mexicans could be heard to whoop and holler. Much "he-ho, ha-ho, he-hoing" could be heard.

I walked as calmly as possible towards the winners' circle. At first the uniformed guard at the entrance stopped me and asked for my identification. Doc Church came by, grabbed my arm and told the guard I was with him.

It was only Doc Church, me and Tad standing next to Knight Errant in the winners' circle. My heart was pounding so fast the sounds filled my ears. I was completely spaced out. As I had suspected, watching my first horse race in my very own colors for the first time overtook my entire consciousness. This so outshone any race I had ever run in high school, college or afterwards. The rush was all-encompassing.

I looked at Knight Errant after his saddle had been removed and his sides were only heaving mildly. He did not look spent. His nostrils flared revealing a bright crimson disc that glimmered in the sunlight.

I watched him walk back towards the test barn. He seemed to be pumped up by his effort. He walked like a proud animal.

I heard some yelling and screaming "Billy Boy, Billy Boy, Billy Boy" and I turned around and looked up at the press box. It was the clockers brigade, early risers who made an exception by coming out in the afternoon to watch a horse race. And no doubt bet their lungs on him.

None of those chanting my name were actual denizens of the press box. The only one smiling down at me was Jasper. Good old Jasper. He was a normal, friendly guy without a jealous bone in his body. He was not really one of the usual press box crowd. I could tell he was happy for me.

Tad, Doc and I hugged each other a few times each, then we repaired to underneath the grandstand to watch the video replay on the display monitors. The three of us decided to drive into La Jolla to dine at a restaurant.

I did not return to the press box. I decided not to stay for the remainder of the card. I phoned the Director of Publicity, told him I had decided to go home as I was exhausted from a lack of sleep, and to send his own feature race recap to the offices of the *DRF* and let them know they should use it instead of my piece. He said he would. He did not congratulate me. Not another word at all. I went down to the parking lot, caught a disappointed look from the attendant, got in my car and drove down the coast toward La Jolla before pulling over into a public parking lot.

As I sat there staring at the expanse of the Pacific Ocean on a glorious summer day at the beach, I was not in the least exhausted. If anything, I was exhilarated beyond belief.

I tried to process what had just happened and wondered what my future might hold.

Money, the lack of which had always been an issue for me, suddenly no longer was. With what I calculated I had made from the day's bets on Knight Errant plus what I still had in my Bank of America checking account, I figured my cash balance to be more than $75,000.

My silks of a white jacket with a single evergreen sash emblematic of prosperity were unbeaten.

I owned a horse with the most uncommon ability anybody was likely to have seen since the great ones.

Today the gelding had raced 6 furlongs in the astonishing time for a debuting maiden of 1:08 2/5. Fractions of :22, :43 4/5, :55 4/5 were uncommon for a first-time starter, no matter that this one was already 4 years old.

Of my immediate concern was my employment at *Daily Racing Form*. I had decided the day before on Saturday that win, lose or draw, I was ready to turn in my resignation.

While in the paddock for a stakes race the day before that served as a prep for the Del Mar Derby later in the meeting, a woman that owned one of the favorites approached me and introduced herself. I thought she was about to thank me for writing my column that day about her horse.

Instead she said "Listen fella, the next time you wanna know something about one of my horses, you talk to *me* not my trainer."

She was a notorious bitch of a woman, with looks to match her sour disposition. Her husband was an extremely successful businessman and this woman fashioned herself as a combination racing guru, part-time mystic and wannabe socialite. She penned columns of her own for a disreputable throw away racing publication.

Apparently she also believed in some sort of voodoo. She wore an outsized ring. When she flipped over her hand to face the ground, small dangling bits of metal were released. She would then rub these bits up and down against the arm of a jockey for good luck. I have never seen an old broad experience an orgasm, but when rubbing the rider's limb she wore an expression that approximated what I fantasized it must look like. It was spooky.

In response to her demand, I responded "Listen to me Mrs. Lipschitz, you won't have to worry yourself with me in the future, as based on this little episode and a few others I've encountered this week, I have decided to quit my job so I will no longer have to deal with raving lunatics and nut cases like you any longer. Have a nice day."

Doc, Tad and I ate dinner in La Jolla at The Cove, a great spot right on the beach overlooking an incredible orange sunset. We ate lobster. Neither Tad nor Doc, himself a noted aficionado of Manhattans before dinner, had a drink that evening. Not even wine was ordered with the meal.

All of us wanted to savor the moment and be clear headed in navigating our future.

"I don't want to get too far over my skis," Doc said, "and both you fellas probably have a better feel about this than me, but we may have a responsibility to treat this horse as something extra special."

We both took in the moment, thought about it, nodded our heads and sat silent for a while.

Tad spoke next. "Look: I am the first to admit that when you guys told me about this horse, I thought you were stark raving mad, especially for guys with as much knowledge and experience as you combined.

"But I have to tell you here and now that I am now officially on board as a true believer. This horse had already done stuff I've only heard old timers like The Jones boys whisper about. And I hear you about responsibility. You have hit the nail right on the head."

Then I spoke up. "Unlike you fellas, I am young and so I lack the experience and knowledge of you two. However, I have read as much as most on the history of the Turf, met and interviewed legendary trainers and riders. So while I am a self-admitted neophyte, I do have a good feel for the enterprise and what being the custodians for a horse like this means to us and more importantly to the sport."

We clinked our water glasses and repaired to our respective modes of transportation to return home and contemplate our futures.

The next morning, on my day off. I decided to drive from San Diego County to Los Angeles County to meet with The Undertaker, but I stopped by the barn to check in on Knight Errant. Tad did not return to the pad the night before and he was not at the barn either. The groom was walking the gelding.

"Bueno?" I offered.

"Si" came the response. "Meester Tad he estopped by early, he feeled the legs, jogged him up I ming, told me to walkening heem for uh hour. Cabayo acts like always to me. He no change, ever. He my pet."

To my relief The Undertaker acted the role of a gentleman and the meeting was both cordial and meaningful.

He told me that he never expected me to last as long as I did in my job. He pegged me as a short timer from the get-go because he said I had too much "on the ball" to stick around in a dead-end job at the *Form.*

Half-kiddingly I told him that if he had not consigned so many of my recent columns to the circular file and made me write new, less-controversial ones that I would have stayed on a few more years.

He told me he admired my courage and willingness to highlight the underbelly of racing and to take the side of the horseplayer in disputes with the stewards and racetrack management. But he claimed that he bucked up against me because that is what he expected the General had wanted.

In a way I had looked forward to a confrontation in which I told The Undertaker exactly what I thought of him and his lame-ass editorial policies. On the 2-hour drive from Del Mar I realized that I wanted to tell him that I was tired of working for a rag that was in fact nothing more than a house organ for the racing industry and that I was leaving to find work at a real newspaper. But he completely disarmed me and my spiel died in silence.

Neither of us mentioned Knight Errant.

In tendering my resignation verbally, I said that I was willing to stick it out until the end of the Del Mar meeting the first week of September, but he said lame duck employees in his experience were more trouble than helpful.

I thanked everybody that I had worked with in the office individually. Before departing I made a point of stopping by the office of Joanie Dechico, head of the credit union at *DRF*, and told her that I would be paying off my car loan in full. I owed about $12,000 on my used BMW. She was grateful, as she said she hated having to chase down ex-employees.

When I went out the front door, walked down the steps and headed to the parking lot, Lief Lindstrom was waiting for me.

"Kid," he said. He was always calling me kid. "Sorry to see you go. You've got a great future in this game. I have to say I envy you. I kind of always hoped that someday I could do what you are starting out to do in racehorse ownership.

"But, unlike you, I was too chicken shit to go out in the real world, so I stuck with my current gig. I don't get paid all that much, but what I pick up on the side through consulting allows me to work very little, play golf at Western two maybe three times a week, and meet some very nice widowed ladies at the 19th hole. Go get 'em Billy," he said, offering a solid handshake. "Call me. Maybe we'll play a round at Western."

I took one last look at the office building before driving out of the lot. I was headed back to Del Mar, but I made a little detour first, hanging a right on Vermont Avenue and heading north. Five minutes later I drove past the athletic field at Los Angeles City College. My dad had gone there, studied journalism and ran track. After high school, I followed in his footsteps somewhat, hurdling and high jumping two seasons at the community college.

I was an okay runner and leaper. But I was never as good as I had hoped to be due to a lack of physicality. But now I had found something even more meaningful and fulfilling in campaigning an equine athlete that possessed everything I lacked, except testicles. I had him there all right!

So I headed back down to San Diego County where that evening I had a date, so to speak, with Murray Stronzo, a staff writer for the *Atlantic Monthly*, an author of several books and the horniest older dude I had ever met.

Murray had about 30 years on me, but I figured I would need every one of them to catch up to the impressive numbers he has racked up in bedding women all over America and Europe. Murray and I planned a night on the town in Del Mar.

Chapter 9

Murray Stronzo technically was a near-brilliant writer, but his fatal flaw as both a scrivener and human being was a need to expose the flaws of others, while ignoring his own. He lacked a soul. Acting as though appointed by a deity on high, he busied himself with exposing miscreants either in print or through gossip. His current project at that time was a non-fiction book about racing, which he would later follow up with several thinly disguised racing-themed mystery novels he used on a retribution tour of the game's lowlifes that cost him (to hear him tell it) untold millions of dollars at the windows.

The New York-born writer formed a friendship with me because I had something he needed and valued: unfettered access to the stable area, a deep knowledge of the machinations of the backstretch and a perceived naivete that suited his streetwise outlook on life.

Now I had become a minor news item around town because the first racehorse I owned won its only start impressively. He tested my new-found celebrity on Monday evening to see if it improved his odds of getting laid.

Murray had set me up with a date. Actually there were two dates, one for each of us. However, when we arrived at the restaurant bar where we met them, Murray quickly sized up the situation and informed his date that she would now be my date.

So instead of winding up with an attractive 40-something hot-to-trot young lady, I instead found myself seated next to a mature woman of an indeterminate age. I felt like I had been set up on a blind date with one of my mother's Mah Jong partners.

That was Murray.

Then he used my good fortune of the day before to demonstrate what a big shot he was because of his close friendship with a budding star. It was repulsive.

Murray and his date slipped away for a minute or two and upon returning informed my mommy-date and me that there was some sort of emergency at his hot-date's home, she needed to beg off and, being the classy fellow he was, Murray had decided to join her for support.

This left me and my mother figure to dine alone. To be fair, she was a trooper, fully realizing exactly what had taken place and empathizing with my plight. She said that I did not have to stay with her, but being the fair-minded individual that I was, I assured her I was looking forward to a pleasant evening.

The meal was all right, but before any talk of dessert I explained what a tiring day I had and asked if we could wrap things up. She drove me back to the Winners' Circle Lodge. I kissed her on the cheek and she shook my hand.

Back in the room I shared with Tad, I found him at 8:30 p. m. completely sacked out, still wearing his entire outfit of the day minus his English Jodhpur Boots that lay on the floor beside his bed. He was flat out on his stomach, head turned to the wall, breathing heavily and filling the room with the acrid stench of booze.

OK, I thought to myself, the fellow was entitled to celebrate. At least he was where he belonged and not out somewhere running his mouth and getting himself in trouble.

We both arose from sleep about the same time the next morning around 5:30. We agreed to visit Knight Errant at the barn before thinking about having breakfast in the track kitchen.

Tad went over Knight Errant's joints while the animal was still standing in his stall, then had the groom lead him out and immediately jog him first down and back in the shedrow and again two times outside in the middle of the circular ring.

"Very nice, very nice," he said to himself, but plenty loud enough to make sure that I had heard him.

Tad instructed the groom to walk him for an hour just as he had done the day before.

"No bringening him I ming to the track today Meester Tad, no eh training?' the groom enquired.

Tad replied, again loud enough for me to hear, "si si senor, no training until day after tomorrow. I see you manana at 5 o'clock and we take him to the beach. Put that cowboy saddle of mine on his back and have him saddled by the time I arrive. Sank you mi amigo."

Doc showed up right about then, suggested that we all head over to Fidele's where we could talk more privately without too many racetrackers clocking our conversation.

After we ordered and exchanged pleasantries I piped up, asking why Tad was taking so long in returning Knight Errant to the track. Tad looked straight at Doc, raised his eyebrows and said "Doc…you're up."

The vet said "Billy, it's because of me. It is not totally my call, but in explaining why I prefer to ease the horse back into training, I think you will get it. This goes back to when I was running the 880 at Stanford. My coach was close with some of the best distance-running mentors of the day and one thing he totally believed in was rest after extreme exertion.

"Back in the day when those gurus from New Zealand and Australia were promoting more miles to produce the best times, my coach took a different tack. He was one of the first to not only realize the benefits of rest, but to insist on it.

"With a superior athlete like we have now in Knight Errant" he said, lowering his tone when uttered the name of the horse, "I suggested to Tad that we try something different with him. That we treat him as an Olympic-caliber athlete.

"So I came up with a schedule to walk him two days, take him to the beach for a mental cleansing as well as some aqua therapy on his limbs, and take him back to the track on day number 4.

"Look," the vet said, dipping a chip into the community salsa, "we still have no idea of what this horse wants to do. We know he can sprint, but we know nothing besides that.

"As fit as he is right now and as good as his bloods looks, I don't think he needs much training at all before his next race. I got the blood results back overnight and there is hardly any difference in them.

"Stress is and will always be his issue and how he handles it metabolically will determine how far we get with him and how long he remains viable as an athlete. Right now all signs say go."

Tad finally joined in. "That's the next item on the agenda, for sure—where are we going to point him for next? I am open to suggestions."

Naturally I had thought about very little else since the race. "I know he has run only once, he lacks experience, he beat thin air in his win, but fast is fast and he ran as fast if not faster than anything on the grounds.

"I would run him back in 3 weeks in the Bing Crosby. We know he fires at 6 furlongs. Why not try him in there?"

Tad screwed up his mouth as though he had bit into something sour and said "What…no non-winners of a race other than maiden or claiming? No small restricted stakes? What's the rush here pally?"

Doc just smiled, as he knew what I was likely to say.

"Meester Tad," I said, imitating the gelding's groom, hoping to bring some levity to the situation. It worked, he laughed, as did Doc. "If we were dealing with a normal horse, what you say would make total and perfect sense. But we are obviously dealing with a freak. So it behooves us to treat him like one. Nobody is going to make fun of you for skipping conditions with a horse like this and, if they do, it would be out of total jealousy.

"The timing of the race is good, with 3 weeks between races. He didn't have a hard race. I know that fast is fast and he went fast so the race had to take something out of him, or he wouldn't be human." I got another giggle from my audience.

"Let me ask you this—how many times would you need to breeze him if he ran back in 21 days?"

Tad rubbed both sides of his face, stroked his prominent jaw and thought for a moment or two before saying "Well, I'll tell you one thing I sure as hell ain't gonna do and that is breeze him back in 7 days like Charlie does."

Doc agreed. "As far as I can tell he is the last old timer to still do that. He tells me he does it because he wants to see how the horse came back from the race. Look: who is anyone to argue with anything The Bald Eagle does? His record speaks volumes, he is a legend and he is an intellectual of the Turf. But as ridiculous as it may sound, Charlie himself may never have put a bridle on a horse like Knight Errant."

That last reverie iced Tad and I, silencing us to contemplate the magnitude of what the veterinarian had uttered.

Then after a while of poking a fork through some refried beans and rice Tad spoke up. "Ok, ok, back to the planet Earth here boys. Ok, when would I work him, hmmmm?

"Ok, probably what I'd do is breeze him only once. I would bring him back to the track on Thursday, when all he would do is jog. On Friday, Saturday, Sunday, Monday and Tuesday I would gallop him. At the end of his Tuesday gallop I would open gallop him like Laz Barrera does, sort of ease him off at the quarter pole and let him finish up strong.

"Then on Wednesday I would give him a proper breeze going a sharp half and let him gallop out five-eighths. Standard maintenance workout. I then would walk him for 2 days and gallop him into the race fresh as a daisy. He is a clean-winded sucker so he requires no pipe openers in the days before the race. How's that sound to you boys?"

Doc Church was writing down the schedule with a pen on the back of an unused paper napkin. Without looking up he said "Tad, I like it. I like it a lot."

I then asked Tad if we were going to stick with the same

rider. "I know he was part of the plan to cash a bet," I said "but are we going to stick with him for the next start or the duration?"

Tad said "Naturally I have been thinking along the same lines as you on this one Billy. Needless to say I have been bombarded by agents ever since the race. We could get anyone we wanted. We could even get The Shoe. Everyone knows he rides first call for Charlie, but when a horse like a Dr. Fager or Damascus comes along, Charlie understands and doesn't pull rank."

I asked "So you are not married to the idea of keeping the kid on the horse?"

Tad replied "No, but he does get along with him. And if we ride him in the next one the other riders might just wonder if we are not high enough on the gelding to seek a big-name jock. It could play to our advantage on both fronts. Me? I think I'd stick with him for one more race."

I asked "Worried in the slightest about somebody getting to the kid before the race?"

Tad gave me the sideways glance. "Kid: you are letting the gamblers infiltrate what's left of your healthy brain tissue. Get real."

So the trainer and the owner headed back to the hotel, grabbed our golf bags, loaded them in the car and headed for some putting, driving range practice and a round of golf at Torrey Pines.

"Tad," I said to him as we waited for a back-up to clear on the ninth hole, "the way I figure it we have about a 10-day honeymoon before the shit hits the fan. In 10 days stakes nominations will be released for the Bing Crosby. Once the word is out that this is where we plan to go with our boy, the press, media, publicity department and everybody else with an outlet is going to start driving us crazy.

"And if the horse is anywhere near what we think he just might be, it will only intensify after that. I am so glad I quit working for the *Form* and have a little money in the bank for a change.

"I am going to spend the next 10 days trying to have as much fun as I possibly can and I strongly suggest you do exactly the same, as if you need any prompting from me to live it up!"

Later that afternoon I got a call in the hotel room from Esther. "I'm standing out near the bar," she said softly. "I am afraid to go in because they might card me. You free?"

I met her in the lobby at the entrance to the bar. She was wearing shorts and a tank top, which highlighted an impressive amount of cleavage that I had never witnessed before.

"Where's your car?" she asked. Then she took my hand and we walked to my car in the hotel parking lot.

I said "You're not going to do it right here right now in broad daylight are you?"

Yep...she was...and she did.

Afterwards she wiped her mouth with some tissue she had brought along for the occasion. "Sorry, but I feel as though I had waited an eternity to do that, even though it's been what? Only 3 days. I was really looking forward to it."

I brought Essie up to speed on events, told her about how I quit my job, cashed a bet, was extremely excited about the horse and I had 10 days of nothing to do but have fun.

She suggested that we go somewhere, get away from the track and racetrackers, and have some fun. She would tell her parents that she was going to spend some time with a girlfriend back up in Los Angeles.

I told her that as tempting as that sounded, the fact that she was not yet 21 scared me and I would not want either of us to get in trouble. Reluctantly she said that she understood.

Before she left to return to the apartment she shared with her parents, she asked for and was granted special permission to have a second helping of dessert before going home for her main meal. I promised not to tell her parents about her upside-down dining habits.

That evening after dinner I sat down to play a few hands of poker at a table underneath an umbrella in the swimming pool area at the hotel. Five guys were seated including a fellow of roughly my age that I had seen around the track the past couple of years. He had been a teen idol on TV, was no longer popular and struck me as a drug user with a big habit. He was loud, flamboyant and a distraction.

I won three of the first five hands I played, which should have told me something, but I was too naïve to figure it out. When I tried to leave with my winnings after half a dozen hands, there were too many protestations from the losers and they prevailed upon me to stay.

I never won another hand and walked away a loser of nearly a grand, which seemed a lot for a pick-up card game near the swimming pool. As I walked through the hotel lobby I was greeted by a Black groom that worked for Bobby Frankel. He used to rub horses for Charlie but left after Frankel offered him more money. That was Bobby's modus operandi and how he landed the best help on the backstretch.

"Billy, you dumb shit," he said, laughing when we started talking. "I figured you for a smarter guy than that."

I asked him what he was talking about. He proceeded to tell me that two of the poker players—one of whom was the former teen idol—were sending signals underneath the table, using a tapping method to first set me up, then fleece me.

I started heading back to the table, but Matlock—that is his name, Earl (The Pearl) Matlock—grabbed my arm to restrain me. "Hey man, they be gone by now," he said, still flashing a big, friendly grin. "Let it go man. Errybody know you gots money now and they all be lining up to take they turn having a go at you."

I was steaming and it took 5 minutes at least for me to calm back down, as nobody likes being taken for a ride, especially by that teen idol jerk. In talking to The Pearl about the ex-TV star I recovered my sense of humor and said "Well I know now not to feel sorry for that guy's acting career having dried up."

We both had a good laugh.

"Wanna go to the bar for a bit?" Matlock asked.

So we sat down in the back in the quietest booth available.

Matlock then broke into a long, convoluted story that at first seemed to be right down my alley and appealed to my investigative reporter instincts. The groom told me that he was fed up working for Frankel, who was winning everything in sight and making winning moves the likes of which nobody had seen on the West Coast.

He said he found out the secret to Brooklyn Bobby's unprecedented success.

"Can we continue this conversation somewheres else, like yo room or yo car?" Matlock asked.

When we got to my room, Matlock sad down at the small dining table and produced from his coat pocket a large "pill" that in size was between a tennis ball and a handball.

He handed it to me. It was not 100 percent solid, a bit soft, with a chalk-like outer layer. Matlock explained that he personally had stolen one of the pills, given it to a pharmacist he had gotten to know and asked if the fellow could find out what it was.

According to Matlock the pharmacist not only was able to break it down to its essentials, but to duplicate it in a compounding lab owned by a guy the pharmacist knew. Matlock and the pharmacist now had gone into business together as partners and were selling the pill for $750 a copy.

"I knows they works," Matlock said. "Because I give one to a friend of mine dat train around here. He gives it to a drowned rat he trains and that sucker bolts up. You delivers it with a ball gun right up the mouth. It works best bout an hour before a race. And the best thing of all it won't test.

"Now I knows that you gots plenty of bread right now and I figures you is a prospect to buy a few of these for your special friends and maybe even that new horse you got.

"And since we long-time friends, I's gonna give you the first one fo free, nothing, nada, gratis. Just because we pals."

Chapter 10

"Hey Bar Mitzvah boy, what's with the bacon on your plate?" a female in the Del Mar backstretch kitchen line behind me said. As I turned to identify the young woman, she still had the needle out for me, saying "don't you know that crap is treif?"

I faced an attractive girl of roughly my age, with a wide smile, perfect white teeth and bright eyes that seemed to delight in rattling my cage a bit.

"Yeah, well, I cut some serious slack to food items whose flavor busts right through the Kosher laws," I responded. I did not know this jokester, was unable to place her accent, but I was pretty sure I had seen her walking around the track that season from time to time.

"Mind if we sit with you?" she politely asked. She was with another girl, not nearly as attractive and sort of a tad boyish in appearance.

She introduced herself. Grace Sindell was her name. Jane Christian was her friend's name.

"Hey, some win with that gelding of yours the other day, right?" Grace said. "Would have been nice to have known something about him in advance. Too bad I hadn't yet had the opportunity of making your esteemed acquaintance, as I have no doubt that we would have become friendly enough for you to have tipped me before the race."

As she was talking away, I got the impression that she had, as my late father used to say, "been vaccinated with a phonograph needle." This girl could talk. Her accent stamped her as growing up somewhere on the East Coast. She had the look of a model, noticeably thin, high cheekbones, high forehead.

The more Grace spoke, the more apparent it became that she was no racetrack bimbo type. She chose her words thoughtfully no matter their rapid-fire production.

"Yeah, well, it was a good day," I said. "I've seen you around the track during the races a couple of times."

"Ooooh, so you did notice!" she said, with her dancing eyes adding further expression to her already over-animated verbal linguistics. "That's quite comforting. Makes it easier going forward to have a nice conversation."

The three of us then got down to the business of eating our breakfast. I had decided to come to the track that morning to find Doc Church, give him the souped-up juice ball and ask him to test it. But first I wanted to have some breakfast.

Grace and her friend, I quickly learned, rode weekends during the season of fall and winter with the East Hills Hunt Club, which in Southern California meant that they went after coyote, the fox long having lost the battle against the encroachment of civilization.

Looking at her friend Jane I reclassified her as "horsey." Interestingly, Grace did not send the same vibe. Still looked like a model to me, although she presented herself as being well educated and articulate to a marked degree.

"Now that we have become fast friends," Grace said, her dancing eyes showing no signs of letting up any time soon, "I feel I can talk to you like a pal. I hope I don't embarrass you, but I want to tell you how much Jane and I enjoy your writing. In fact last week after reading a piece of yours in the *Form* I showed it to Jane and said 'hey, this guy is different from the others. He's got style and, more importantly, he's got a brain.'"

Pretty much sounded to me as though Miss Sindell was cultivating me to pass on future winners at the track, but it was always nice to get a compliment about my work. However, as with most positive remarks of this type at the racetrack, it fell into the same basket as the others—the one making the compliment at some point in time wanted something in return. It was a softer version of quid pro quo.

Outside of the racetrack environs, if a young lady complimented a writer in person, it was either genuine or an introductory remark prior to jumping into the sack as its ultimate goal. Murray Stronzo had wised me up about this and often talked about rarely turning down a chance to speak at a writers' conference because it was the easiest pussy available to a writer no matter how unattractive they may be. Murray, by the way, was no bargain in the looks department and always came across as needing a haircut, a shave and a shower.

"Thanks Grace," I replied. "Compliments hardly ever arrive without somebody in racing wanting something in return."

Grace never flinched, taking the comment in full stride, and agreeing. "Yes, I can only imagine. But, as you say, still nice to hear, right?"

I was definitely getting an East Coast vibe now, because many of her sentences ended with a question mark. Bobby Frankel spoke in the same way.

Grace and Jane had decided to go racing at Del Mar on their day off and would be headed back to Los Angeles after breakfast before stopping off to visit a fellow fox hunter in nearby Rancho Santa Fe.

"You going back to the barn now?" said Grace, firing yet another question. "If you wouldn't mind terribly much, Jane and I would certainly like to join you and have a quick look at your gelding."

Since I was headed to the barn, I invited them to join me. I had the rocket ship ball in a small brown paper bag and brought it along with me.

Jane was my height. She was able to look me directly in the eye when she spoke. She walked with the posture of a professional runway model, square shoulders, easy gait, swinging arms.

Damn, I thought to myself, she was thin but she had a helluva body. And she was dressed so smartly for a visit to the backstretch, with teal dyed leather pants and a rust-colored tight-fitting top. She was very nearly completely flat-chested, but that did not detract from her overall sexy vibe.

Back at the barn, I introduced the gals to Tad Smithwick, who took Knight Errant out of his stall so the young horsewomen could inspect him. As the groom presented the horse, I asked Tad about Doc, whom he said had gone back home for a couple of days.

It was evident, once the ladies had been presented with Knight Errant, that they were dyed-in-the-wool horse lovers.

The softened expressions on their faces, their easy body language, their approach to the gelding—it all added up to horse lover.

It got me to thinking about the difference between horse lovers, horse players and racing folk. Most generalizations wind up being an exercise in futility, but it seemed to me that horse lovers, especially women, had a connection to the animal itself. And I would not attribute it to any maternal instinct, as many female horse lovers feel closer to their horses than the rest of the humans that populate their lives, including their husbands.

Horseplayers, on the other hand, mostly could give a rat's ass about the animal itself. This is why during a race you will hear many of them yelling "c'mon with that 3 horse," not even bothering to identify or invoke the name of the animal itself.

Racing folk—me being among them—are drawn to the enterprise for many reasons, the most compelling of which–at least in my case—is the sheer athleticism of the Thoroughbred racehorse, its bred-in will to win and its overall majesty. Racing folk look at these steeds as players on a vast canvass and not as pets. The real old timers look upon their horses as stock.

"Can I touch him?" Jane asked Tad.

The trainer replied "Absolutely. Docile as a lamb and well mannered."

Jane gently rubbed Knight Errant's forehead in a slow, circular motion. Then she placed a palm up against one of the horse's nostrils, then the other. She then stroked the gelding's neck from the just below an ear and all the way down to where it joined his shoulder. Then she put that arm around his neck, moved her face right up against his body just above the shoulder and drew in one very long breath through her nostril, held it, stepped back and gradually exhaled slowly through her mouth.

With a heavenly expression taking over her face, Jane smiled widely and exclaimed "is there any better smell in the entire world than that of a horse, I ask you?"

Yet another question from these two I thought to myself. Perhaps Jane had been hanging around Grace too long!

Grace thanked me profusely for being allowed to have an "up close and personal" gander of Knight Errant. She handed me a business card and said that she hoped to hear from me.

I told her that I was going to drive back up to L. A. to visit my veterinarian for a day or two and she said "who knows, maybe I will get a call from you, right?"

Later that afternoon I arranged to meet Doc Church at his ranchito in Bradbury Estates. I relayed the tale Matlock the groom had told me, handed the bag with the ball to the vet and watched him gently finger it to extract the white object from its kit.

Doc held the ball lightly with just two fingers. For a second I flashed on how a physician will palpate a guy's testicles and ask you to turn your head and cough when performing a health exam before a school will let an athlete participate in a sport.

Doc Church moved the ball around at various angles to take in its perfectly round shape. He sniffed it, put it down on his leather covered deck, gently stroked it and checked his hands to see if any residue had come off the thing.

"Crazy story, no doubt," Doc said, looking at me with a sincere expression. "I am not going to pooh-pooh this sucker out of hand, although I must tell you that I am skeptical it contains anything that will move up a horse."

I asked Doc if there was a way to do what the pharmacist purportedly had done, which was to break it down, list its properties and try to reconstitute it. He told me to leave the object with him.

"I have to visit the lab this afternoon with some more blood from the gelding, so I will show it to them and see what they might be capable of doing with it," Dr. Church said.

When I told Doc that I might meet up with a girl I had met at Del Mar, he asked me to tell him about her. I did not get two sentences out of my mouth before Doc leaned forward across his desk and said "I think I may know her."

The old rascal, I thought to myself, still checking out the talent at his age and after so many years of devoted marriage.

"Is her name Grace, Grace something?" he asked.

"Sure is," I replied. "How in the heck to do you know her?"

"Ha! Danced with her at the Hunt Ball…the East Hills affair at the Beverly Hills Hotel," he explained. "By the way, she's a helluva dancer for a young lady. She knows all the old steps, unlike practically anybody her age out here. I am guessing she has gone to cotillion and probably back East."

From Bradbury I drove west half an hour or so to Pasadena's main branch library on Foothill Boulevard, where I spent an hour or so looking through a few newspapers and periodicals to see what might have been written about the stunning debut of Knight Errant. Naturally I had not written a word, as I was no longer employed by *DRF* and, besides which, it would have been a conflict of interest. Same was true for my weekly racing wrap-up for the *Thoroughbred Record*.

Interestingly, but unsurprisingly, the lone mention I was able to ferret out of my search was a single line in the *San Diego*

Union in which the Turf Writer Nelson Fisher noted that the gelding appeared to be a lightly raced animal of considerable promise. That's it…end of story…end of coverage. Had the horse still been owned by Ellerslie Farm and trained by James Maloney the Del Mar press box habitues and publicity department ass-kissers would have been all over him.

Back at my cottage on West Huntington Drive just down the street from Santa Anita, I sat on the only chair in the single-room dwelling and recapped events of the last week in my mind.

I have long been in the habit of doing this, dating back to my days as a jumper and hurdler, when I would go through every track meet in what amounted to my career in Track and Field.

It helped me to focus on which elements of each performance were significant and memorable.

When my recap had brought me back to present time I was ready for dinner. Out of habit I returned to Pasadena, dined by myself at Beadle's Cafeteria, drove back home to Arcadia and relaxed.

I could not stop thinking about Grace.

Around 9:30 p.m. I phoned her. She picked up on one ring.

"What took you so long?" she said out with an air of incredulity.

I told her that I had a busy day and she advised me to relax, as she was just "jerking my chain."

When I asked her what she was doing, she said "just sitting around, waiting to go to bed. Mind if I drive over and join you?"

I was taken aback. "Not too late for you? Don't you have to be at work tomorrow?"

Quick as a wink she said, "Never too late to see you my fine young Maccabi. I can be there in less than an hour. As for work, the shop where I sell clothing doesn't open until 11, so no problemo Billy Boy."

When I let her in the door to my cottage she was more subdued than I had seen her. She appeared to be taking everything in stride. She placed her small night bag on the bed.

In appearance she struck me as being a cross between Ali McGraw from the movie "Love Story" and Diane Keaton. She favored the former but dressed like the latter. All she was missing was the hat.

She leaned with her back against the wall. I approached her, put two fingers between her leather belt and the black pants she wore, then pulled her towards me. She closed her eyes for our first kiss.

It was reserved, tender and exciting.

"Shouldn't we get in bed?" she said.

Right in front of me she undressed in nothing flat, dropped her clothing right where she stood and got under the covers of the double bed. She faced the wall with her back towards me.

"No boobs…sorry. They didn't arrive with the rest of the package at birth," she said. Her legs were smooth as silk, freshly shaved and well-tended, like all of her. After about 10 minutes of togetherness, we both fell asleep.

By the time we crapped out it was midnight. At the crack of dawn I felt her reaching out for me. This time my back was facing her. We made love twice, cleaned up, showered together, dressed and drove up the street to have breakfast at Rod's.

"I've heard you interviewed on the radio, read your stuff incessantly and heard the racetrack chatter about your wit and sense of humor," she said. "How do you think you will like having a relationship with a female that can go toe to toe with you? Intimidating? I intimidate the bejesus out of most people, especially men and most notably Jewish men."

I told her that I found it delightful so far and had no fear about holding my own. She smiled, obviously okay with my response.

As was her wont, she then peppered me with one question after another, asking a lot about exactly what the plans were for Knight Errant and closing with "when can I see you again?"

We arranged to have a meal after she got off work at her shop on Melrose Avenue just down the street from Fairfax High School where I used to complete in track meets. We met on Fairfax Avenue in L. A.'s borscht belt at Canter's Delicatessen.

Grace, full of piss and vinegar as always, turned out to be a big eater despite her tiny frame, which according to her weighed in at 104. She knocked off a Billy Gray's Band Box Special, named after the famed Jewish comedian that operated a night club two blocks south of Canter's until 1967 across the street from CBS Television City. The dish featured four open-faced sandwiches of chopped liver and egg-salad, with all of the trimmings including cole slaw, sliced onion and a half-sour pickle. For dessert she devoured a tall and full slice of chocolate cake filled with whip cream. She ate fast, but with table manners fit for royalty. She obviously had been well raised.

"I'd invite you back to my house, only I live with my mother," she said. "I don't have to but I choose to because she needs the company, I love her and want to be there for her."

We kissed long and passionately out in broad daylight in the open-air parking lot at Canter's and promised to meet back at Del Mar on the day Knight Errant would make his second start in the Bing Crosby Stakes. We planned to spend that night together and the next day at the seaside. We both wondered aloud if we could stay away from each other for that length of time.

CHAPTER 11

Jenny Lipscomb stood on the left side of Knight Errant at the Del Mar barn. Before giving the exercise rider a leg up on the gelding, Tad Smithwick softly and patiently explained exactly what he wanted.

"Jenny, this is not a normal horse," he began. "What I am going to tell you will sound far-fetched, but you've known me long enough to know I am not crazy. I want you to take a good holt of the horse, keep him on the bridle all the way around and let him pick it up down the lane on his own. No urging, Hand me your stick. I'll keep it for you in my tack room."

Puzzled, the young blonde girl said, "So what's the crazy part?"

Tad smiled, then said I want you to go in about :58 3/5.

Jenny laughed out loud, then said, "Yeah, right. Like that's going to happen."

Tad said "I've seen you in action enough to know you are going to hit your mark right between the eyes. We're counting on you not to let this sucker go down there in :56 or :57."

Jenny could only close her eyes and shake her head from side to side.

Tad took the shank and stood beside the gelding as he escorted him to the track. This was not an early or late morning work, the type that Tad has cut his eye teeth on setting up betting coups. This was a well-watched, well-known move in broad daylight right after the 8:15 renovation break.

Jenny, on loan from Charlie Whittingham for the move, was well used to being in the first set on the track, as was The Bald Eagle's wont, because he preferred the freshest ground possible to ensure safety and an even surface for his breezers.

Knight Errant would be working on a spectacularly brilliant morning with sunny skies and no usual marine layer to fog up or cloud the Del Mar racetrack from view. Up high in the press box and the adjacent clockers' stand the top deck was crowded, something none of us had ever seen.

When I glanced up from the apron, a lot of guys waved to me, giving me thumbs up and ok signs.

Knight Errant entered the track on the backstretch gap, jogged the wrong way around the track to the wire, paused for about a minute and a half, then was allowed to jog back around the first turn toward the backstretch.

Jenny did not give the dark-coated 4-year-old much of a run to the pole. As usual, when he broke off there was hardly any perceptible change in his stride, cadence or posture. As the Kentucky-bred ambled his way down the back side he seemed to be simply breezing along at a useful if not particularly speedy clip.

"Twenty-three flat" yelled one of the clockers from on high.

The gelding was working alone, Jenny was perched high in the saddle. When he switched leads heading into the far turn, again the change in legs was accomplished so smoothly it was undetectable.

Knight Errant, working right along the fence, seemed to be going steadily at the same pace, as he approached the quarter pole at the turn into the home stretch.

"Forty-six flat" a clocker blurted out.

I looked up at the press box and people were now leaning over for a closer look at the first truly public workout for the budding star Knight Errant.

The gelding had been programmed to accelerate turning for home. He was taught to fire down the lane. So after changing leads into the stretch, there was a barely perceptible motion from Knight Errant to lift his body and try to surge a bit.

Jenny, however, being the seasoned morning rider as she was, never gave up an inch of rein on the death grip she had on the gelding. When he hit the wire a clocker yelled out "fifty-eight and three, fifty-eight and three for fuck's sake, if you can believe it. Whoo-hoo!"

Tad confirmed the clocking on his stopwatch. He turned to me with a very satisfied-looking smile. "Whad' I tellya? I am really starting to understand this ole horse. Like breaking sticks out there today. Cannot wait to see the reaction from Jenny," Tad said.

Tad picked up Knight Errant at the gap and we walked back to the barn without a word being spoken. Not a peep was heard out of Jenny, who was merely whistling gently on the trip back to Tad's barn.

As the groom went about his job of cooling out the horse, Tad, Jenny and I went into the tack room and shut the door.

Jenny widened her already large blue eyes and said "Lordy, lordy, lordy what in the name of the Father, the Son and the Holy frigging Ghost was that! Lordy, lordy, lordy. What an absolute treat *that* was.

"But Tad, how'd you know that was exactly what he'd do?"

Tad duly explained that he had already worked him in :57 2/5 over at the little five-eighths training track at Rancho Santa Fe, so he pretty much knew what the horse was capable of. And he was infinitely fitter and sharper now than back in July. And Tad purposely had lightened up on the gelding's workload and he figured to be fresher and faster this morning.

"Yeah, yeah, yeah I get that, but how'd you know he would keep up that pace without any urging or not being allowed to have his head?" she wondered.

Tad said that from seeing great horses like Ruffian and Forego train he had a pretty good idea of what a horse like Knight Errant was capable of in the morning. Of course, Tad pointed out, that was while I was on the ground.

"The reason I wanted you to get on the horse was to hear from somebody that had breezed top horses day after day for the top horseman in the nation. I want to hear what this one felt like to you," he explained. "And I know, from having talked to you enough at Bully's bar, you pretty much have a clock in your head."

Jenny thought about how to reply before speaking again, as she organized her thoughts. "Well, first I would tell you that while Charlie has some of the best stock in the country year after year, he has trained precious few sprinters, so my frame of reference is not all that great with speed horses.

"As for this one, I don't make him out to be a sprinter. Not that he cannot sprint. Lordy, lordy no. He strikes me as a horse capable of anything. I am taking no credit here for hitting that :58 3/5. I give it all to you and the horse. Tad, my friend, you know your horse.

"Overall my assessment is that he just may be the most impressive horse I've ever sat on. I wonder what in the hell he'd have done had I let just a notch out—57, 56, 55? What the fuck? I cannot believe that I am actually saying these things out loud. Glad we've got the door shut."

Jenny hugged Tad, thanked him for the "opportunity" and "trust," then assured him that her lips were sealed about her impressions of the work. She winked at me on the way out of the door.

On the other side of the door was Freddy Glickman, the guy that was now doing my old job at *Daily Racing Form*. Standing right behind him was none other than Murray Stronzo.

Freddy had done a notes column for *DRF* for a couple of years before returning to teaching at the junior high school level. He missed the track, had let The Undertaker know that he was once again available should something come up, and when I departed The Undertaker unearthed and propped him up in my old stand. Nice guy—maybe too nice, if you get my drift—but boring as a blank sheet of foolscap.

"Nice work on that gelding of yours Billy," Freddy began. Freddy was pear-shaped in build, about as couch-potato-looking a fellow as one would ever be likely to meet, so his alacrity in getting downstairs from the press box and down to Tad's barn was surprising and a bit refreshing. Surprising, that is, until I noted Murray right behind him. I gauged that Murray had glommed on to my replacement to have a backstretch savvy journalist he could attach himself to in order to finish his book. I figured with Murray's ear to the ground at the bars in and around Del Mar that he had egged on Freddy to be Johnny on the spot.

"Yeah, yes it was. Nice work, as you say Freddy," I responded in as dead pan a manner as I could muster.

Freddy then peppered me with a few questions, trying to glean some info to fill his column. Freddy, as I say, was a very nice fellow. But whereas it took me on average about 25 minutes to knock out my column, Freddy on the other hand would situate his big, wide and flabby ass on a chair in the press box for hours at a time as he agonized over completing the 750 or so words it took to fill a *DRF* column.

"So what's next for him? Non-winners of a race other than maiden or claiming, I assume," he said.

Then, staring directly into the evasive eyes of Murray, I said "No, actually, we are thinking very seriously about the Crosby…the Bing Crosby."

Murray pipped up, unable to control himself, and addressing his new backstretch tour guide. "Whad I tellya, whad I tellya," he said. "Classic mistake, but one that apparently is unavoidable among the dreamers and amateurs in this sport."

"Seriously…the Bing Crosby?" Freddy asked. His voice indicated that he was starting to think that he had found the subject of today's column and would have to look no further.

"So, like, huh…the Bing Crosby. I don't have to tell you that you will be facing the top older sprinters on the grounds, and for that matter, some of the best in the nation." He uttered "amazing" under his breath, then continued. "What's the thinking here Billy?"

Now addressing Freddy directly, I said "Freddy boy, to tell you the God's honest truth, I in fact have lost my fucking mind." Then I looked at Murray and continued answering Freddy. "You see, since the gelding won last week I have been getting so much pussy down here at the beach I really think it has started to affect my brain. My medulla oblongata has been unable to properly process all my recent increase in sensory input. So, in a sense, I have fucked my brains out."

I honestly thought Murray was going to bust a gut he began laughing so hard. He has this nutty, reflexive laugh that was high pitched and throaty at the same time. It went something like this "Ah hooo-hoooh hooh."

Freddy never changed expressions during this part of our exchange.

"No c'mon now Billy, be real with me," Freddy said. "I am getting ready to devote my entire column today on this. What's your actual thought process behind a daring move like this? This could be a big story for both of us."

Without even realizing it, I had before my very own eyes morphed from being the one asking the questions to being annoyed at the press for trying to get me to answer them. I was finding out under this baptism by fire what my interviewees had felt like. And I must say that I was not comfortable with the process and my instinct was to fuck with the reporter and make his job harder, as I found it to be mildly amusing.

"Geez, ok...I'm sorry pal...I get it...yeah, I can really see where this could be huge for me," I lied. "So, this morning before the work, Knight Errant was telling me that pending a complete physical after the breeze that Tad and I might want to seriously consider skipping the allowance race and going right into the Crosby. The Knight, you see, is my very own Francis The Talking Mule."

Freddy never had much of a sense of humor and what limited capacity he had for tomfoolery was rapidly becoming exhausted.

"One last time you fucking idiot," he pleaded with a smile. "What's the idea here?"

Murray had moved back several paces, because he was unable to control his giggling and hoo-hoo hoohing.

I started to feel sorry for Freddy. I knew his dilemma and I had had my fun. So I said "Ok Freddy. I'm sorry for being such a dick, but I never realized until just now how much fun a guy being interviewed by the *Form* could be.

"All I can tell you is that this horse is different. Rather than try to explain why, I will let the gelding speak for himself a week from Sunday. Don't bother trying to wheedle more information from the trainer, because he is actually less responsive than me and detests people that try to meddle in his business. Unlike Francis, he will do his talking on the racetrack."

When Freddy walked away, scribbling notes on a large yellow pad he carried with him all the time, Murray moved forward to engage me.

"So are you really getting a lot since your horse won so impressively?" Murray asked, his eyes bright and wide open as he awaited any good news on the pussy front. Murray, you see, lived for pussy. Not from his live-in girlfriend of long standing, but strange and unexpected pussy.

I had only seen Murray one time since I dated a peer of my mother thanks to him commandeering my actual younger date. One morning, when I had slept in late and Tad was at the stable, I heard a loud, rapid fire knocking on the door of my hotel room. When I answered I was still wearing my pajamas and was not wearing any slippers.

Murray Stronzo was getting ready to use his knuckles to knock on the door again when I opened it.

"Ah, Billy...Billy Boy thank fucking God you are here," he said. He grabbed me by the arm and started to escort me to his room down the hall at the Winners' Circle Lodge.

"Wait a damn second willya, let me grab my room key for fuck's sake," I said.

I slipped into my shoes and followed him down to his room. He stood on one side and I stood on the other of his unmade bed.

"Look, Billy...I am desperate," he said, explaining that his girlfriend was on her way to meet him at the hotel and she was due to arrive any moment. He said he had slept with some 'strange' that night, she was a particularly hairy woman with a bush so hairy it looked like shrubbery and there was pubic hair all over his sheets.

Murray said that his girlfriend Mary was a nurse, very observant and a freak for cleanliness. She was certain to notice even a single pubic hair on the bed. He implored me to get down on my knees with him and continue his task of finding, removing and flushing any pubic hair down the toilet.

Damned if I was going to be picking up any unidentified body hair with my bare hands, so I walked down to the front desk, borrowed some Scotch Tape, wrapped some in a small bundle and used it to arrest any errant pubic hairs. When we finished I brought the soiled tape to a trash receptacle and returned the tape dispenser to the front desk.

Murray, at one point during Operation Pubic Hair Removal, looked up at the ceiling but in reality way, way above it and said "Jesus H. Christ on a pogo stick what in the hell is wrong with me? I have a wonderful woman who loves me, puts up with all of my selfish, ridiculous shit, and here I am on my hands and knees extricating wild pubic hair off my bed so Mary won't find me out and leave me. I am sick, do you hear me sick, sick sick."

Without telling him so, I was inclined to agree with him.

So after Freddy left the stable, Murray naturally wanted to glean any gossip from me about Knight Errant that he could spread around the Del Mar bar scene, thereby making him look like a knowledgeable insider.

I was not interested in enabling his gossip and I was loathe to tell him anything about my new friend Grace that could be used against me or get back to her in any way.

"Murray," I began my evasive fiction, "to tell you the truth I have been so busy I haven't really had any time to do much of anything. I have not made a bet since the horse won, I've only gone out with one girl and mostly I have been going back and forth between Del Mar and L. A.

"I did meet a young lady that I really, really like. She will be coming down here when Knight Errant runs in the Bing Crosby. I'll introduce her to you. I am dead certain you will like her and find her as interesting as I do. Never met one remotely like her. She is an absolute trip."

I did not want to completely blow Murray off, as I had an idea to write an article in a general circulation magazine about how little racing officials and Turf Writers do to uncover unscrupulous practices in the sport. I had no standing outside of racing to warrant any such publication, but Murray did and he could help me.

Murray said he missed seeing me and walking around the backstretch with me and hoped we could get back on course so he could gather enough info to complete his book.

Then he told me that the talk of the town focused on where Knight Errant would race next. Few if any seasonal denizens of the beach racing scene expected to see the gelding reappear in the Bing Crosby, as it was a huge ask for a once-raced 4-year-old, but plenty said that I would let my ego run away with me and force my otherwise sane trainer into doing it.

"I don't know if racing Knight Errant in the Bing Crosby is crazy or not," he said, "but I know that you are not crazy, so if you wind up doing it, I am sure that you have a better handle on it than anybody else."

Chapter 12

When I returned to my room after completing my variation on muff diving at Murray Stronzo's quarters, I found an envelope stuck under the door. It was from Doc Church. "Analysis of ball remarkable only in that it contains common plant fiber. Typical backside scam I'm afraid. Talk later. Doc."

When I answered the ringing room telephone, Hank Shuman introduced himself.

"You likely have no idea who I am," he said. "I went to University High School like you, but I'm a dozen years older than you or your brother. I'm an ex-stockbroker and I have been trading for myself the last several years. More importantly, I am a dedicated horseplayer. It is in this regard that I am contacting you."

I listened intently for the next few minutes as Hank explained why he wanted to chat with me.

"I am calling in regard to your stance on performance enhancing drugs," he said, fully riveting my attention. "I am not going to chat about this on a phone line.

"But I want to invite you to hear more about what I suspect, what I know and what I think needs to be done. I have a place on the beach down here at Del Mar. I am right next door to Fat Barry's place. I am assuming you know where that is."

I told Hank that everybody knew where Fat Barry lived and that I had been to his pad, which was located on the most expensive residential strip in the entire beach community. Unless this guy Hank was renting, I figured he must be very well-healed if he owns a beach property next door to Fat Barry.

He asked if I had eaten yet. When I answered in the negative, he invited me over for lunch. Coming right on the heels of just learning about Matlock's $750 magic performance-enhancing ball I was not in much of a mood for yet another cock n' bull story, but because this guy obviously had wherewithal of some form or another, I accepted his lunch invitation.

Unlike Fat Barry's pad, which resembled what I would imagine the United States Military Command Center at The Pentagon looked like, Hank Shuman had a beautifully decorated and laid out luxury home.

The first thing anybody would notice, however, was that in a space that normally would be used as a family room, Hank Shuman was sprawled out on his back atop what looked like a long-haired lambswool rug. He was dressed to go jogging in grey sweatpants and a white T shirt.

Hank was flat on his back looking straight up at the ceiling, where a gigantic television monitor was staring right back down at him.

Mrs. Shuman, whose first name was Alice, asked me to be seated on a white leather sofa adjacent to where Hank lay prostrate on the floor in front of me.

"Lunch will be served in a bit," she said. "Shrimp salad on challah ok for you?"

OK, so Hank and Alice appeared to be Jewish like me. All the shiksehs I knew would never refer to egg bread as challah. Unlike students that had attended Hamilton or Fairfax High Schools on the West Side of Los Angeles, being Jewish was not a given for a kid from University, which was closer to the Pacific Ocean and just south of the UCLA campus.

Hank muted the TV and began to speak.

"So Billy, about a year ago I threw my back out playing too much tennis," he began. "I suffered a couple of slipped discs. Rather than risk the debilitating post-operative issues of surgery, I am following the advice of an Asian doctor I met. He told me to lie on my back for between 6 months and a full year. Lie on a hard floor with no padding. This lambswool skin is my lone point of deviation from the plan. I use it not so much for cushioning but for its ability to filter the air and so I won't feel the coolness of the marble flooring or stick to it. Looks nutty and sounds even nuttier…I agree. But welcome to my life."

Hank said that when lunch was ready his wife would prop up his back so he could eat, but then he would have to resume lying flat on his back. He hoped this would not inconvenience me too much.

"Inconvenience me?" I thought to myself. Here is this poor bastard forced to lay flat on his back for up to a year and he is worried about inconveniencing me? This fellow struck me immediately as being a cut above the norm.

Hank told me that he had enjoyed considerable success in the business world, first as a broker, then as an investor for his own account. He had no clients, he refused to involve friends or family, because he wanted to take his shots without any worry about how his decisions might impact those for whom he cared.

Shuman said that, like me, he had been a longtime devotee of horse racing and playing the ponies. He described himself as a pretty big player. "Not in a league with Fat Barry," he assured me, "but in my prime I bet ten grand a day." However, Hank said in the last year he had toned down his gambling because he became convinced the game was no longer on the level, as too many key participants looked to be juicing their horses with PEDs.

"Six months ago, as a complete and total indulgence," he explained, "I asked my wife if I could spend a hundred grand for a short period of time to satisfy my theory that certain Southern California trainers were juicing. She is a wonderful gal, she knows how much this means to me and, frankly, she was sick and tired of hearing me complain about it. She told me to stop moaning and groaning and do something about it. She green-lighted my plan."

I thought to myself "Wow...this guy is a man of conviction and action." I was in awe of him and his tale.

Shuman did his due diligence, found an investigative journalist with ties to the intelligence community, hired him, educated him on what he might be looking for, and turned the guy loose.

After 6 months the investigator handed over his professionally generated report. Before Hank made his next move, which potentially might involve law enforcement or racing regulators, he wanted to share the report with me to make sure he was not barking up the wrong tree.

During lunch, my mind raced with the infinite possibilities

of what might be done with the gift I was about to be presented. I probably rushed through my meal because I felt like I had some challah crust stuck in my throat, so I calmed myself down and sat quietly for about 10 minutes.

Hank was eased down on his back again and ready to continue with his presentation. "As you can well understand," he began, "I don't want to let this potentially volatile report out of my possession.

"It is about 120 pages. You can read it here at your convenience, but I don't want you to take it off the premises. And no photographs either. Farshtaist?"

"Yes," I told him, "I understand. Unless you have anything else you want to tell me right now, if it is all right with you, I'd like to start reading the report as soon as possible."

Addressing his wife, who was tidying up the lunch plates in the kitchen down the hall, Hank said "Darling, was I right or was I right about this young man? He wants to start reading the report right now. Right now for goodness' sake. Show him into the lanai."

Alice Shuman motioned me with a finger to follow her. She took me to a large sunny room decorated in a Tiki Hut motif. There was a table already set up with the report, a pencil, a pen, an eraser, a notepad and a large glass, which Alice would fill with ice water and a slice of lime. It was quiet in the lanai except for the lapping sounds of the surf outside the door that led to the beach.

The report indeed provided a treasure trove of damning materials and a blueprint for law enforcement and racing authorities to catch, convict and imprison some prominent individuals in racing in the United States. Amazingly by dint of sheer will and creative thinking, Hank and his journalist pretty much got the goods on their subjects.

Because of a limited budget, the dynamic duo decided to focus on only a trio of local trainers, namely Russell Zane, Vinko Cindric and Paulie Diller. Initial surveillance convinced the investigator that all three of the trainers employed various forms of monkey business, but only two were likely using PEDs of one form or another that they had imported internationally.

Paulie Diller was not surveilled after the initial two months of the initiative, but the other two did have packages containing what was believed to be illicit materials delivered. The stuff was not delivered directly to them. Instead they were brought to assistants, owners or girlfriends to muddy the evidentiary trails of these mules and enablers.

The investigator regularly duked Federal Express drivers, taxi drivers, neighbors, deliverymen, private couriers, part-time teenage help, undocumented Mexicans, racetrack security staff, retired exercise riders and grooms…the list went on and on.

Illegal substances likely had been designed and made mostly in China, and sent either through Mexico or Canada, but some were likely made in Mexico or Canada. Most of the drugs took circuitous routes from where they emanated through foreign lands before reaching Southern California.

The journalist was able to produce video and photographic evidence exhibiting airbills, travel documents, courier receipts and the like. Unfortunately, although the actual drug materials had been photographed and filmed, none had been obtained.

Around 5:30 p.m. I had read or skimmed enough of the voluminous materials to learn what I thought I needed to know.

I went back into the family room. Hank had fallen asleep with the TV still on.

Alice came out of her room to raise an index finger to her lips as a sign for me to be quiet. I tiptoed out of the room towards the front door.

"Thanks for coming over and reading the report," she said. "He does this most afternoons around this time. Craps out right there in the middle of a race sometimes. It's probably from a lack of physical activity. He used to be very active before this back issue. Played tennis every day for hours. Used to play a lot with Murray, uh, what's his name…you know, the writer. Stronzo.

"You know Hank ran the 1320 at University. We both went to University. When you were such a revelation there, we both followed your career. So Hank has always had an interest in your goings on. I hope you two can put your heads together on this and come up with something."

I nodded my head and said I would await Hank's call at his convenience.

I stopped by Roberto's taco stand just up the road from the racetrack in Solana Beach. Back in my room I devoured a green chili pork burrito, a red burrito with refried beans and an order of taquitos with that string beef one only seemed to be able to get near the Mexican border anymore.

I found it amusing that the Shumans followed my track exploits, because it's not like I was a Mel Patton, the Uni High grad that became an Olympic Gold Medal-winning sprinter and was the first guy to run the 100 yard dash in 9.3, breaking Jesse Owen's world record.

Around 7:30 p.m. the phone rang. It was Hank. He asked

if I could return to his beach house for a quick recap. I drove over there immediately. Once again I found him on the floor atop his lambswool fleece.

"It's all very compelling," I answered when he asked what conclusions I had come to from reading the report. "However—not to put a damper on the awesome work your investigator generated—but, as the TV commercial asks—where's the beef? Without any evidence of the PEDs I don't see the FBI, the CIA, a district attorney or any gutless racing official picking up on this to carry it to the next level."

Rather than seeming to be put off by my critique, I was surprised to learn that Hank totally concurred with my thoughts.

"This is precisely why I wanted to bring you in on this Billy," Hank said. "You understand what I am after. You live this reality every day at the track. You see Russell Zane claiming a rat for $12,500 and winning classified allowances with it, claiming one for $35,000 and winning feature races, ekcetra, ekcetra, ekcetra, ad infinitum.

"Billy, I brought you in on this little exercise because, frankly, I think you can help me bring this thing home, bring it to fruition. You understand the dynamics, you know the players, you know the stable area, you have contacts in the backstretch community, you are infinitely familiar with the front side and the executive offices."

While Hank was brilliant, dedicated and energetic, he lacked the fundamental understanding of exactly how trainers cheat and what drugs could do to aid in their quest of gaming their honest rivals.

"Hank, basically cheating is engaged in to alter four aspects of performance," I started to explain.

"First there's pain management. Secondly there is physical enhancement. Then respiratory enhancement. Finally, there is delaying the onset of fatigue..

"OK, so pain management is simple. If an animal feels pain it protects itself and stops moving fast. Eliminating pain by using a drug is very possible. This is especially important with low-level claiming horses, as they usually hurt the most.

"As for physical enhancement, this is accomplished by using steroids, just like the East Germans and Russians have been doing with their track athletes for decades.

"The last two are the most important. Red blood cells bring oxygen to the lungs. Oxygen fuels a horse. If one can increase the number of red blood cells they can deliver more oxygen to the lungs, so that a horse will be able to run effectively for a longer period of time.

"Finally, lactic acid build up in the muscles slows a horse down in the stretch. If one can use a substance to buffer that lactic acid a horse can continue all the way to wire without tiring as badly."

I explained to Hank that scientists, racing officials and veterinarians know exactly what can be used to achieve improvement in all four areas. There are tests and rules outlawing the use of any number of pain killing drugs.

"Steroids are still in full use. They increase the size and density of muscles. This allows a horse to train harder than would otherwise be possible. Olympic sprinters have benefitted from illegal use of steroids.

"Blood enhancers are the new kid on the block. They have been designed to aid humans with cancer, blood disorders and circulatory conditions.

"Erythropoietin or EPO for short is a hormone produced by the kidneys to stimulate red blood cell production. EPO treats anemia, especially in kidney disease or cancer patients, by boosting red blood cell counts. It's powerful stuff and can transform a Division 3 cross country runner into a freaking Olympian.

"The dreaded lactic acid build up is most seen when an athlete or horse ties up late in a race. This acid can be neutralized by a simple solution of baking soda and sugar given a few hours before a race. It is delivered by a running the liquid through a tube inserted up the nose. It can delay the onset of fatigue.

"It is not legal, but many trainers seem to get away with using it. It's called milk-shaking. And there is talk about a paste that takes more time to become activated but eliminates the use of a tube, so it's more surreptitious and safer, as tubing an animal sometimes can nick the vocal cords causing a cyst that impairs a horse's wind.

"Now the trouble with each one of these performance enhancers is that science has devised synthetic variants that are hard to identify unless the manufacturers have developed a test for them. This is rarely the case lately because of costs.

"The one thing any regulatory lab vet will tell you is that unless they have a test, they are unable to identify what substances are used for cheating. Even using the most sophisticated modern-day microscopes, finding the properties of a drug without a test would be like looking for a star in the night sky. Impossible.

"So our task would be to find samples of drugs, get them to a lab that can break them down and devise a test to find them in the future.

"Track and Field, cycling and other sports have been waging

this battle for years. But the Germans, the Russians and lately the Chinese have been able to stay a step or two ahead of the regulators.

"Beating the bad guys has become hard because a shadow industry of rogue chemists that are always devising new and more powerful drugs has come into play. So just when one new PED is identified, another one already has found its way into the bloodstreams of athletes and horses."

Again, rather than act discouraged, Hank was already coming up with ideas on how to best come into possession of samples of the illicit drugs being used by at least two trainers in Southern California.

"Well, if we—that is either you or me—could convince somebody in authority with standing to help us, we could figure out when a drug delivery was going to happen, have the enforcement personnel at the ready and pounce on a package as it is being delivered. We need a law enforcer with an interest in racing that is impressed by the investigative report."

Then I piped up and said "I think I may be able to help with that. Give me a few days to work on it."

In the meantime, the next day being Friday, stakes nominations were due to be released after about 4 p.m. at the backside Racing Office, where trainers with horses pointing for the Bing Crosby Stakes were obliged to file their intent with Del Mar Thoroughbred Club's officials.

As it had been an action-packed couple of days, I fell asleep soon after my head hit the pillow. I wound up falling asleep with my clothes on except my shoes, which I must have kicked off at some point during the night. I never even heard Tad come in during the night.

CHAPTER 13

Grace and I spoke every evening, usually around 9:30 when her mother was safely off to slumberland. Tad was usually out at a late dinner or early bar-hopping tour. So it was perfect for both of us.

On the phone, at night, Grace was much quieter and more subdued, as if the energy in her battery had drained during the day. She was much more pleasant, not as acerbic and definitely not nearly as much of a wise acre. The wit apparently hit the old sack before she did.

During the few weeks between the races of Knight Errant, I learned a lot about Grace's background, as the conversations allowed me to fill in many of the missing blanks about her.

Her dad, apparently a world-class asshole, was Jewish. He blew off the mother and daughter shortly after they moved from New York to Beverly Hills, as he figured he needed an upgrade from the reserved, quiet Lutheran gal he had married.

Grace grew up in West Los Angeles, where after school she would start making dinner for her mother and herself, doing homework and tidying up the house. The routine wore on her to a point where her resentment for her father intensified all through high school and college. She had received a scholarship to Stanford but was unable to attend when her wealthy father refused to help her with room and board.

She went to high school in Beverly Hills, a community with a strong Jewish presence. Although she had friends, she took out her angst against her father by giving the Jewish boys a hard time.

Grace studied English literature at USC which she attended on a scholarship, continued to live on the other side of town with her mother, then upon graduating spent 2 years in New York, modeling for department stores and absorbing the Manhattan lifestyle. When her mother began developing medical issues, Grace returned to California to be a dutiful daughter.

Before her dad completely blew off the family, he did pay for lessons at an expensive riding school, where Grace found her love for horses. When she became involved in the Hunt scene, she found that most of the riders were mounted on warmbloods, quarter horses or mixed breeds. Thoroughbreds were shunned because they were considered too high-strung.

A friend gifted her with a Thoroughbred gelding that she still rides. It is because this ex-racehorse was so dear to her that she started following horse racing after riding him one day on the main track at Santa Anita as part of an amateur day of sport.

Named for Ichabod Crane's horse from the Washington Irving story *The Legend of Sleepy Hollow,* Gunpowder hit the Santa Anita main track running as his subconscious and muscle memory simultaneously kicked in. She admitted to being scared shitless but was also thrilled beyond belief and when she was able to gather him up down the backstretch and stay aloft all the way to the gap, she was greeted at that track entrance with a round of applause from the other riders on hand that had witnessed the wild event. Grace was officially hooked on Thoroughbreds from then on.

Sometime over the weekend before the Bing Crosby Grace told me that she would not be able to spend the entire weekend with me because Saturday was always the best day to sell clothing at her shop and she could not possibly leave her boss alone, as she was the only other worker.

"But I will be there on race day and can stay with you on Monday as well," she said. "If you want, I can drive down and we can be with each other on Saturday night. If that might interest you."

I scored a reservation for our own room at the Winners' Circle Lodge, which was completely sold out, except for one room an enterprising front desk clerk always kept aside because he knew he could get someone to duke him for late access to it. I slipped the guy fifty bucks to close the deal.

The next morning I awoke to find a note from Tad on the nightstand near the phone. He asked me to meet him at the barn.

Once again, Tad motioned for me to join him in the tack room in a closed-door session.

"I am hearing rumbles from the hinterlands about our Mexican jockey," he said. "A nigger in the woodpile tells me he is getting pressure from someone high up at Caliente."

First of all, I absolutely detest it when somebody, especially somebody with whom I have a working relationship, uses the "N" word. Keep in mind that the main reason I chose LACC to start my higher education was to be able to run track with

Black guys. But having lived in Kentucky, I realized that people my age used the "N" word as their default description because it had been uttered as a matter of course in their households. I met enough of these crackers that had no bone to pick with the Blacks and they were quality folks that meant no harm.

I had read a novel by John Knowles named "A Separate Peace" that taught me one could form a meaningful friendship or relationship with another that was grossly flawed by simply isolating that unacceptable aspect of the affected individual and focusing on the positive parts of the friend. This became very helpful as I traversed the tricky landscape of horse racing, which is peopled with a lot of poorly educated rednecks of one stripe or another that are always looking to scapegoat anybody available to blame for their own failings. So making a separate peace became a matter of survival for me in this atmosphere.

In horse racing if one wins one of 4 or 5 races they contest they are deemed to be a genius. So even the top horsemen routinely lose. This can be deflating, leading to depression as well as drink and drugs to ease having to deal with the daily grind. So scapegoating was part and parcel to this climate in which the "N" word was used.

Tad explained that his acquaintances had strongly hinted to him that our Caliente rider might be subject to pressure not to let our horse finish among the contenders.

"So, yeah, I am worried a little bit about that," he said. "Tomorrow being entries I am wondering if we want to make a change. What say you, Billy?"

I actually had thought about that myself earlier. "Without knowing the source or sources, I wouldn't have a clue if there was any validity to a tale like this," I said. "Also, and I've thought about this for a while now, this could be the work of agents for jockeys that want to ride Knight Errant. You know how dodgy and back-stabbing some of these guys can be. That guy Black Heart didn't warrant that name because he was a Boy Scout that helped little old ladies across the street."

Tad took in what I had said. I could see I had made my point. "Ah, shucks Billy, you are probably right," Tad said. "But I did have to relay the info. After all pal, you are the horse's owner.

"I will say this, though…and this is something that I have been ruminating over…at some point, if the gelding is what we think he is, it will behoove us to replace him with a top jock. That is only fair to the horse, to you, to me, to Doc and, in a way, to Bear Harwood. So think about who you might want to land on before we race him again, okay?"

Friday before Sunday's running of the Bing Crosby, entries were drawn for the 6-furlong race. Nine horses were entered. Knight Errant drew the number 6 stall in the starting gate. The Caliente jockey was named by Tad to ride again.

Standing in front of the backstretch Racing Office was Freddy Glickman from the *Form* and Guy Harlow from the Del Mar publicity department. When the Bing Crosby draw was completed, I turned around and started to walk back to the barn where Knight Errant was back in his stall.

Freddy caught up with me halfway back to the stable.

"Hey, Billy….Billy, hey, wait up wouldya," Freddy called out.

Unbeknownst to me I was once again assuming the role played out by countless horsemen when I had wanted to glean some information from them for my column or my advances.

Freddy wasn't a bad egg, so I slowed down until he caught up with me.

"What up Freddy, what it is?" I said to him, using a dialect my track team pals at college would immediately have recognized.

Freddy said "So can you give me anything for my advance that I might not already know?"

I thought about it and said "You can quote me as follows Freddy. You ready? Here it comes. Our camp is happy with the draw, as we like being more outside than inside. Our boy leaves the gate fast, so other than an inside draw he will always be ok with the draw.

"There are some tough older sprinters in the race with loads of experience. A few have been freshened since contesting the sprint stakes at Hollywood Park.

"It will be interesting to see what odds Bernie Bokun puts on him. I am guessing without even looking at the past performances that Knight Errant will come in somewhere between 8 and 12 to 1.

"I make him 4 to 1 based on what I have seen from him and what I think he is capable of.

"How's that? Good enough for you Freddy?"

Freddy was relieved that I didn't jerk his chain as I most always did. After he stopped writing down what I had told him, he looked up and asked "Billy, just between us…and I swear I will not tell a soul…how good do you think this horse really is and should I make a bet on him?"

As Freddy was tight with a buck, was married with a kid and did not earn much at *DRF,* he was not in the habit of asking interviewees about betting information. But we were both writers, so he felt he could ask for the tout without embarrassing himself. And I believed him that he would tell nobody else. He had witnessed firsthand what happens when you do or do not share betting information in the press box. And at Del Mar it seemed worse because there were more characters that could be a total pain in the ass at Del Mar than either Hollywood Park or Santa Anita.

"Freddy bet your money," I said to him in low tones.

Then he said "Billy, are you betting him?"

I thought about it and suddenly realized that I had not made a single wager at the track on a horse since I cashed on our "Big Horse."

"Freddy, here is something I hadn't realized until you just asked if I was going to bet. I have not bet a horse since Knight Errant broke his maiden. Haven't even thought about it. This is a first for me. But, truthfully, I have been so busy with a variety of things that betting a horse had not even crossed my mind. This would be like a smoker telling you he hadn't lit up a cigarette in a couple of weeks. Hard to fucking believe ain't it pal?"

I sensed Freddy believed it when I told him to bet, but that he was highly skeptical about my not having bet another race the past 3 weeks, which probably made him suspect of my tout. But that was his problem to work out, not mine.

The Del Mar publicity writer never looked for me. He did not contact me at the hotel. He never talked to or contacted Tad Smithwick. When the *Form* came out, the in-house Bing Crosby advance contained one sentence about Knight Errant. That was it.

The selectors at *DRF* did not include Knight Errant from their 1-2-3 picks, the Graded Handicap had him at 12 to 1 and Bernie Bokun told a friend of mine that he would put him at 6 to 1.

Bernie Bokun was a true piece of work. If he were an animal he would have been a hog, because he attacked his free press box food like he was hitting a trough. And his thick mustache bristles glistened with grease and gravy. He was built like one of those weightlifters you would see in the Olympics representing a Balkan nation. He had thick heavy arms, covered densely in dark curly hair. I used to fantasize that if Bernie tapped out one day, he could sell those mustache hairs to an artist for use on a specialty paint brush.

When he spoke, Bernie lisped a bit and wound up spewing spit when he emphasized a particular point he wanted to make. It was challenging having any sort of verbal interaction with him.

Bokun was a sick, totally addicted gambler. But he was a dynamo when it came to churning out his graded handicaps for a dozen Southern California newspapers and doing the morning line for Del Mar.

Truth be told Bokun would have done the line without pay, because he manipulated his prediction of the day's probable betting line to get the best odds possible for his own personal bets.

When my friend told me that Bernie had put Knight Errant at what we both recognized as artificially low odds, I said "He's at it again. Everybody knows that double those odds are truer to the mark than his absurd odds," I said.

"So, as per usual, Bokun wants 12 to 1 or better. He knows that if he plays it straight and puts the horse at 12 to 1, any betting that brings down the price will be perceived as strength and he will likely only get 8 or 6 to 1. So he is using a bit of reverse psychology here. Another guy paid to serve the public using his position to screw rubes to feather his own nest.

"Bokun has him at 6 to 1, knows it is too low, and that when the gelding drifts to 9 or 10 to 1 nobody will realize what has occurred. And he will have a better chance to get his 12 to 1 than if he had played it straight."

I did not return to the barn, instead I found Maria Sanchez, the wife of a groom that every morning brought a tin containing tacos and burritos she made at home. Few on the backstretch trusted the ingredient list of either the tacos or the burritos, and referred to them as kitten tacos, suggesting that Maria was stuffing feline meat instead of beef or pork between her steamed corn tortillas or inside her big flour tortillas. I bought four tacos and two burritos and brought them back with me to the hotel.

In the lobby of the so-called "Losers Circle Hotel" I bumped into Alphonso Jenkins, who as it turned out had been lying in wait for me to arrive. I can never remember how or when I first met this Black dude, but he had been around ever since I first started working in the game.

Ostensibly Alphonso was employed on the night shift of the *Los Angeles Mirror* as a copyreader. When he managed to get any sleep I would never know, because when his shift ended, we would all see him at the track every day.

Because this gambler was such a likeable fellow, he was able to score a spot on the *Mirror's* horse racing page that featured any number of handicappers' selections. He had ingratiated himself to the sports editor, who let him put up one selection per day. Alphonso chose the handle "Man in the Mirror" under which he "released" his vaunted singleton pick.

Alphonso earned everlasting fame on the Southern California racing circuit when he was the lone public handicapper to tout Destroyer before he won the 1974 Santa Anita Derby at odds of 44 to 1.

On those rare occasions when a horse he selected won a race, Alphonso would magically appear as if rising from a sarcophagus. He could be seen slowly marching up and down the length of the press box, both arms stretched out in front of him like a zombie and chanting in a deliberate sing-song manner "Hey now, who had dat winnuh, who had that winnuh, who, I say who *had* dat winnuh...winnuh winnuh chicken dinnuh... oh, yeah dasssss right...I say, who *had* dat winnuh."

So Alphonso came up to me, gave me a high five, a low five, a normal handshake and a special homie handshake he reserved for his friends that consisted of a regular handshake, followed by grabbing of the thumb and then tamping above and below a clenched fist.

"Hey, yo, Billy...Billy, Billy, Billeeeeee...Billy Boy. What it be?" Then he leads me behind the bar where it is quiet and private.

"Kuh Night...Kuh Night...EEEE Ront...yeah, what you think about yo boy here using this geegee as my longshot for Sunday? Has it got any chance...ehhh nnny chance whatsoever?"

I started laughing and had trouble stopping. "Alphonso when did you ever need information for one of your crazy-ass picks my man. I thought for sure you just pulled them off the wall or straight out of your big booh-tay."

Then he started laughing. "Yeah, you know me all too well Mr. Billy. But I ain't picked an actual winner in so long I really needs one to keep my credick-ability intact. So what you say Big Boy...Knight Errant? Got a winning chance?"

When we both stopped laughing I said "Look, here's the

deal. I really don't know. We are taking a shot. You know that. And as far as how good he is and if he even belongs in this company. Well, the bottom line is nobody knows. Take your best holt my man and for both of our sake let's hope he runs a blinder."

Chapter 14

Before Grace's car arrived in the Winners' Circle Lodge's back parking lot I started to get that tingly sensation under my tongue that I used to experience before a track meet. I was excited to see her.

It was after 10 p. m., her eyes looked tired from the 2-hour drive and work week, but her smile was as wide and bright as ever, as she tried to put her best face forward.

Rather than engage in a long, deep kiss one might have expected from her after a physical absence of a couple of weeks, she lightly brushed my lips with hers, reached down to pick up her suitcase and walked toward the hotel entrance.

I had already moved some things over to our new room and Grace put her stuff away once inside the room. Then, with her back towards the king size bed, she spread her arms out fully to the sides like wings and allowed the weight of her body to tip her backwards onto the mattress, sighing on the way down with an extended and breathy "Ahhhhh." A king-sized bed, she noted. "Luxury. Wonderful!"

Rather than luxuriate in that position alone for a while, she quickly popped up and was once again fully wide awake with her normal energy accentuated by her bright, dancing eyes. She quickly undressed. She wore no panties under her leather slacks. She must have rushed to get on the road to Del Mar for her to have gone commando like that.

We made love twice before falling asleep.

She proved to be a brilliant distraction, as I had not thought about Knight Errant running in the Bing Crosby Stakes until I had awakened in the morning. We lay there in bed, in each other's arms, saying nothing…not even good morning…for some minutes.

"Where'd you learn so much about sex Billy?" she began. "You're not that old, you don't strike me as being a horn dog, yet you are quite a skilled lover. How'd that happen?"

Actually, I was thinking the same about her in terms of being such a skilled lover, but unlike me, she gave me the impression from the first time I saw her that she was a young lady that had been to more than a few parties.

"I lived with a girl for nearly a year that basically taught me most of what I know about sex," I told her. "She herself had not been that great at the enterprise until she met a horse trainer from the Midwest who she claimed was the greatest lover of all time. He taught her, she taught me.

"I thought I had gotten pretty good at it. She was an exercise rider. Used to get up at 4 in the morning. She wanted sex before heading out to the track. She wanted it when she came back to our apartment after breakfast. And she wanted it before we went to sleep at night.

"If, God forbid, I missed one of the three daily sessions, she took that as a sign that I had fallen out of love for her.

"One evening, after what I considered to be my best

performance with her, I dared to ask if I was as good as her mentor. She didn't answer for a while, then sweetly caressed my head in both of her hands, as if I were a child, and said that while I had come a long, long way, that neither I nor anybody else could ever expect to match Lover Boy. It was pretty deflating I've got to tell you.

"I wound up losing more than 15 pounds during my time with her and was back weighing what I did the day I graduated high school. I was in great shape. I even thought about starting to high jump again."

She cast a skeptical pair of eyes at me as I explained to her about my journey toward becoming proficient in the sack.

"Well, why are you not with her anymore if she was that hot in bed?" Grace asked.

I explained that the exercise rider decided to quit the track and pursue a career as a NASCAR driver. She actually wanted to be a jockey, but she enjoyed food too much and was unable to make riding weight. Race car driving, she said, was the only other sport she had found that provided her with the same thrills and feeling of speed she got from riding horses.

I turned the tables on her, asking how she learned so much about love making.

"Somewhat similar," she said. "I had a mentor, but it wasn't a lover of mine and it wasn't a male. It was a young woman I shared a flat with for a while in New York. She had learned everything she knew while working in Japan as a hostess and part-time sort of Geisha girl in one of those dodgy clubs where sexy young women hold out the promise of a liaison as a means of getting customers to buy one expensive bottle of champagne after another.

"While employed there, she was taught the ancient art of love making as practiced by some of the girls. When not hawking champagne bottles she freelanced on the side to earn more money as a high-class hooker. Back in New York she was taught about love making by an Englishman that had spent many years in India.

"For about 5 months she showed me the book of Kama Sutra, explaining things about sex and regaling me with some of her wildest encounters. The relationship came to a screeching halt one night when she went after me in my bed right when I was about to fall sleep. She turned out to be bi and had been grooming me for all those months. I never saw the signs until it was too late."

Grace then got out of bed, stood naked before a long mirror, checking herself out from one angle after another. She was quite thin for sure, but she looked fit. Her stomach was flat, her arms were beyond toned, exhibiting strength from horseback riding.

She had the legs of a rider. The thighs were ample and her calves tapered. Seen from the front and back, the calves were somewhat bowed.

It only struck me then that she had the same shaped limbs as a ballet dancer. When I was a junior in high school, I was one of a few boys that took ballet lessons for a while, as the best high school jumper in the nation had revealed that ballet was one of his secrets to success.

Ballet dancers, because of their extensive and intense work at the barre, developed those same calves as riders, whose limbs become a bit distorted because of how they are positioned on a horse.

"You've got the legs of a ballet dancer," I told her.

She turned toward me, parted the hair that hung down over her eyes so that she could see me better and said "Really…a ballet dancer? How so?"

I explained my theory to her.

"Nobody had ever mentioned this to me before, nor have I ever heard it explained this way," she said. "Makes sense I suppose. Makes me feel good, as I *am* a bit self-conscious about being bow-legged someday like those cowboys that walk like they are balancing a turd between their thighs when they walk.

"Now I can think of myself as a ballet dancer. Much preferable than an old cow poke don't you think?"

I said "What I think is that we should take a quick shower, beat it over to Fidele's for some breakfast and visit Knight Errant at the stable."

When we walked outside the room, coming toward me was Esther, carrying a small bouquet of flowers. When we made eye contact, she casually repositioned the flowers behind her back, was obviously flustered and tried to put on a happy face upon seeing me.

It was still fairly early in the morning, an odd time for an unscheduled visit, but there you have it.

I introduced Esther to Grace. The mutual stares were chilling. Esther's eyes began to well up with tears. She suddenly threw the flowers at my feet, then shouted "So this is why I haven't seen you for so long. You've got someone else. You don't need me anymore, is that it?"

Then she marched off in the opposite direction, back toward the lobby, before stopping and yelling out at the top of her lungs "Is she spreading her legs for you Billy…is that it? You complete piece of shit you."

She started marching off again, only to stop, turn around once again and scream "And I hope that piece of shit horse of yours runs dead fucking last today you asshole."

Grace turned to me with her widest-eyed look and said "So, *not* a fan?"

Just then the door of Murray Stronzo's room opened and the *Atlantic Monthly* writer stepped out partially into the hallway with a bleary-eyed expression.

"Billy can you kindly consider stacking your poontang in a more sensible manner? In the past you've always been so good about doing this with your secret pussy. Get back to that wouldya?" He then went back into his room and gently closed the door.

Grace and I burst out laughing as we walked down the hall, went into the parking lot, got in my car and drove a few minutes away from Del Mar racetrack to Fidele's Mexican restaurant for breakfast.

Near what should have been close to the end of the meal none other than Arturo Fugazi sat down at our table right next to Grace. A bear of a man with the athletic body of a onetime athlete, Art put his arm around Grace and, wearing a smile that promised to adorn his fat face all through the night, said "You know how long I've known your boyfriend here? I was clocking his action since he started out in track at junior high school when he could not have been more than 11 or 12."

If Grace was taken aback by Fugazi's overwhelming personality or familiarity it did not show. That, I soon learned, was part of what she gained from living in New York. Nothing ever seemed to faze the young lady.

"So how long have you two been going together?" Art said. "Does your family love her as much as you do Billy?"

Grace and I both laughed a lot while Art was going through his over-the-top shtick.

"Art, we only just recently met, we are not boyfriend and girlfriend, Grace is a racing fan and rides to the hounds, and my family has no clue, nor would they likely approve of anybody I hung out with that was involved in horse racing---let alone a girl—because they think our pastime is made up of nothing but degenerate gamblers and people that shun their families and keep them broke because of their constant addiction to betting. Answer your questions Art?"

Most folks given that barrage would have been at the very least somewhat taken aback, but not The Fugazi.

Art then switched seats to take the chair next to me. He did not make the move to get a better look at Grace, but to be able to whisper in my ear, as he sought information about Knight Errant and his chances later that day in the Bing Crosby.

Grace leaned forward to better hear the soft-spoken words.

"So, Billy, my boy," he said softly. Then he turned to Grace, returning to his booming voice. "You know how hard I tried to recruit this kid to come over and let me coach him at Pierce College instead of running and jumping for that right-wing A-hole, excuse the language, at LACC? I had him all set up."

Then returning to the sotto voice again, Art whispered "Like I say Billy, so today, you know what I mean...today, can I bet? Can I bet with confidence? Of course whatever you tell me I would never pass on to anybody, least of all my crazy-ass cronies. You know you can trust me Billy."

If anybody possessed a larger megaphone or pipeline to those involved or on the fringes of horse racing that was not a member of the media I never met the individual.

Art himself never wagered that much, because as a community college track coach his salary was low. In fact, to make ends meet, fund an apartment every summer at the beach and dine out most nights at the Italian restaurant of his choice, Art had set up a scam that allowed athletes with poor grades or insufficient class credits to gain college units toward either graduation, eligibility or scholarships by signing up for classes that did not exist. He was able to earn a nice buck from both the athletes or their coaches or future coaches until a rival coach outed him. Amazingly he was allowed to maintain his position at Pierce.

"Coach you crack me up," I began. "You keeping some gossip or betting information under your hat? That's a joke if I ever heard one. C'mon, get real here."

Art nodded his head up and down in a knowing gesture. "Yeah, of course you know me," he said in what probably was his most normal voice, before slipping into a new tone, one that exuded false sincerity to a near perfect degree. "But I'd sure love to cash a nice bet down here this weekend to beef up my bankroll Billy. I know that if you knew something and felt strongly about it, you would do the right thing and tell your old Coach Fugazi, right? That is right, isn't it Billy. Billy Boy?"

Grace waited exhibiting considerable interest in hearing how I would answer the plea.

I did enjoy and like Coach Fugazi. To remain friendly with him, though, I had to use my separate peace technique to set aside his criminal behavior when he gamed the entire collegiate eligibility system. So, I actually tried to give him a sincere response, without really telling him what I thought about Knight Errant's chance later in the day.

"Coach—look—you above almost anybody else I know should be able to fully understand what I am about to tell you," I said, keeping my voice at a low range. "Imagine you have a kid. He didn't come out for the track team until he was 22 years old, never ran track in high school and was only a bit of a legend in the Watts area for what he had shown in gym class or on weekends when kids got together on their high school tracks.

"So you train him, he shows uncommon speed in wind sprints, you enter him in the first meet of the winter in a hundred-yard dash against a weak out-of-town school, he freaks, wins by 7 yards, runs in 9.8.

"You are so enamored of his native talent that you decide to bring him along with your team to the Santa Barbara Relays and put him in the open hundred there. The field includes a few seasoned guys that have run 9.5 and 9.6 and done it against NCAA finalists.

"So the morning of the meet at Balboa Stadium I see you dining with your wife and sit down with you. I ask you the very same things you have asked me. What's your answer gonna be Coach. What's it gonna be?"

He listened to me without showing much expression on his face. I could tell that I was making some key points.

After about a minute of thinking about it, Fugazi rose from his chair, shook my hand with a rugged grasp, leaned over to pat Grace gently on a cheek twice, winked at me, and started to walk off. He turned, smiled, and said "Billy, I get it. I do get it. Good luck son."

Knight Errant was at the front of his stall when Grace and I arrived at the barn. Tad was not there. The groom was seated on a bucket in front of the stall reading the *Form*.

"Eas all goo, eas belly goo," he said. "You want see him aqui?"

I said no and told him that I would see him in the paddock later.

Back in the room, as Grace and I sat on separate chairs looking at the *Form*, she turned to me and said "You were very patient with Mr. Fugazi. That was very kind of you."

I said "Yeah, well, when I like somebody and I've known them since I was a kid, I tend to cut them plenty of slack. Coach is a racetracker through and through. He's owned a few in his day, so he knows the ropes. But the lure of betting a winner never leaves and I understand that as well as any, believe me."

Then Grace, given the opening by me, said "How much are you going to bet on Knight Errant today Billy?"

I surprised the young lady when I told her that I had not really thought about it at all. Which was true. But now that I did, I figured that if he was 6 to 1 or more, I would have a dabble. But with all the wise-guy money out there fueled by private clocker reports I told Grace I could see him being hammered down to 4 to 1 or even less, despite all of the weekend money being bet by unknowledgeable rubes.

Then she asked me what I expected to see that afternoon.

"Grace, strictly between us girls, I expect to see something I've rarely if ever witnessed," I answered. "None of us—meaning me, my trainer Tad Smithwick, my vet Dr. Jim Church, our riders and our jockey—has ever been close to a horse this talented. So I could see anything...*anything* happening."

Her mouth was parted as she took in this information.

"I cannot wait," she said. "This is so, so exciting!"

Chapter 15

Around 11 o'clock on race day of the Bing Crosby I received a call from Tad Smithwick, requesting that I drop over to our joint room for a strategy session.

I sat in one of the two chairs in our room, while Tad stood the entire time. He was quite animated during this strategy session, as he wanted to emphasize some of his key ideas.

"Billy, you've been around long enough and talked to enough people to have heard a trainer say that one of his horses acts like it's been here before. Ring a bell?"

I told him that I had heard it a couple of times and understood it to mean that the horse acted like it had more experience than it should have given its relatively short time in training.

"Yes...precisely...that's it in a nutshell," Tad said pointing an index finger in the air to bring home the point.

"Now, I think that this expression has been used to death by some guys that heard it, liked the way it sounded and put it in their repertoire for clients and the press.

"My dad has been around as long as any horseman alive and been deeply involved with some of the greatest of his or our time. He knew Louis Feustel, the gentleman who trained Man o' War. That's how far back he goes.

"Well, according to him, he said the first guy that ever used that line about a horse acting like he'd been here before came out of the mouth of George Conway, specifically when telling a friend that his unraced 2-year-old, a colt by Man o' War named War Admiral, was so fast and wise as a juvenile, that everything seemed to come so easily to the colt, that he acted as though he had been here before."

Tad paced the floor of our small room, gathering his thoughts to drive home his final point, then said "I don't want to sound foolish and I know you will get what I am about to say because you are the one that found Knight Errant for chrissakes, but this horse really strikes me as having been here before.

"So, what does this mean for today's race…that's the question? If in fact, either literally—oh my God I cannot even believe I am saying this out loud—or figuratively this gelding of ours has been here before or acts like it, he probably knows more than either of us how he wants to be ridden.

"We have a young rider that has lots of wins to his credit, but he's never ridden a good horse, or a potentially great one like Knight Errant. So I would like to place my faith in the strategy for today's race in the lap of our horse and not our jockey."

He took a deep breath, not for dramatic impact, but because he had been talking so fast he was out of breath. "So, here's my plan," he said "I think we tell the jock to be a passenger. Don't say a word other than that. Let the horse run his own race and just sit on him until he feels he needs to be ridden, if in fact that even comes into play.

"I would let the horse completely dictate where he wants to be during the race and when he wants to make his move. What say you?"

It was a brilliant spiel, one that Tad obviously had been thinking about deeply for a while. I liked it and I told him so.

We shook hands and told each other that we would see each other in the paddock.

When I returned to the temporary weekend room, I found Grace putting the finishing touches on her lipstick. She had already dressed for the track. She looked smart in a tailored peach colored linen suit that accentuated her usual tanned skin and reddish-brown hair.

"So, what's the plan, man?" she asked.

I told her that while I was looking forward to the race as much as any other I had ever been involved in either as an athlete or a reporter, I dreaded having to spend the hours leading up to the race in a fishbowl. I was so tired of the chore of having to deal with everybody in my circle and on the fringes of it that I needed a break.

"What would you say about driving down to Coronado Island and having lunch at the Del?" I asked. "Ever been there?"

She had not, obviously had known all about it from the movie "Some Like It Hot" and relished the idea of seeing it.

"But what is it with you Billy?" she said with a genuine look of puzzlement on her face. "Who in your position would not want to be the cynosure of all eyes at the track on a day when everybody had your name on the tips of their tongue?"

I tried to explain that I love the horses and the game, but not the attention it brings with either having a good horse or when my picture used to run alongside my *DRF* column.

"When I used to go racing, other than some friends I made there, nobody knew who I was. I could walk around anywhere at the track, listen in on conversations, have lunch, bet and, simply put, 'be a fly on a wall.' By nature I am a writer and an observer. I prefer to be anonymous."

I could tell that while she was very interested in seeing the Del, she was disappointed not to be able to parade around at my side as my plus-one on a big race day when a horse I was associated with was the talk of the town. She liked the attention, I did not.

Post time at Del Mar was always 2 p. m., a civilized hour that allowed beach goers, brunch lovers and margarita imbibers plenty of time to wend their way to the track. The feature race was always run about 5:30 or so in the afternoon. This gave us plenty of time to drive the half-hour down to the Del, have a leisurely lunch in the restaurant and get back in time to walk into the paddock.

I still had my press parking pass for the meet and the attendant was a pal that would always find a spot for me, so there was no anxiety about getting to where we had to be on time.

Although I had managed to provide the best possible diversion from having to think about all the possibilities of the day's race, all through lunch and walking around the fabulous Del my mind raced with thoughts of what might occur at Del Mar around 5:30 p. m.

After we perused a collection of memorabilia from the estate of L. Frank Baum, who was described as a "frequent guest of the Del, where he wrote at least three books of his series about *The Wizard of Oz*," I admitted to Grace that I wanted to get to the track as soon as possible.

Normally on a race day, as a reporter but more importantly as a gambler, I needed to see an entire day's card unfold to get a line on how the track was playing. Was it favoring speed, or stalkers or closers? Stuff like that. But on this day this information was not relevant, as our strategy had already been decided. Our jockey, in essence, was none other than Knight Errant himself.

I escorted Grace through the paddock and into the area behind it that was enclosed and served as the first stop for horses when they arrived before being saddled and walked around the ring.

We were both impressed with the coat condition and suppleness exhibited by Knight Errant, even indoors.

When the horses were walked outside to enter the stalls where they would be saddled under the iconic ivy-covered overhang, Grace studied the head of my horse quite intently. Grace was a true animal person, whether it came to dogs, cats or horses. She never planned to marry or have children. So animals got the love she normally would have reserved for people.

"Your horse has a most interesting eye Billy," she said, drawing out the word interesting and pronouncing it "inn-tressting." She explained that it had the same sweetness and kindness of a dog at her riding stable named Buddy.

"You cannot help but fall in love with a horse whose eye is so expressive. In my limited experience this is an eye that speaks to generosity. It is the kind of eye that in the Hunt field promises that a horse will give you everything he's got despite the peril of the ground and fences. The eye of a dedicated hound that will never give up the chase no matter what obstacles might get in its way.

"I expect this is one very big indication of why Knight

Errant is such a wonderful prospect and may explain why so many insiders are high on him."

Seemed a bit esoteric to me, but I deferred to her judgment on a matter that frankly was beyond my understanding. As far as I was concerned Knight Errant was what he was because of his easy way of going, his sheer athleticism when in full flight and his purple-blooded lineage.

Instead of going into his stall, watching him get saddled and talking to the trainer like a lot of owners do, I stayed in the center of the walking ring with Grace. Nobody came up to chat with us, which was fine with me. Everybody was intent on focusing on their own horses.

Then Murray Frigging Stronzo tapped me on the shoulder blade while simultaneously saying "Big day for Billy Boy. Big day." I did not even turn around so as not to encourage him to begin a conversation. Out of sheer courtesy I introduced him to Grace. I did not even look at him as he chatted her up. I was watching Tad straighten out and smooth the saddle cloth after one final tightening of the girth strap.

Knight Errant's coat glistened in the late afternoon beach-town sunlight. He looked to be in magnificent condition.

"Murray, I've got to talk to my trainer now," I said to him.

He said "So what, is that my hint to move off?"

I curtly replied "You got it."

He hung around for a bit, then moved back a step or two. When I turned to him with a look of exasperation, he finally moved away. "Sick bastard," I thought. All he wanted was to be part of something potentially exciting in which he had no standing. Wanted to play the part of a guy in the know, when he was not nor ever would be.

Smartly dressed as usual for the races, Tad came up to us. I introduced Grace to him. "Very good to meet you Grace," he said. "For some reason I feel like I've met you before, maybe at night at a bar. I meet so many people that in my alcohol infused state I rarely remember them. Sorry if we've met and I forgot."

Grace assured Tad that this was, in fact, their first meeting.

"Billy, we're all set, we're all good," Tad said. "I've got Charlie Wacker's box for us to watch the race. He's not here. Take these two ducats and I'll meet you up there."

Tad gave the Caliente jockey a leg up and accompanied them around the ring once just behind the groom.

I held Grace back from leaving the walking ring until all the horses and people had cleared out, to further avoid being harassed by anybody hoping to elicit betting information from me. We had an easy passage to the box, which was right on the finish line, high up enough for a good panoramic view, but low enough to see the horses well.

Once again I had forgotten about betting. A quick glance at the tote board showed, amazingly enough, that Knight Errant had been bet down to 3 to 1 and was the second favorite to track-record-holder The Blizzard at 6 to 5.

Grace said "Mind if I place a bet?"

It was 3 minutes to post time.

"Hurry up if you do. Big crowd today," I said.

Grace disappeared and when she came back the horses were starting to load. I said "how much did you wager?"

"Actually the lines were too long, so I just skipped it and came back so I wouldn't miss the race," she reported.

Tad used his long field glasses. I had inadvertently left mine back in the room.

When Knight Errant's odds dropped to 5 to 2 Tad, moving his binoculars to look at the tote board, wise cracked "I see you bet your money Billy."

Knight Errant walked in the gate like a champ, no hesitation whatsoever, which I always consider to be a good sign.

Like a big cat going after its prey, Knight Errant sprung from the gate on top and immediately was nearly a full length up on his opposition, which was made up of the fastest horses on the grounds.

Quintana, riding to exact instructions, sat high up in the saddle, gradually leveling off so his shoulders and butt were on the same plane. Knight Errant, like an adult playing with children, eased himself back, let most of the field pass him and wound up just past mid-pack.

Ding-donging up front two horses set what looked like a wickedly fast pace, which was confirmed by a glance at the tote board that read :21 2/5. At that point of the race Knight Errant was 5 lengths back in fifth, with clear sailing outside and off the rail.

Around the turn the two leaders kept up their tempo admirably until they reached the quarter pole, when race caller Harry Henson said the half was reached in a speedy :44 2/5. A :23-second middle split was fast, but it should have meant that both leaders could still have something left for the drive to the wire.

Knight Errant, still being allowed to race on a loose rein, had inched to within 3 ½ lengths of the dueling leaders. He took himself wide around the stretch bend and positioned himself in the middle of the track for his expected challenge.

The Blizzard had wrested command and was in front by himself as he hit the furlong pole in 56 seconds flat. Knight

Errant, still content to track, moved into third, but still had 3 ½ lengths to make up.

Then it happened. He did something sprinters are not supposed to do. He both quickened and lengthened his stride. Most horses can either quicken or lengthen their stride, but not both. When it is seen, it is usually on the turf, hardly ever on the dirt. Only a horse like Secretariat was capable of that.

The barely perceptible increase in quickness and power propelled Knight Errant down the center of the track at what can only be termed a phenomenal turn of foot. He managed to erase the deficit in a matter of a sixteenth of a mile. Once in front by half a length at the 110-yard marker he never let up, scooting in electrifying fashion to win clear by nearly 3 lengths.

So taken aback was I by the brilliance of the move, that despite Grace screaming at the top of her lungs into my ear and Tad pounding me on the shoulder, I never felt the urge to cheer, as I looked on dumbfounded by what I had just witnessed. I felt a sense of being shocked rather than excited.

What the fuck, I thought to myself, had I just seen?

Walking down the stairs to the ground level toward the winners' circle I was vaguely aware of racegoers slapping me on the back, trying to shake my hands, yelling my name and people flashing winning tickets in my face.

Grace led the way to the winners' circle.

"You had to bet so much Billy? Couldn't you leave some crumbs on the table for the rest of us you greedy bastard?" Coach Fugazi blurted out at me as I entered the winners' circle. I looked back at him and he was grinning like a fool. He was happy.

When the horse returned for the photo next to Tad, me,

Grace and the groom, he amazingly did not look to be all that tired. But that softened look in his eye was gone, replaced by ones that radiated with what in that late-day sunlight can only be described as fire.

I thought to myself that the blood of the mighty Bold Ruler had kicked in big time. Only the ancestry of the horse could possibly begin to explain where that effort emanated from.

When I finally came out of my stupor, the first thing I said to Tad was "can you believe what we just witnessed? Can you fucking believe it and can you believe that he is our horse?"

I was born into a Jewish household. We were never religious like our grandparents. My father became an atheist because of what he had experienced as a bomber pilot during World War II. He forced me to have a Bar Mitzvah to honor his mother. But there was nothing spiritual in our upbringing.

However, as I stood there in the winners' circle after the Bing Crosby I started to wonder if for some reason I had gotten it all wrong, that maybe there actually might be a deity of some sort, because nothing in my experience could possibly explain why a young guy like me, with a trainer more interested in improving his golf swing than getting up early to condition horses and a jockey that barely spoke a word of English from the wrong side of the border would wind up with an animal like Knight Errant.

Freddy Glickman was milling around on the edge of the enclosure, as was the Del Mar publicity director, but they went to Tad for the post-race interview. I was no longer one of their peers, or even friends, now that I was involved in a Big Horse.

I steered Grace back towards the paddock, underneath the receiving barn, out the back exit and towards the parking lot, leaving behind a post-race toast from the higher-ups of the Del Mar Turf Club in their Directors' Room.

I felt that I needed some time to process what in the hell had just happened.

I knew that I was spoiling Grace's fun, but I felt strongly about getting the heck off the grounds, going back to our room and analyzing what I had just seen with my own disbelieving two eyes.

Final time for the 6 furlongs of 1:06 4/5 shaved three-fifths of a second off the previous track record, which runner-up The Blizzard had most likely equaled on the day.

The Blizzard ran a blinder, as they say, performing too well to get beat and losing his track record in the bargain.

A quick calculation told me that Knight Errant ran the opposite fractions of a normal sprint race in the United States. He actually ran faster at the end than in the beginning. His fractions were reversed. This had long been considered impossible.

It happens all the time abroad, where sprint races lack pace and upside-down fractions—or negative splits—are commonplace. He came home his final split, his last quarter-mile in an unheard of :21 4/5. Even more amazing was the final furlong that I worked out to be 10 2/5 seconds.

We had a world beater on our hands. We had, as The Rabbi would say, a real "ferdle."

Chapter 16

Doc Church had decided to return home to Bradbury and watch the race on TV. He came back to Del Mar the next afternoon, took some post-race bloods and couriered them to the lab.

When I saw him at the barn he asked me to visit him before lunch at his beach rental. He seemed more serious, less jovial than usual. Something seemed to be on his mind.

When he let me in the front door of his small house, I saw Tad sitting on a chair. He also was preoccupied with something. I was starting to get the feeling I had been invited to an intervention. And, as it turned out, I was not entirely wrong.

First Doc gave a brief summary of the physical condition of Knight Errant, the state of his tests and what the immediate future held for the gelding. All was in line in terms of the blood and metabolic readings. That was good news.

Then Doc said that he had not totally thought through what might happen if the horse turned out to be as good as he was and what the unintended consequences might be from his fiddling with his metabolism.

"What I've done, first in being able to identify the horse's issue, then figuring out how to address it and finally treating the horse, all fall within legal and ethical parameters.

"But you guys both know what this game is like when somebody is doing too well...they look for an explanation. When a horse does what our boy did on Sunday, this scrutiny only heightens. Sure as shit right now somebody suspects the horse might be getting juiced and they are going to start asking questions and looking carefully at our every move.

"You guys have not been involved in any problem solving, only me. And, as I say, I am confident that I am standing on solid ground. But, because this sucker looks for all outward appearances to be the Second Coming, I have to admit that the potential scrutiny and questioning is something I would not be comfortable with.

"So we need to be careful in what we say, in our movements in an around the horse and who we share information with, if anyone. This horse will never fail a drug test, because what he is given and what it produces are part of the horse's normal biology. It is produced by the system of the horse. We are not drugging or juicing him. And the benefits of his treatment are not in any way enhancing what a normal, healthy horse produces. It is merely correcting a deficiency and allowing him to compete on a level that biologically is as normal as any other horse out there.

"So—bottom line—I will be as circumspect as possible, I will watch my movements around the barn, I will not share my actions or thoughts with any colleagues and I suggest that you guys follow my lead."

I deeply appreciated both what Doc had been able to accomplish with the horse and his candor and trust.

But that chat was not really why Doc invited me to his beach house, or why Tad was present.

Doc began his spiel. "Billy, you know who is the most excited about the horse? Bear. Bear Harwood. That race has re-ignited his passion for racing to a degree that I never would have believed. He sounded like a kid when we spoke this morning.

"Billy…Bear is so thankful for you taking the initiative to put the horse back in training, elevating the immediate family of the mare and placing the focus of the entire racing community on the family's Ellerslie Stud."

I smiled and took it all in. Bear Harwood was a giant, towering over the entirety of the Bluegrass. For him to be grateful to a speck on the wall like me was gratifying beyond belief. This being especially so because I was without a job. Thanks to Knight Errant money was not an immediate issue for me for the first time since I left home at 18.

Doc was only getting warmed up. "Billy…Billy, Bear is so pumped, so psyched, so jazzed he wants me to ask you, as a favor to him and his family, if you would allow the name of Ellerslie Stud to be listed along with yours as a co-owner of Knight Errant." He stared right into my eyes when he uttered that last part, not to intimidate me, but to drive home the importance of the request.

"Well, huh…that is something isn't it…that is interesting," I said, fumbling for words as I tried to process the impact of such a request.

I had to admit having the brand of Ellerslie Stud next to little old insignificant me, Billy Richards, was ego massaging for sure. But a competing thought quickly emerged, which was that in a game dominated by the super wealthy and powerful, it looked as though I was possibly being taken advantage of and being moved aside by a big shot.

Doc spoke after a bit. "So what say you Billy? Good with that? It's a great opportunity."

I was trying to figure out how being asked to share the spotlight and potentially being marginalized by the most powerful industry player in Kentucky was going to morph into a great opportunity for me.

"Doc, I really need to think about this," I said slowly. "After all, you just sprung this on me. I need to think it over."

Tad then chimed in. "Think about it? Really. You need to think about having the name of Ellerslie Stud—the preeminent breeding outfit in the entire country—next to yours?" Tad said. "You've got to be kidding. There are millionaires, titans of industry and members of the President's Cabinet that would be bending over forwards and backwards for an opportunity like this."

I got the bending over backwards part of the equation, but frankly I started to wonder more about the bending over forwards, because the big shots in racing and breeding have a long history of taking over everything once they become involved.

This was a huge dilemma for me, as I was just starting out in the game as an owner and being associated with Bear and Ellerslie could make any career I chose to follow. On the flip side of the coin, my involvement and my name could soon be winnowed down to nothing more than a footnote in history.

Doc said "Yes, take your time Billy, there's no rush. But if you agree it would be prudent to make a change to the ownership line with the racing officials well in advance of the gelding's next race. So think about it, but don't drag your feet on it."

Tad said "Doc, don't worry about it…I know Billy's too smart not to snap up this opportunity. I am sure we…I mean you will be hearing back from him real soon on this subject."

Doc said "Billy, just spit-balling here, but if it would sway you I'll bet I could get Bear to let you keep the purse from the Bing Crosby. You do recall that the bonus clause in your purchase agreement calls for him to receive 100 percent of the net purse from the first Graded stakes win."

On the drive back to the Winners' Circle Lodge I remembered that my dentist used to buy a reject at the end of each racing season for a pittance from Calumet Farm in Lexington, Kentucky. His trainer used to gallop horses for Ben A. and his son Jimmy Jones who trained Citation for Calumet. If one of them came good like Knight Errant, would one expect the owners of Calumet to ask if their names could be returned to the ownership line? I seriously doubt it. A deal is a deal, after all, and if it had not been for my enterprising moves the gelding would still be loping along the trails of Bradbury under a stock saddle.

When I got back to my hotel room I had a message from Fat Barry that he wanted me to drop by for lunch at his fabulous beach house. When I arrived a Latina welcomed me at the door and led me to a round room that was set up like a war room at the Pentagon.

Shockingly Fat Barry, seated on a large cane-back chair with wheels that allowed him maneuverability, wore only shorts and flip flops. No shirt. A man of perhaps 50 years of age, the handle Fat only began to describe him. Without any real frame of reference, I am guessing the guy weighed around 650 pounds. He literally had bags of fat hanging from his sides just under his arm pits. It was a disturbing sight to say the least.

However, thanks to Barry's outsized personality and infectious way of speaking, I soon was focused strictly on what he had to say and not his overwhelming adipose tissue. Man, each bag of fat was the size of a child. Grossed me out!

Ringed around the round room designed by Barry were 8 TV monitors. They were all on and, at various points from morning until night, they would be tuned to sporting events on which bets could be placed legally or illegally through bookmakers or employees at the track.

Barry was nationally renowned as a baseball expert and gambler. Apparently he was one of the first to realize the tremendous advantage Major League Baseball pitchers enjoyed when throwing at home. Winning these bets formed the base of his fortune. He also bet heavily on racing. Football completed Barry's preferred menu of contests on which he placed bets.

Sitting on his very mobile chair, Barry would maneuver between all the sets as he followed the action in a non-stop fashion. One wondered when and how he found time to eat and maintain his weight, so to speak.

"Kid, I gotta congratulate you on that Knight Errant," he said, as the Latina entered the space with a pair of mobile trays on which the lunch spread was carted over to Barry and me. Barry grabbed what looked like a tuna on rye. His was a quadruple decker, mine a normal two slices of bread.

"That was some performance. Never seen anything remotely like it. I don't know exactly how you were able to pry away such a steed from Bear Harwood, but more power to you young man. More power to you."

After polishing off three sandwiches and not wiping the crumbs off his chest or around his mouth, Fat Barry said "I'd like to buy the horse from you. Of course, there is a limit to how much somebody can give for a gelding of his age. He must have issues otherwise why would he not have raced until past the middle of his 4-year-old season? But I can pay you cash. Cash that you can hide. Now that you have no job, the cash can keep you in clover for quite a spell, unless you gamble it all away unproductively. But I can help you there."

Fat Barry was trying to reason with me. He was no dummy. As a junior at Hamilton High School in Los Angeles he got a part-time job after school working for an illegal bookie. Barry spent afternoons in a single room apartment that included a folding card table, a folding metal chair, a phone on an end table and a refrigerator.

The table had a glass top on which at the start of each afternoon Barry would spread a thin layer of Bon Ami, covering the glass with a pink liquid that when dry would allow him to scratch in all the bets he would receive on the phone. At the right corner of the table was a bowl of water with a sponge to wash away any evidence of illegal gambling should the cops arrive to bust the operation.

After doing this for a year or so, Barry realized that he did not need his boss, as he knew all the customers and figured he could cut the vigorish they had been paying and set up shop for himself.

So Barry moved out of his parents' house upon graduating high school, rented his own apartment under a fictitious name, managed to get a phone number through help of one of his new customers and he was in business.

So much dough did Barry make that within a few years he had managed to pay cash for a home in Beverly Hills. One day when an IRS agent arrived to ask exactly where he had obtained funds to purchase such a tidy home at such an early age, Barry came clean.

Barry paid his back taxes, opened up a couple of clothing shops that catered to big guys similar to himself, and promised the authorities he would clean up his act.

When the Pick 6 came into being in Southern California and offered multimillion-dollar payouts on days when a carry-over occurred, Fat Barry came up with the idea of having a trio of employees circulate around the track, seeking out horseplayers with live tickets. He started buying these if he liked the remaining horses on the tickets in the later races on the card. Fat Barry hit so many of these multi-million-dollar Pick 6s that by and by he was able to buy the beach house and start his very own racing stable.

That Fat Barry would land on Knight Errant as one to acquire for his Big Bad Barry Stable was not surprising, as few knew the game better than him.

"Barry, I am flattered that a guy as astute as you would want to buy my horse," I said, with as much sincerity as I was able to muster while still eating my tuna sandwich and trying not to stare at the man's outsized body, "but the truth of the matter is he cannot be bought. He is not for sale."

Barry laughed out loud, some food dribbling out of the sides of his mouth. "Billy, you are young but believe me when I tell you that unless you are the Queen of England, everything is for sale," he said. "That is the given. The only question is price. So I can give you a hundred grand in cold hard cash. In round numbers that's 8 times what he earned on Sunday. A hundred grand. Handled correctly you won't have to work, if ever, for a long, long time."

I tried to explain that money was not a consideration. Of course I could not share the exact details, but eventually I convinced him that my hands were tied and no sale was possible.

"Aha, I get it now…you are fronting for someone or some entity that wants to remain anonymous. I get that," he said. "I knew when I saw your name on the ownership line that there was no way in hell that a guy like you could possibly be the real owner. Ok, but Billy please promise me that if things change that you will give me first crack at him. He is a marquee horse and these are very fucking hard to grab onto in this game."

I knew what a seasoned racetracker and horseplayer like him had uppermost in mind. How good would Knight Errant be if there was a switch in trainer and jockey. Let's face it, Tad Smithwick and Rafael Quintana were not exactly names on the tip of the tongues of owners looking to scale the heights in horse racing.

Back in the room I got a call from Grace, which was unusual for the time of day, as she should have been at work in the dress shop on Melrose.

"Just checking in pal," she said in as cheery a tone as possible. "Everything good with you? How's the horse today?"

I told her that all was fine, that I had been busy with a couple of meetings already during the morning and at lunch. I said the horse was fine. I still felt bad for whisking her away from all the post-race hoopla, which I knew she would have reveled in as a co-center of attention with me. But she took it in stride, which was a relief.

She asked "so what's next for the Big Horse?"

I told her that neither Doc, Tad nor I had even broached the subject yet, which surprised her. "I would have thought this would have been the first topic of discussion this morning," she said. "Huh. Shows what I know, right?"

I told her that I had to go because Tad and I had a late tee time to play the back 9 at Torrey Pines. But she wanted to keep on chatting. "I suppose you've got some offers to buy the horse, huh?" she said.

So I vaguely told her about one offer. I did not disclose which party had made it, nor the amount of the offer. She sounded interested in learning more, but I pressed to get to the golf course.

"OK, but please keep me posted on any sale gossip or news," she said. "I find this aspect of the game to be utterly fascinating."

During our golf game, Tad never brought up Bear Harwood again. But he did engage me in conversation about Grace.

"I remember where I saw her before," he said. "Of course, one has to consider that I was in an alcohol-infused fog at the time, but it was at the Brigadoon Bar up the road on the Coast Highway. She was there with a much older guy. You will undoubtedly know him…Chester Sherwood…you know the big-time downtown L. A. lawyer that's on the board of the Autumn Racing Association.

"I eventually remembered because it struck me as out of place for a guy his age…he's got to be what, early 70s…playing kissy poo with a girl in her 20s."

Sherwood was a distinguished looking elder statesman of the Turf, well connected, suave, wealthy and owner of an increasingly prominent racing stable he formed with 3 of his pals.

Chapter 17

I am the kind of guy that when something important needs to be decided or resolved, I want to work it out sooner rather than later and I tend to jump right on it.

So the day after Doc Church and Tad Smithwick tag teamed me about sharing my name on the ownership line in the racing program and *Daily Racing Form* past performances with Bear Harwood's Ellerslie Stud, I decided to drive up to L. A. to seek the counsel of the one adult I knew that I thought might be able to provide me with the advice I was looking for.

My dad died when I was 18 and he would not have been able to help me anyway because he despised horse racing. I had a wealthy uncle that started his own extraordinarily successful business during World War II, but I did not see him understanding my dilemma either, as he was pro-Establishment all the way down the line.

After going over everybody I could think of that might be able to help me make a sound judgment that could impact my career in racing and conceivably the rest of my life, I kept returning to my old buddy Steve Prince's dad Hugh.

Hugh was in his late 50s. He had lived in the same house

half a block down the street from Rancho Park Golf Course for more than 30 years. He obviously was a very steady fellow. His wife had died when his son Steve was a teenager. After Steve moved out to join the professional golf tour, Hugh stayed on in the house.

The father was a hero of mine because he was the only adult I had ever met that followed his dreams, stood up for himself when challenged, took shit from nobody---and I mean *nobody*—and he treated Steve and all of Steve's friends like they were pals of his. He was the coolest adult I had ever met.

Hugh had his life down to the essentials, he mastered every aspect of his existence that was important to him and he seemed to enjoy everything he did. Hugh wrote the half-hour TV situation comedy "Hobson's Choice," for which he had written the pilot and was the comedy show's sole writer.

The show was about a doctor and his take on life in dealing with his own family and the lives of his patients from his own unique perspective. The main movement in the script came from soliloquies in which the lead character would look directly into the camera and give his take on a situation. Viewers simply could not get enough of it because the lead character had such a simple yet unique take on life. In fact, every time the doctor opened his yap, what came out was pure Hugh.

Hugh was tangentially involved with some of the writers that had been blacklisted in Hollywood during the McCarthy era. Hugh was in no way either a Communist or a Socialist, but some of those that were or might have been were his close peers in scriptwriting for the movies.

When he was interviewed and investigated, Hugh never flinched, never got flustered and perfectly stonewalled those looking for dirt or actionable deeds that might land him in trouble. As I said before, Hugh never took shit from anybody.

Hugh once told me that he knew from an early age that he wanted to write, that he wanted to play golf and he wanted to work on whatever car he had at the time. "Golf and working on my car give me time to think about my next script," he once told me. So, Hugh golfed, worked on his VW beetle (which he told us had a motor design that was as simple as a washing machine), wrote scripts and cooked his own meals. That was his entire life.

When Hugh was ordered by the Navy to be stationed in Jacksonville, Florida, he had such a cushy assignment that he was able to play 18 holes of golf everyday...sometimes 36. So he became quite proficient spanking that white ball around with his sticks (as he called them).

The home he bought was a one-minute walk to Rancho, which although a public course was home for decades to the Los Angeles Open. When Hugh's son and I were in high school, the father, his son and I would slip onto the golf course after the last foursome had teed off to play 18 holes. We never had to pay and we got in a good dozen holes before night set in. In the summer we sneaked on the course at first light and began at hole 11 so as not to get in the way of those playing the back 9. So we would get in 7 holes for free. Hugh was very good, his son was great and I was just so-so. But we had a great time.

Sometimes after dinner we would visit a neighbor's house and shoot pool. They had a snooker table. Hugh had been stationed for more than a year in England, where he learned to play the game and he taught Steve and me the ropes and we enjoyed the heck out it.

Before I got involved in horse racing, I had always thought

about having the same exact lifestyle as Hugh. He was my role model.

So I phoned Hugh and asked if I could take him to lunch as I had something important going on in my life that I wanted to talk with him about.

Sitting in a corner booth at Biff's Café on Pico Boulevard half a block in from Westwood Boulevard, I explained in excruciating detail exactly what my dilemma was, fleshing out the characters that were involved, what their roles were in the industry, where the power rested, what being in league with a big shot like Bear might mean for me, etc.

I must have done a very thorough job of it because Hugh grasped the salient points, the conflicts, the upside, the potential downside and why I was torn between sticking up for myself or caving into pressure.

"Billy my suggestion is that you consider the big picture but focus on the smaller present issue. Yes, of course your career path is important, but more important is making the best decision on the day, not down the road. Don't get bogged down worrying about how it will impact the long run, try to think about today," Hugh said.

"I have known you for more than half of your life Billy, so I think I have a pretty good grasp of how your mind works, what is important to you, how you relate to people and what might be suitable for you down the road.

"And, without any ego on my part, I think I know why you chose me to counsel you on this problem. You may or may not be a lot like me, but you would like to. I get that. But we are all different Billy. This is your issue, not mine, however I want to help you reason it out.

"So, first, a couple of inevitable long-term questions: any idea yet where you might want to be in 10 or 15 years in terms of your career?"

Well, I had been thinking along these same lines, running different scenarios through my mind, trying to figure out where in the hell I fit in out there. I had not been able to form an answer.

I explained this to Hugh, who nodded his head as though he completely understood. "Your young still Billy," said Hugh. "I am 56 and I am still young in my thoughts, so I get it.

"Let me ask you this," Hugh said. "Do you see anybody in the racing game whose lifestyle you would want to emulate?"

I told Hugh that the man I had admired most so far was my old editor at the *Thoroughbred Record* magazine. He was a man of great integrity, wit, humor, he stood up for himself, but because he had to answer to a board of directors he was frustrated and began drinking too much.

"One thing I have learned lately," I told Hugh, "was that I preferred playing the racing game rather than writing about it."

"Well, let's draw a line though working for a magazine as a staff writer then," Hugh said. "Anybody else? A trainer, a bloodstock agent?"

I told Hugh that I did not grow up with horses, even though I loved to watch them move and made my grandparents drive me out to farms on the weekends so I could watch them in the fields and whinny to them. I did not think I was qualified to train horses.

As for being a bloodstock agent, my old magazine editor once wrote a story that compared agents with child molesters and posed the question in print "which one was worse?" Too many bloodstock agents have bad reputations and generally are held in low regard by other players in the industry.

Hugh said "So what about being part of management at the track or in a racing organization?"

He knew pretty much what my answer was going to be, but for the sake of thoroughness, he probably felt that he had to ask.

"No. Neither would be a good fit for me," I said. "I don't fit into the corporate mold or structure because I cannot survive mentally as a 'yes man' or tool. And as for an organization in racing, too many politically motivated decisions are made about the lives of its employees and constituents that hurt them. As far as I can see they are no different than federal, state or municipal politics. Again, not for me."

Hugh said "This is good for you to verbalize right now so that when you get down to the nitty gritty you can make an informed decision. Billy, I think you are ready to make that decision right now.

"The decision on the table today is not what exact position within your industry you might wind up in, but how what you decide with Mr. Harwood impacts your immediate future.

"I am positive, having seen you in action all these years, that like me you have a problem with authority. Not everyday garden variety authority, but the type that is troublesome, unfair or not on the level.

"I am like that as well. Look at me, though—I work in a collaborative form of entertainment peopled by some of the biggest assholes in the history of show business. But I made sure that I had an iron-clad form of independence that shields me from having to deal with putzes like producers or studio heads or major network bigwigs.

"Billy, I don't see you ever working for anybody but yourself. Exactly what form this takes is unknown by either of us at this time. More importantly, with regard to Mr. Harwood, I think you don't want to have to give up your sole ownership of your horse, am I right?"

I told him he was right.

"OK then, for a moment, just imagine how you are going to feel about yourself if you cave in," Hugh said. "You are going to feel played, you are going to feel emasculated, and you are going to be disappointed in yourself for giving in. Am I right?"

I told him he was right.

Hugh then said "And if you cave in are any of those involved going to have respect for you going forward?"

I said "probably not."

Hugh said "I can guarantee you they won't. Once they break you pal, you are done. You will resemble a shriveled-up balloon the day after somebody let all the air out of it.

"However, while the players involved might temporarily be pissed off if you stand your ground, in the long haul they *will* respect you. And, in real life, they will admire you because they know damn well that they would have caved."

I sat there for a few minutes, not talking any more, just thinking. Hugh had helped me. I guess I always knew the answer, but I needed him to help bring it forth in me. He did not tell me what to do, he elicited the answer from me.

After I thanked him profusely, he smiled and said "Got your sticks in the car? Wanna play a little golf?"

"Actually Hugh, I am going out with a young lady and I am anxious to see her, so I better get moving," I said.

I dropped Hugh back at his house and drove East toward

the dress shop on Melrose where Grace worked. I decided to surprise Grace and just pop in the shop.

She was with a customer, espied me out of the corner of her eyes, at which point a small smile appeared in the corners of her lips. But she never lost focus on selling a tight-fitting skirt to a young customer.

"This skirt fits you perfectly and accentuates your figure beautifully. Boys will not be able to keep their eyes off of your ass, believe me. Want me to ring it up?" Grace said walking to the cash register.

The customer retreated to the changing room to take off the garment. When she closed the curtain behind her, Grace motioned for me to move toward her. She kissed me hard and fast, moaning a little as her tongue sought out mine.

"You rascal, why didn't you tell me you were coming up here? Wanted to surprise me? Couldn't stay away, right?" she teased. "So what's up?"

I told her we could catch up at dinner. She said she would have to check in with her mother before committing. "It's 3 right now. Call me at the shop...here's the number," she said handing me a business card. "Call me just before 5, okay Billy?"

I guess that was pretty presumptuous of me to assume that she would be available and I felt like a jerk. But when I phoned her at 5 she asked where we could meet for dinner and when.

"If you get cracking we can just about find something at the Farmers' Market before they start shutting down," I proposed. The Farmers' Market is a world-famous L. A. tourist attraction a mile south of Fairfax High School, so a drive of less than 8 minutes from Graces' shop.

While most people were starting to leave the property and

some vendors had already started putting away their wares, Grace and I were able to get what we wanted. She went for the New Orleans fare and I stuck with a favorite Chinese stand.

Nobody was seated near where we landed with our trays, so I was able to speak freely.

"I am going to stay at my place in Arcadia, kind of a trek for you," I said, getting right down to brass tacks. "I'd like to spend the night with you. I wouldn't ask you to drive all the way out there, but we can get a room near where you live if that interests you."

It was immediately apparent she was game. She said that when we were finished eating, she would go home, check in on her mother, then meet me at the hotel of my choice. She would bring an overnight kit and head to work the next day straight from the hotel.

Flush in my bank account and my wallet from my gambles, I felt I could splurge on a nice room, so I booked us at the Bel Air Hotel, which I figured would impress Grace. It did. She always tried to embrace luxury and this picturesque celebrity enclave nestled in a prime residential area of Bel Air was romantic and high end.

We made love before falling asleep and when we awakened. Before showering we just stayed in bed for a while and talked. Grace and I both were relaxed, off the muscle and subdued.

"Billy, have you received any feelers about selling Knight Errant?" she asked. It was not the voice of a nagging wife hungry for a sale to bolster the family's finances, but more like one of genuine curiosity.

I reiterated that I had the one solid offer.

"Well, would you be interested in selling if the right one came along?" she asked.

I explained that I was unable to sell because my hands were tied by a deal I had struck with Bear Harwood, the master of Ellerslie Stud.

"Even if it turned out to be a lot of money?" she asked.

I told her it was an impossibility.

"What if, for example, someone or some group came out of the blue and proposed a partnership. Would that work?"

I thought I could close the subject by turning toward her, looking her directly in the eyes, and saying "Grace, honeybunch, I don't know how many ways I can say this before you believe me, but there are absolutely no circumstances under which a sale of all or any part of Knight Errant can be accomplished."

She fell into silence. After a couple of minutes she asked "So, have you decided yet where you might race the horse next? I am curious because of scheduling, as I want to make sure I can be there."

Once again I told Grace that it was too early to think about the next race for the horse. There were just too many variables.

"Well, taking into consideration these multitude of variables," she said in sort of a mocking, smart-ass tone of voice, "would you imagine that, for instance, the horse might run again before the end of the meeting? Or would you wait for the fall meet at Santa Anita?"

I liked that I had a relationship with a young woman that was so into horse racing and especially my horse, but the line of questioning—coming so early in the morning—was becoming more than a bit tedious.

"Don't know, don't want to think about it, just want to get ready and have breakfast," I said, terminating the conversation. Unfortunately it would not be the last of these chats in the same vein.

CHAPTER 18

Back at Del Mar when Doc Church, Tad Smithwick and I were in the same place at the same time, the vet invited us to a small outdoor barbecue at his house, where we could talk candidly about future plans for the gelding.

Before any talk about the future, I bluntly stated that I had decided to pass on the opportunity to share the ownership line with Bear Harwood. "Maybe I am cutting my own throat for my future in the game," I said. "But I basically have always been a loner who followed his own path and if I entered into this new arrangement with Ellerslie Stud I know that I would not be happy."

Both acted like they were fully expecting a revelation like this. Doc said that while he would have readily accepted the overture from the master of Ellerslie Stud, he understood that I had to be true to myself. Tad could only shake his head and mutter under his breath "Jews, Jews, Jews…what is one to make of them?" Then aloud he said "I thought Jews were supposed to have superior intellect and business acumen. Well, shows what I know. Maybe you are God's chosen people, but you chose wrong this time buddy boy. Moving right along."

I said "Look, you two have a long-standing relationship with Bear. You work for him for chrissake. Of course you feel as you do and I understand where you are coming from.

"But, as close as you are to Bear and as talented and smart as you are, if not for my initiative none of what we are now experiencing would have taken place.

"So in this instance, I hope that you two gentiles take a moment to reflect on the fact that without this here Yiddle, we would not have the opportunity to work with an animal like Knight Errant."

They both nodded in the affirmative during this little outburst that was delivered with as little emotion as I could muster.

"We are a fine team and none of us could have gotten to where we are now on our own," I said as sincerely as I could. "We each have a role to play and so far we are a cinch to receive Academy Award nominations at the very least. And on one final note, I for one would like to say that it is an honor just to be nominated."

Doc and Tad laughed. The air had been cleared. Now we were able to move forward.

Then we talked about Knight Errant's future.

Tad made the first offering, which was to inform us that the gelding had exited his Bing Crosby win in excellent shape.

Doc confirmed that the bloods all came back in good order, pointing out that there were no red flags in his chemistry.

Then I said "As far as the next start, I would be for skipping the rest of the Del Mar meeting. I would get the horse back to Santa Anita so he could refamiliarize himself with the surface and get him away from all of the hullabaloo down here in crazy town.

"How many accidents do we have to witness at this stand to realize how fraught with danger the place is. You have exercise riders out all hours of the night, coming to work either with a lack of sleep or still hung over. There are too fucking many gaps to the track. Under ideal circumstance this poses a constant danger, but when you add in the late hours and booze it makes for an accident waiting to happen."

Doc did not have all that much business at Del Mar, so he embraced the idea.

Tad said "Personally I like it down here because it gives me a chance to see my friends and meet new people. And I don't have to stay at home with a wife that clocks my every move. But, hey, it's your horse, I want to be a team player, so yeah we can blow town I guess."

I asked the other two if we should sprint the gelding again or try to stretch him out. I said I had no feeling either way, but that the next logical step was a race going 7 furlongs around one turn if we could find one.

Tad said "I have been waiting a while to bring this up, but I have been thinking about this deeply. This horse is by Bold Ruler out of a sister to Round Table. Just because he can sprint doesn't necessarily mean he is only a sprinter. It tells me this sucker has such a high degree of talent that he sprints without having the pedigree to do so.

"Nobody seeing him for the first time is going to say he is built like a fast horse or a sprinter. He has the look of a middle-distance horse. He broke the track record in a sprint only because he is a total fucking freak.

"The more we sprint him the greater the chances he will start to show stress from running so fast and we are apt to lose him. Sprints take more out of a horse than route races and they place more stress on the horse.

"So if I owned him I would prepare him to stretch out. When and where exactly we do that I have not investigated, but in my mind he should be prepared to run long in his next start."

Doc listened intently to Tad, then said "There is no right or wrong direction with a one-off animal like ours. All racing and training boils down to trial and error. We all know that. But now the ante has been upped because the horse is, as you say, a freak.

"From a veterinary perspective, given the gelding's issues, stretching him out sooner rather than later I feel is a positive step in the right direction, because anything that will cause added stress to Knight Errant should be avoided, as his metabolic issues worsen with racetrack related stress. So stretching him out is an idea I like."

My turn to chime in. "I too have been thinking about the future, but I have been trying to avoid it for fear of us making a mistake. Whatever we decide to do is going to be scrutinized, criticized and debated by everybody in the game from coast to coast.

"One thought that keeps popping up in my brain is the Big 'Cap," I offered. Before that comment both Doc and Tad had been looking away from me, but when the words Big 'Cap were uttered, both of their heads jerked sharply towards me. "I know that's a mile and a quarter against some of the best animals in the country.

"But the timing seems right, as we could get at least 3 route races into him before the race in March. He could stretch out once at the fall meeting, then have two preps at the main meeting next season.

"And Tad, as you say, he is bred for the trip more than he is for what he has been asked to do so far."

Doc said "In principle what you say sounds good out loud and probably on paper. And we would have more than enough time to set the schedules both in terms of medicine and training for the gelding.

"But let me just point out two important potential hurdles I see standing in our way. I would be lying if I told you that I am not worried about what I have been doing to correct this horse's metabolic deficits in terms of having my methods scrutinized. As I've told you two fellas from the outset, nothing untoward has been done.

"However, in using experimental treatments that have been developed for humans, I am operating in uncharted waters. Friends of mine in human medicine have stuck their necks out to help me. The last thing I need is for them to be exposed or to get in trouble.

"Right now we have won a maiden race and a sprint stakes. Once we go hunting for bear, so to speak, and start knocking heads with the big boys, their connections—and I mean both trainers and owners—are going to start zeroing in on what we have accomplished. They will start asking a lot of questions. Rumors will start flying. State racing officials could start poking their noses into our affairs.

"So I am not advocating keeping a lower profile and staying in less publicly watched races, but before we dip a toe in the big lake we should know what we are potentially letting ourselves in for. The big boys don't like to lose. They spend the most money and they expect to win. And anything that gets in their way is going to sound alarm bells."

Back up in Arcadia, where Knight Errant once again was stabled at Santa Anita Park and in full training less than a mile from my cottage on Huntington Drive, I received a call out of the blue from of all people Chester Sherwood.

I knew Sherwood from my writing jobs in racing because he was a partner in a high-profile racing stable with a few friends and he was a big shot in the organization that presented racing in the fall at Santa Anita. He was a well-known corporate lawyer in the top oldline firm in downtown Los Angeles.

"Billy my friend, how are you, like I need to ask?" he bellowed. "You're the talk of the town aren't you? I just want you to know that I for one couldn't possibly be happier for your instant success. We all know that there is no such thing as instant success. Whatever you are now starting to achieve is the result of a lot of hard work. Congratulations to you."

Man, that mouthpiece had some line of chatter. I was sure that if I never responded or said a single word, that Sherwood would have upheld my end of the conversation just to keep the ball rolling.

I thanked him.

"Billy, can you have lunch with me tomorrow?" he asked.

Not knowing what on earth he could possibly want to chat about, I said I could, and he invited me to meet him at the Jonathan Club on the beach in Santa Monica. The Jonathan Club is a famous hub where Los Angeles' most influential WASPS conduct power meetings and historically, at one point in time, had been infamous for excluding Jewish members.

Dressed in attire that would have been suitable for an

owner in a big race, I duly arrived at valet parking and, after checking in at the front desk, was escorted to a table for two where Chester Sherwood had been seated. He took off his pair of half-reader glasses, stood up to greet me with his big smile and shook my hand firmly.

"Billy, so good to see you fella," he said warmly. He invited me to sit down. I fully admit to having had more than a slight case of the "willies." Coming from a Jewish middle-class family and not having spent much time at private or country clubs, I was on guard. It did not take much time for me to notice that the only people of color on the premises were the Black service staff. That did little to lessen my willies.

After chatting about mostly inconsequential stuff, Sherwood got down to business. "William, sir, the reason I have asked you here today is to explore what can be done to allow my friends and I in our Classic Racing Stable to be part of your magnificent animal going forward. We would like to buy in and race Knight Errant in partnership with you.

"We of course would be even more interested in buying the entire animal, however, I would imagine after what he exhibited last weekend this might prove to be infinitely more difficult."

So, once again, I was forced to inform someone that Knight Errant could not be bought. And, once again, I explained that money could not change the situation.

"Billy, as you undoubtedly know, I am a lawyer,' he began, "and not just any lawyer. I deal with the most prominent investors, old money, movers and shakers in all of California. Our firm controls much of the old wealth in and around Los Angeles and we are politically entrenched to an unnerving degree.

"So what I have to offer you is not just cash...which would not be an insignificant amount...but entre to some of the most powerful brokers in business and politics in our region. The doors that we could open for you are wide and deep.

"As you may or may not know, two of our stable's partners are members of The Jockey Club and I am on the board of directors of the Thoroughbred Owners and Breeders Association as well as the Thoroughbred Racing Association—both national outfits. Should you someday aspire to membership in The Jockey Club or think you have written something that deserves an Eclipse Award, we are not beyond helping you achieve these goals."

Jesus H. Christ these guys really wanted a piece of Knight Errant badly to make these sorts of overtures, I thought to myself.

"Mr. Sherwood...Chester, if I may call you that..." I began. "You have no idea on earth how flattered I am to hear all of this, but my hands are tied and I am unable to deal on any part of Knight Errant. You, sir, are not the first, nor I suspect will you be the last, to enquire about the availability of the horse, either all or part. And because of an arrangement I have with the gentleman from whom I acquired the horse, nothing can be altered in this agreement.

"Now I know from having dealt with a few lawyers in my time that every attorney feels he is capable of working out a deal and clearing away any barriers that might stand in the way of doing a deal, but this one is different."

Sherwood listened, not moving his head or changing the direction of his eyes. His mouth was slightly ajar, as he was apparently in disbelief about the message I delivered to him.

At some point in time, I forget exactly when, he said "Okay, I get it. No soap then Billy, right? Hey, at least do you want to hear the figure we have in mind?"

I told him that I really did not need to hear it, but he felt that he really should finish his offer, so he said "two hundred and twenty-five thousand dollars."

He was right, that was some kind of offer. A record for a 4-year-old gelding I would have imagined.

"Wow, you were not kidding, that is a whole lot of money, the type of money to change the direction of my life," I said. "If a miracle occurs and I somehow find a way to do it, I will definitely get back to you."

Once Sherwood realized that he was getting nowhere with me, he switched gears to discuss plans for the horse to find out at the very least if there was any chance the gelding would be gracing any card presented at his race meet at Santa Anita in the fall.

"Can I at least return to my partners with some good news that Knight Errant will run in a big race at our meeting?" he asked.

Sherwood was very happy to learn that the horse would indeed stretch out in his next start in a big dirt race around two turns at his meeting. I made him promise not to breathe a word of it to anybody until after the Del Mar meeting was over early in September, so as not to ruffle any feathers among those horsemen in charge of conducting that summer meeting, as they had been very accommodating to Tad, me and Doc. He shook hands on it.

Since it was kind of a drawn-out lunch and I was not back in my car until half past 2, I decided not to buck the traffic back to Arcadia. So I pulled over to use a phone in a booth and called Grace.

I told her that I was on the West Side of town and wondered if she wanted to catch a bite of dinner. "You're having difficulty eating dinner without me these days, huh?" she said. "Yes, I can do that, but afterwards I have to get back to my house."

We met at El Coyote, the Mexican restaurant on Beverly Boulevard, just a few blocks south of Grace's dress shop on Melrose. We shared a large guacamole. I ordered tacos with string beef and she ordered enchiladas with chili verde sauce. Crunching sounds made by chewing the thick house-made tortilla chips filled the dead air between us. I could sense something was amiss.

"So what's new on the Knight Errant front Billy?" she said, breaking the silence. "Any decisions on any front?"

Her interest in the short strokes about the horse was starting to feel out of place. Suddenly I flashed on what Tad had told me about her playing kissy face with Chester Sherwood and suddenly her game became quite apparent. And, as I thought about her, it dawned upon me for the first time that her timing in engaging me at the Del Mar backstretch kitchen a day after the gelding's maiden win was nothing if not suspicious.

"Why ask me? Why not ask your friend Chester Sherwood?" I answered.

The color drained from her face. "Busted!" I thought to myself.

After calling up a puzzled expression for her pale face she said "What…huh…what's he got to do with this?" she said as if reading a script for a screen test.

I looked down at my tacos so as not to see her expression

any longer. "I had lunch with him today in Santa Monica, but you already know that," I said. "I am sure that when you see him later tonight he will tell you all about it."

She slammed the palm of a hand hard on the table, making the plates jump and some red salsa splatter. "You bastard," she said. "You pathetic bastard. You and your horse can both go to hell. I did nothing wrong."

She stood up, turned toward the front door of the restaurant and walked out.

Chapter 19

Seated at my all-purpose kitchen table-working desk in my studio cottage in Arcadia, I began to think about which horses and what connections Knight Errant might have to worry about most in the Chester Sherwood Stakes.

There were two obvious contenders. First and foremost was Charlie Whittingham-trained El Bestia del Bosque. He had been imported from Argentina, where "The Beast of the Forest" had wreaked havoc on his peers at 3 by taking the Triple Crown. He further etched his name in history by adding a signature victory over his elders when scoring a memorable triumph in the Gran Premio Carlos Pelligrini.

"The Beast" not only was classy, he was versatile, winning between a mile in the Argentine Guineas and up to a mile and three-quarters. His races on the deep sandy dirt at Palermo racetrack in Buenos Aires pointed him out as a horse of both speed and stamina.

As was his wont, Charlie liked to give these Southern Hemisphere arrivals plenty of time. Consequently, the horse did not make his Northern Hemisphere debut until a year and four months after his Pelligrini score. He raced twice at

Hollywood Park, winning the Inglewood Handicap going a mile and a sixteenth and the Hollywood Gold Cup going a mile and a quarter.

As has been Charlie's practice with a tip-top horse, he skipped the Del Mar meet in favor of waiting for the fall stand at Santa Anita. Charlie could prep him once before the Chester Sherwood Stakes as it was not carded until the last week in October.

El Bestia del Bosque was owned by a 4-man partnership consisting of some of Whittingham's most loyal and successful patrons.

Then there was trainer Russell Zane's former claiming horse Redeemed that had been haltered at the end of last year on opening day of Santa Anita's winter/spring meeting in the sixth start of an otherwise undistinguished career.

The $20,000 claim had lost only once in 6 starts since then, climbing the class ladder to account for the Californian Stakes at Hollywood Park and the Del Mar Handicap.

A California-bred by a modest stallion out of a mare with no family to speak of, Redeemed was just the latest example of Zane pulling another rabbit out of a hat, turning an ugly duckling into a swan.

Zane always could train. He proved that time and time again, taking others' rejects and improving their form, sometimes in startling turnarounds. His father was a good horseman, but he finally gave up on Russell and would have nothing to do with him after his son got in one jackpot after another.

When Zane hit bottom, his wife took matters into her own hands, bringing him down to her Catholic Church, introducing him to the priest there and finally convincing him that accepting Jesus Christ as his personal savior could be his salvation, both as a human and a horseman. Russell bought into it.

As the younger Zane got his act together, started winning and gathering clients, there was plenty of talk about using performance enhancing drugs. Whether this was in fact the case, the simple fact is that nobody has been able to prove it.

The rumor mill indicated, as they very often do when too many wins are unexplainable, that Zane was using something that did not test. When presented with these rumors by an occasional Turf Writer with a pair of balls, Zane only laughed in that full-throated way of his.

"Yes, I have an edge," he would say. "God. God all mighty. The father of Jesus and the father of all of us. I am on the straight and narrow these days and my excellent results are the result of a lot of hard work, a lot of time spend at the barn and a new focus on my craft."

But the available data told a much different story.

A brilliant New York handicapper named Len Ragozin began generating speed figures a few years ago. Some enterprising customer of his was able to get the Manhattan-based genius to send him some of his "Sheets" on horses that had been claimed by Zane. An analysis was not really required, as immediately or very soon after Zane started training a new horse, its figures not only improved out of all proportion, but they consistently hit their new marks with a regularity unseen before.

Far be it for me to cast doubt upon the religious commitment of Zane or anyone else that believes in God or Jesus, but the numbers do not explain how this new-found spirituality allowed a horse that could run no faster than a 14 on the "Sheets" to suddenly hit a 7 race after race after race, no matter the trip, the racing surface or the company. The Lord God All Mighty, if he truly can impact performance of racehorses to this degree, would surely cause a dramatic increase in attendance at local churches, especially in and around racetracks near Del Mar, Inglewood and Arcadia.

Both Redeemed and El Bestia del Bosque were formidable horses, they were proven at the top level, they were at the top of the game and they figured to be hard to beat by any horse, let alone a twice-raced, inexperienced gelding that had never raced around 2 turns or competed beyond a sprint.

The good thing for our team and me is that few if any members of the press would have us on their radar and, if they did, it would only be to make light of our chances or to make fun of us. That took a lot of the pressure off us.

Knight Errant's performance in shattering the Del Mar track record for 6 furlongs in becoming the first sprinter to shade 1:07 around a turn, on dirt at a major racing venue had been scrutinized to the nth degree.

Few seasoned racegoers were willing to accept the bare result. Del Mar, being located right on the beach, is subject to wild racetrack variants based on the tides. This has been known among sophisticated handicappers for many years since Bing Crosby, Jimmy Durante and Pat O'Brien opened the gates of the seaside track back in 1937, four years after Doc Strub started Santa Anita.

So some naysayers attributed the brilliant effort and bullet-fast final time to an anomaly with the racing surface due to the movement of the tides. Others doubted the accuracy of the electric teletimer. A few wondered if the run-up was elongated.

In North America, as opposed to racing in the British Isles and Europe, the electric timer is not activated precisely when the gate opens. The starting gate at each track in the United States is placed a number of yards in front of the electric beam that kickstarts the timing device. Each track at each distance of a race places the gate in a different spot. There is little uniformity. Consequently, if a horse gets a running start of 60 yards versus 20 or 30 yards, that horse builds up more of a head of steam than if the run-up is shorter, and he will record a faster race time because of the longer head start. So run-up distance is a viable feature that can seriously impact the final time of a race.

Because I used to travel to different tracks around the country, The Indian used to seek me out upon my return to ask what I gauged the run-up to be at various distances at certain racetracks. He kept a log of such stats and used them in his handicapping. There is no end to the esoterica involved in trying to take an edge in gambling on racehorses.

Soil samples, water content in the surface, wind gauges, amount of sunlight—all have an impact on the racetrack. Another little known but extremely impactful aspect of the game involves how much water the trucks put on the track during each renovation of the surface between each race. Yet another is the length of the harrow that serves as a comb over the track following the watering.

All of these variables not only impact the final time of a race but can impact performance. Trainers know what their horses like and need. This is why the smartest, most seasoned horse trainers try to buddy-up to the trackman as much as possible.

However, the trackman charged with maintaining a safe

racing surface told me he doubted very seriously that the sea movements had made the track any faster on the day. Others timed the video replays with a hand-held stopwatch and concluded that the time was one-hundred percent legit.

Being a Track and Field buff I am very familiar with suspect times. In track, as pure a sport as the world has developed, there are no run-ups. Races are timed when the gun is fired. The Olympics, which first timed races with a stopwatch in 1896 in Paris, began using an electronic timing device as far back as 1912.

However, when I ran the hurdles in high school, most meets still were hand timed with a watch. Consequently, we got used to seeing high schoolers clock times for the 100-yard dash that would have made them Olympians if accurate. In Texas, high schoolers ran times faster than the world records because the meets did not have a wind gauge and gale-force zephyrs propelled the youngsters down the track faster than a speeding bullet.

Peers of mine, when we were alone, all wanted to know if I thought Knight Errant's final time was real or not. What I told them, and what I believe, is that I did, for the simple reason that when Secretariat shattered one record after another enroute to his Triple Crown success, we learned and accepted that when a horse that superior comes along, we have to alter our normal thinking to accommodate the new phenomenon.

I decided to drive to Pasadena and have lunch by myself at Beadle's Cafeteria. When I loaded up my tray with deep-fried halibut, green peas, red stewed tomatoes and a slice of lemon meringue pie, I was suddenly joined right behind me at the cash register by none other than the infamous Apples McGonagle.

I told the cashier to please add the gentleman's tray behind me to my tab. Apples smiled that mostly toothless grin of his and nodded his head at me. "Much obliged, sir, mucho obligato," he said, as if mucho obligato meant anything in any language on the face of the Earth.

"Mind if I join you young man?" he asked.

I nodded in the affirmative.

"Follow me kid," he said and headed for a secluded spot way in the back with which I was unfamiliar even though I must have eaten at the cafeteria 75 to 100 times.

It was still August, the dead of summer in Southern California, so it was in the 90s outside, yet as was his style Apples donned a long winter overcoat and wore the type of flat tweed cap preferred by Newmarket horsemen. He was dressed for winter.

"Apples, surprised you're not at Del Mar," I began.

"Geetus my friend. A lack thereof dontcha know," he said, employing a word for money that trainer Farrell Jones introduced many moons ago and came into general usage on the backstretch of Southern California.

"I had a tidy little nook that I had discovered several seasons ago down there where they used to store equipment for the San Diego County Fair that is conducted just in advance of the meet at Del Mar," he explained. "Wuncha know security found me and unceremoniously evicted me early one morning. So here I am."

Although he looked for all the world like a vagrant, Apples was a well-educated fellow, extremely well-read, knowledgeable about the goings on from the front side to the backstretch of a racetrack, perhaps more than any man alive. But he was loony tunes and had the insane asylum receipts to prove it.

"Say, if you don't mind me enquiring," he began, "what in the hell kind of trick does that drunkard Tad Smithwick have up his sleeve? The effort put in by that Ellerslie cast off was just—you should excuse the expression—a tad too cute for my tastes."

I did not respond and kept on dipping my halibut in the tartar sauce and eating away without reacting to his absurd question.

"Sonny boy, as we both know, I've been around the block more than a time or two, seen every stunt in the book, watched as the miracle men have done their voodoo acts, pretty much seen it all," he said. "But never have I seen a transformation like this or a horse literally run that hole in the wind we hear so much about but have never really witnessed until last week.

"So my question, simply put, is what gives here fella?"

When I finished indulging in my pie with the homemade crust that was a Beadle's specialty, I looked up at Apples. He was a very tall older man. Even seated he towered over me. Do not know his age, but it could be anywhere from 85 to 105, that's how long he has been on the scene. He was there in New York when the modern game began.

Apples was always verbal, always in somebody's face. But he was respected because of his vast knowledge base. He even talked Belmont Park President Alfred Gwynne Vanderbilt into letting him position up to 16 patrol judges on the roof of the racetrack to individually watch each horse and how it was ridden to ensure integrity in the sport.

"Apples, I understand what the horse did is hard to fathom and even harder to process," I said is subdued tones. "None of us, young or old, have seen anything like it. Even Secretariat, the modern day 'Big Red,' never sprinted like that. Only a horse like Dr. Fager approached something like that. But surely no horse we can call up for comparison would have been able to produce an effort like that in the second start of its life as a 4-year-old in August. It was mindboggling and defies precedent or adequate explanation."

Apples stared me down. "Your brand of chatter is quite good for such a young fella Billy, I'll give you that," he said. "Very well put, very eloquent, but in the final analysis--unpersuasive. I know you've seen my plant and herbal book, the one I carry around the backside in case a trainer needs to fix some ailment using natural means and not injections or pills.

"Well, in all of my years of collecting samples of everything ever grown on God's green earth capable of altering the physique, glands, circulatory and respiratory systems of the equine, I've yet to come across anything that can make a horse run like that. No siree Bob.

"I've seen the best voodoo-meisters in the game back East and occasionally out here that can surely alter the state of a racehorse. But eventually they all test. I am certain that some chemical trick that enhances breathing in a horse can make a difference, but not over 6 furlongs. So Billy, what am I missing here pal. You can tell me. It stays with me."

Affecting a voice not unlike that of a Southern Belle on a plantation in the ante-bellum South, I said with a flutter of my eyelashes "Why sir, whatever are you implying?"

Apples could only offer a look of exasperation on his furrowed, thickly set brows. "For goodness' sake Billy," he said. "Can you at least give me a ride back to Arcadia?"

When I pulled up to where Apples said he resided, which

was an alley behind some shops off Huntington Drive on the far East end of town, he turned to me and said "Wanna come up and see me book?"

Wryly I replied "If you said etchings you might have had me, but an invitation to check out your shriveled up weeds for the umpteenth time, I will just have to pass on this rare opportunity. You stay safe and take care Apples."

He got out of the BMW, bent down so his head was at my level and through the window uttered "I will figure this out Billy. I will find out what in the hell is going on here. You mark my words. No freaky performance of this magnitude and import is going to slip by Louis Apples McGonagle, I can promise you that fella."

As soon as I departed the alley I drove directly up to Bradbury to report my conversation to Doc Church. When I arrived at the gate, the guard said he had no permission slip for me to enter. I asked him to phone Doc Church and tell him it was Billy Richards.

"Sorry I didn't give more advance word of coming up here," I said to him from my rolled down window when Doc met me in the driveway of his ranchito. "But I knew you would want to hear about a conversation I just had at Beadle's with that nosy Apples McGonagle."

I recounted the entire conversation, Doc listened intently, thought about what I had told him for a few moments, gathered his thoughts and then said "Billy, I wouldn't give it a second thought. Look: there is nothing in Apples' frame of reference or old-timey plant book that can even begin to explain what I've been doing.

"Sure, a lot of drugs used on humans and horses have a

basis in the plant world, but what we are relying on is new world medicine that is light years ahead of anything Apples, a Chinese herbalist or African witch doctor could even get close to.

"On the other hand, you are right about one thing, we don't need anybody nosing around at odd hours trying to figure out what is being given to the gelding or who is administering it.

"Like I told you just the other day, all eyes and ears are now on us, so we need to be extra judicious about what we do and what we say and to whom we say it.

"And once again, to set your mind at ease, we are doing nothing wrong, we are using no illegal substances and we are not breaking any rules. But, as I also have pointed out, I would like if at all possible to keep what I am doing under wraps to protect my sources. Stay chill Billy, stay chill."

Chapter 20

Later that evening I received a call out of the blue from my old girlfriend that quit the racetrack—she exercised horses for Charlie Whittingham—to become a NASCAR driver.

"You still interested in writing investigative pieces?" she asked. She was nothing if not blunt.

"Of course. You got a hot tale about a juiced racecar driver?" I said.

"Billy, this is serious," she said and I was easily able to discern from her tone that she was on to something, possibly something important. "I don't want to talk about it on the telephone.

"Can we meet? I am out here near Pomona. How about meeting somewhere quiet and then getting a bite to eat?" She volunteered to meet me in the parking lot of Celia's El Loco Taco, our favorite Mexican hangout about half a mile East of Santa Anita.

Jilly Grant arrived just after me, exited her old Karmann Ghia and got into the passenger seat of my car. She leaned over and gave me a peck on the cheek. She looked healthy, had her usual excited girl smile that promised fun was just around the corner.

"Soooo…and Billy, obviously what I am about to tell you is highly, highly hush hush and you have to treat it with all of the sensitivity it demands," she began. "So," she said, clearing her throat, "last weekend I was at Flintridge visiting some of my old jumping friends and I ran into one of my old exercise-riding friends from the track. She invited me back to her apartment after we finished riding our horses.

"At her apartment was a tall blonde girl in her twenties. She had been seated on a chair in a dark corner of the living room. Her face indicated that she had been crying. She had bags under both eyes, her face was blotchy red and her posture was that of a defeated individual that had just lost a competition or something. I don't know, but she looked too sad for words.

"My friend introduced her to me, oddly no mentioned of her name, but just describing her as a friend from the track. I had never seen the girl around the track.

"After some small talk, my friend asks the girl to tell me what she had told her. In a very methodical manner and measuring her words, this girl proceeds to tell me about her relationship with a horse trainer. It was deeply personal, sometimes extremely hard to listen to and then unbelievably revealing.

"Based on the story the girl told me, I could understand why she looked so wiped out emotionally. It took a lot of courage and trust for her to say what she did, because it involved spilling the beans on an older extremely prominent trainer at the track.

"Frankly I was shocked that she would tell a complete stranger what she did, so I am guessing it had been painful for her for so long, she just could not contain herself any longer."

What the tall unnamed blonde young woman told Jilly was incredibly damning to the horseman involved. She was still in college. She did not say where, but Jilly guessed it was a very prestigious school. She said the girl came from money, was very well spoken and she came across as sincere.

The trainer in question met her at a Halloween party the year before. She was there with some other college girls. While still wearing their masks, the girl and the trainer—a fellow that had a daughter roughly the same age as the girl—hit it off.

When they removed their masks the girl was stunned to find out that she had been chatting away with an adult more than twice her age. The guy had the voice of a much younger man, had an infectious laugh and was charming in an off-handed way.

"Rather than move right along, the girl became more intrigued with the trainer," Jilly explained. "Long story short they became lovers. She sounded to me like a vet or a pre-vet student, so they both could relate to each other about horses.

"Well, when she visited Southern California, which became more and more often, she spent time with the trainer, who arranged for an apartment for her in Arcadia. It was their love nest.

"The trainer and the girl became so close that the trainer drew her into his inner circle, a group that consisted of the trainer, his assistant and the girl. One night the trainer woke the girl up at 2 in the morning, had her get dressed and join him in his car for a short ride to the Baldwin Avenue gate of the track.

"The security guard at the gate waved them in, the trainer drove to his barn and they got out near the office. The foreman showed them to a stall that the assistant entered, snapped a shank on the animal and waited for the trainer to take out a syringe from his jacket pocket.

"Before injecting the substance into the jugular vein of the animal, the trainer kiddingly asked the girl if she wanted to do it. She said she was still sleepy, had trouble even knowing if she were awake or dreaming, and declined."

On their way back to the apartment, there was no conversation. They both climbed back in bed. When she awoke in the morning the trainer had already left for the track. When he returned around 11 a. m. she asked the trainer if she had dreamt about going to the track in the middle of the night or if that really happened.

Jilly said "They smoked a lot of grass, so I believe her story about dreaming. Well, again…long story short…this became almost a nightly ritual. I asked the girl what she thought the substance was and she said she didn't know, but guessed it was something off-label that made horses run faster."

That was the sum total of what Jilly had been able to glean from her lengthy chat with the girl. The blonde and the trainer had only recently broken up, she said she was through with him and did not plan to see him ever again.

I asked Jilly if the trainer had abused the girl and she said "not physically but emotionally. The connection was purely sexual. The girl admitted to having a huge appetite for sex and the relationship persisted because of the trainer's insatiable libido."

Asked if Jilly thought the young woman was able to obtain any of the substance injected into the horses, she said the girl had heard enough from the trainer and his assistant to be afraid of getting any further involved. She was frightened enough to strongly consider transferring to a different school in a different state.

Then Jilly delivered the bombshell. The trainer was Russell Zane. Yes, that is correct…Russell Fucking Zane…God's own boy…cheating not only on his wife but trashing animals and horse racing in the bargain. Wow.

Jilly and I then ordered our Mexican food, which we ate outside on one of the picnic tables at the taco stand. I know it is not fancy, but they feature homemade food cooked by the mother of the younger proprietor and it is flat out the best Mexican food on the planet, especially the taco de carnitas and green poblano pepper burrito.

I answered all of the questions Jilly asked about Knight Errant except for my deal with Bear Harwood. She knows Tad as well as anybody and thanked me for giving him the opportunity of a lifetime. Doc was best friends with Jilly's jumping mentor, so it was a tight-knit little group.

Before departing Jilly updated me on her career advancement in the world of racecar driving.

"Billy, even though we aren't together anymore," she said "I just want you to know that I am not the least bit surprised you are in this position of having the most exciting unexposed horse in the land. You have always thought outside of the box and that is how you landed Knight Errant. Know always that I will be rooting for you and your horse's success."

Another peck on the cheek and she was out the door and driving back to NASCAR land.

As soon as I arrived back at my pad I phoned Hank Shuman. I asked if we could meet for lunch the next day. I did not let on what I had learned because I wanted to see the look on his face when I told him.

A smile grew on the face of Hank Shuman and exploded in a full-faced grin. His wife had propped him up for my revelation.

"So Hank your instincts are spot on," I said. His supportive wife beamed with satisfaction at her husband's triumph. "So what do you think is next. Do you need more evidence before sharing this with authorities?'

Hank was lost in thought. His eyes were darting back and forth and his lips were moving slightly. Then he looked at me and said "I think I need to contact my forensic guy and have a meeting. We need to do some brainstorming, come up with a plan to obtain the evidence we need to drive this baby to the finish line. Then we can figure out which entity is best to deliver the goods to."

During lunch Hank asked if I could stay local for a day or two until his guy was able to meet, because he wanted to introduce him to me and have me participate in any discussions that might be deemed useful.

A couple of days later I returned to Hank's beach house for lunch, where I was introduced to Conrad Squires, the "investigative journalist with ties to the intelligence community" as Hank described him.

"Connie," as he asked to be addressed, did not fit what I would have expected to see in a combination investigative journalist/private dick. He had an everyman appearance. He looked more like a car mechanic than well-established journalist.

Short, with curly hair and a round face, he was bland as a

piece of untoasted white bread. He listened more than he spoke and when he did talk it was succinct and directly to the point.

I retold what Jilly had imparted to me. Connie took notes without looking up at me and occasionally nodded his head.

When I finished my summation, Hank immediately piped up, saying to Connie "So whaddya think. What's our next move Connie?"

Connie looked at Hank, then went back to studying the notes he had taken. "Hank, what I think is that we have been handed a wonderful present right in our laps, that's what I think. Do I think we have everything we need? No. But with this information we should be able to bring this case to a quick resolution.

"Give me 10 days to 2 weeks to finalize a few things, tidy up some loose ends and we should be ready to kick some ass my friends.

"As far as what we do with the evidence and how far we want to take this, that will be strictly your call. Our options are the FBI, the State of California Attorney General, the San Gabriel Valley DA, the California State Horse Racing Board, Santa Anita racetrack or even the Arcadia Police Department. The choice, as I say, is yours.

"I have worked with the FBI and the State AG, but not the others," Connie said. "But I don't think the FBI will move fast enough for you fellas. They will use what I share with them, but they will want to basically begin from scratch. The State is a bit better, but they also don't move with a whole lot of alacrity.

"Local jurisdictions have priorities and this sort of thing is a bit like inside baseball stuff that may or may not float their boats.

"My suggestion based both on my experience and my gut reaction to the likely evidence, the players involved and the amount of expertise required, would be to involve Santa Anita in some way.

"In the final analysis it is the integrity of the industry that is at stake and any hits to the viability of the business negatively impacts the track's bottom line and adds an element of sleaze that they should find abhorrent. Do either of you have any solid contacts at the track."

Buddy Hillenbrand's name immediately sprung to mind. He was the director of racing at the track. He always complimented me on my PED articles. He cares about the integrity of the game like few others. And he could be trusted as a confidant.

Connie became more animated when I talked about Buddy. "That's our man, that's exactly the type of individual we need Billy," Connie said. "But I suggest you two sit on this for a couple of weeks until I iron out a few wrinkles that I see cropping up. That will tighten our case and make my presentation of evidence all that more credible."

Before leaving I turned to Hank and said "As a journalist, I have to tell you that if there is any one horseman I would like to see get his comeuppance it is Russell Zane.

"Ever since Jilly spilled the beans about Zane, I keep harkening back to the interview he gave a colleague who asked why he was able to move up so many horses, even on top trainers like Whittingham and Tom Pratt. Russell paused, then in his cocky manner said 'Well, some trainers are what I would call enlightened.' Enlightened my ass! Whatever happens to this creep he deserves it."

On my drive back to Arcadia from Del Mar my thoughts raced with all the possibilities the nailing of a drug cheat might achieve. Ever since I began going to the races, first as a 7-year-old kid tugging on my aunt Ethel's skirt and as a journalist covering the sport for *Daily Racing Form,* there has always been rumors and chitchat about trainers giving secret substances to horses to make them run faster to cash a big gamble.

Over the years, in jurisdiction after jurisdiction, what amounted to the racetrack cops were always chasing the cheaters, but by the time they were ready to pounce, the bad guys had found something new to hop a horse and new ways to deliver their magical potions

As in Track and Field and Cycling, the chemists were always a step or two ahead of the authorities. Occasionally an enterprising jurisdiction would try to bust a cheating trainer by hiding in the haylofts above a horse's stall and jump down at the appropriate time to catch somebody in the act of juicing a horse. Invariably, however, word got out and the cops came away with only a lot of straw, dust and horse pucky on their clothing.

There are so many ways to cheat and beat the system, they make catching the crooks very difficult. For years there have been rumors of one trainer in that plied a worker at Southern California's McKinley Laboratory with money, vacations and yacht excursions just for letting him know the schedule of which drugs were tested on what days of the week so that he could juice an animal with a banned substance and know the lab would not be testing for it. Whether true or not, the stories created and fed a rumor mill that had operated non-stop from, as my grandmother would day, the "year alef" or the year 1.

When I returned to the San Gabriel Valley I made a beeline for the Bradbury Estates so that I could share my newfound knowledge with Doc Church, as this topic had dominated most of our conversations before the advent of Knight Errant.

Doc Church listened to my updates.

"This is better than the movies for chrissake," he said when I finally wrapped up my report. "And it is all plausible. That's the best part. It all makes sense and does not sound fanciful, exaggerated or made up.

"Let's face it, we've all been suspicious of Zane. Wrapping himself up in all that Jesus talk to shield himself, his sleaze-ball owners and that preppy assistant of his. Makes me wanna puke just thinking about them.

"When your father kicks you out of his house and your surrogate father can only shake his head, you know something is not on the level."

I asked Doc what he thought Zane might be using and where he was getting it.

"Very hard to tell in this day and age," Doc said. "Could come from across the border or even across the street. Shipped across from Mexico or Canada, or from a local hospital supplied by a pharmacist. Or it could come from a chemist in the Midwest. All are possible Billy. That's what makes it so difficult.

"But, based on how his horses run, how they not only do not tire but re-break in the stretch I would put my money on some form of oxygen enhancement delivered by amped up red blood cells activated by some form of EPO. That's where I'd put my money. There's plenty of it around, but knowing how, when and what amount to give, separates the men from the boys. And finding a synthetic form of it that won't test is the gold standard.

"Hey, back in the real world, the Big Horse is going to breeze tomorrow after the break," Doc said. "Tad is just going to take it nice and easy with him he told me. See you out there Billy."

Chapter 21

Knight Errant, as was his unique characteristic when breezing, imperceptibly moved into another gear when breaking off at the five-eighths pole. The naked eye was at a loss to tell that he had increased his speed, because even using binoculars from my perch in the Cupola there was no discernable change either in stride frequency or length.

Yet the clock told a different story, as usual. On this morning the gelding would have the first of 3 workouts in advance of the October 16 renewal of the Chester Sherwood Stakes.

Tad planned to breeze the horse 3 times on September 25, October 2 and October 9 in advance of the race. Distance of a mile and a furlong would require special preparation for a twice-raced horse that had only sprinted.

Rafael Quintana had come up from Tijuana, Mexico for the breeze. The gelding was among the first workers on the freshly renovated track. He broke off alone and appeared to be cruising the entire way around. When he hit the wire he gradually eased himself down without the rider having to take a new hold of the reins.

I caught him going the five-eighths in :58 3/5, which was

the bullet move of the morning and which, for a normal horse, would have been a smoking-fast workout. But not for Knight Errant. He went from the furlong pole to the wire in :11 3/5, which as stated earlier was "motating."

When I took the stairway down towards the apron, Fishel (The Rabbi) Friedman was seated in his normal spot.

"Boychick, long time no see," he said, more matter-of-factly than friendly. "You tricked me. You left your job at the *Form* and never wrote about me."

I explained that it was not intentional, it just played out differently than I could have predicted. 'I am sorry," I said. "Hopefully, what you got betting made up for any disappointment."

"You know me," he said, using the same monotone voice as always. "I don't bet that much. And when a bet is made, I don't like to use my own money. I want my clients to bet for me. Since you silenced me and I honored my commitment I couldn't arrange for one of the gamblers to bet for me. So I cashed a modest bet."

I did feel somewhat bad about the situation, even though I had bet a grand for him. "Geez, that really depresses me to hear this. How much did you get down on him?"

Fishel, not hesitating, said "Nothing, just a couple of grand."

I laughed so loudly that it echoed through the hollow unattended morning grandstand in uproarious fashion.

Even Fishel could not contain himself and started laughing heartily.

"Fishel, you crack me up," I said. "So you made a nice hit then. Congrats. I am happy that your word was rewarded, as it should be. Fishel, you are a man of integrity. You should have become a Rabbi."

Fishel said "Explain to me how any horse can work as fast as Night Errands and look like he is out for a mere gallop. I don't get it. I ain't never seen no ferdle do anything like him."

I told Fishel that it was the mystery of the ages. The Argentines would call him a white fly…a once in a lifetime freak of nature.

Fishel said that I must have done some very special indeed in my previous life to receive such a mitzvah. He started explaining that reincarnation, although not mentioned in the Torah, was embraced in the mysticism of the Kabbalah.

"Yeah, whatever," I said and started walking away, so as not to encourage The Rabbi to go off on one of his religious tangents. Once he got rolling, he would start rocking back and forth, getting in a verbal rhythm that did not stop until I started to walk away. I was his reclamation project.

On the apron I ran into Laz Barrera, the Cuban refugee who moved to Mexico seeking a larger canvass for his training career and eventually came to the United States, where he gained a well-earned reputation as a great trainer.

"What kind of freak is this you got?" he said. "You know that I always breeze my horses fy-yay. That's my style forever. I have breezed thousands of fy-yay in my time. But how is it I never seen one do it like this gelding you got? Splain this to me."

I knew Laz well. He was sincere. He had trained some of the fastest horses to grace the American Turf. And five-eighths, or as he pronounced it fy-yay, was his shtick. I have seen him breeze a horse in :57 2/5 and decline to run it because he said the horse should have gone faster and done it easier. He was the planet's leading five-eighths expert. He was genuinely puzzled.

"Laz, I wish I could explain it, I really do, but I can't," I said. "It is probably the easy way he moves. His stride is frictionless."

The instant I uttered that word "frictionless" I knew it was a big mistake, because it was a word few would ever use in casual conversation and Laz was an immigrant with a limited English vocabulary.

"Free-shawn-lease? What in the hell does that mean?" he said with a good bit a laughter surrounding the word.

I explained to Laz that friction results when two things rub together. I said that when Knight Errant runs he is like a horse whose legs have been sprayed with WD40."

Barrera contorted his face up in a knot, which told me he thought that I had either lost my marbles or was just jerking his chain.

"Free-shawn-lease. Humph. Ok," he said. "I will tell my foreman to go to the hardware store and get me some WD40." He winked and walked off.

I took a detour from the apron through the grandstand and decided to take a shortcut through the paddock to enter the backstretch just past the Association Gate between the executive offices and the receiving barn.

Leaning against the walking ring's cream-colored railing was none other than The Bald Eagle himself, Charlie Whittingham, the dominant trainer of top horses in Southern California.

"Hey scribe, or should I say ex-scribe," he said. "You know, now that you gave up writing all that bullshit in the *Form*, I can talk to you as though you were a regular person."

I told him that is something I looked forward to.

Whittingham nodded. We had become a bit more friendly

when I was dating his exercise rider Jilly Grant. But now I sensed I had been elevated to an even high place in his ranking of those who peopled the racetrack.

"Just between us, what you did in giving Tad a nice horse like yours is something that I really appreciate. Class move my boy. And so far he couldn't be doing a better job."

I nodded my head. Charlie was close with Tad's father.

Whittingham started walking back towards his barn in the stable area. He cranked his head to one side, motioning for me to join him.

"What's next for that rocket ship of yours if I'm not being too nosey?" he asked.

I told him that we were pointing for the Sherwood.

He did not change his demeanor, just nodded and said "I see."

Then as he neared his barn he said "You know that's where I'm going to run The Beast. I'll tune him up 3 weeks out then go in the Sherwood. Might be one or two steps too early for your horse Billy. Could cook him. Don't get in Tad's way if you can help it."

When I explained to Whittingham that it was Tad's idea to run in the Sherwood, he looked over at me, furrowed his brow and mumbled something about how that was interesting, very interesting.

Back at the barn, Tad was acting a bit pensive for a guy that should have been gratified to see Knight Errant work so fast so effortlessly. But something was up, I could tell.

"Billy, you know as well as I do that fast is fast," he began. "I wanted the horse to go around there in a minute and change. That's what was called for this morning. I know he did it like breaking sticks, easy as pie, but fast like I say is fast and speed tells on the physique of a horse."

I asked how the gelding's breathing was and what the rider had said. "Billy, you don't need to question me on these fundamental short strokes. Everything you would want to see that would provide a trainer with comfort I saw and heard. I just will never, ever be able to get used to training a horse that just keeps doing the unexpected at every turn. I guess it is just my problem."

I told Tad that when a light-weighted jockey like Quintana breezes a horse it is apt to work much faster than a trainer expects. I see it all the time with The Shoe on Charlie's horses. That's why some trainers won't even let a jockey breeze a horse, especially on the eve of a race.

"Yeah, you're probably right," he said, but I could see he was not buying it and was sticking with his own thoughts on the subject.

I told him about my chat with Whittingham, how Charlie thought I was pressuring him to run the horse in the Sherwood and then was pretty darn taken aback when I told him that it was Tad's idea.

Tad smiled and let out a strong "Ha!" He then said that Charlie was always advising him to stop being so conservative in his placement of horses, so when Whittingham heard that Tad was bold enough to point for the Sherwood, it must have struck a chord and forced him to recategorize Knight Errant in his pigeonholing of horses at Santa Anita.

On my way to my car I ran into Timmy (The Limey) Broadhurst, the ancient trainer who had come from England when racing went legal at Santa Anita in 1933. I nodded, trying to keep up my pace to the parking lot, but The Limey would have none of it. In his normal daily life at the track he sort of shuffled around, but I found out right then and there when he wanted to he could really pick up the pace.

"Good day young man," he said, in a voice that indicated years of living in Arcadia, California had not Americanized his English accent. "I've been meaning to talk to you about that gelding of yours. Where are you headed, if I may be so bold as to ask?" He pronounced ask as "ossk."

I made a huge frigging mistake by telling him that I was headed to Beadle's for lunch before stopping off at Bank of America.

"Want some company?" he sheepishly asked.

What he really was angling for was to be treated to a meal. He was a well-read fellow, with plenty on his mind at all times on various subjects concerning not only horse racing, but the world in general. He had more stories and remembrances than anybody on the racetrack.

"Sure Mr. Broadhurst" I said. "My car is right over here."

One would have thought that I was his jailer and this was his last meal the way The Limey loaded up his tray at the cafeteria. He placed not one but two entrees on his tray, saw that it was taking up too much room, then grabbed a second tray so as not to short sheet himself on the meal.

I paid for all three trays, carried two of them to a nearby table and The Limey followed in close pursuit with the other tray. Beadle's was packed with the usual luncheon crowd, peopled by local workers in the many business offices in and around downtown Pasadena. But it was not so loud that we could not carry on a pleasant conversation.

"Something I've been meaning to chat to you about since hearing you planned to try Knight Errant over ground," the old guy said, with a twinkle in his faded baby-blue eyes. "It's about his pedigree. As you know I worked the yards in England from a very early age and I saw quite a few prominent horses before I came to Santa Anita.

"The fastest male and female I ever saw are in your lad's sire line. These of course would be The Tetrarch and his daughter Mumtaz Mahal. You have impressed me in the short time that I've known you with your knowledge of the history of the Turf, so I don't have to tell you who these horses are.

"The Tetrarch, as you may recall, cared very little about the act of breeding mares, he then developed fertility issues and consequently sired very few foals. But in Mumtaz Mahal he gave us the grandam of Nasrullah, the sire of Bold Ruler and Bold Ruler gave us Secretariat.

"So you may not know this, but I was fortunate to see both The Tetrarch and Mumtaz Mahal race. I can tell you that in all my years around racing no faster horses ever graced the playing field at Headquarters than these two animals.

"But, for the purposes of this conversation, I must tell you that neither one of them could carry their speed beyond a sprint in top company. The colt never ran beyond a sprint so we are not truly sure about how far he could run. His races, though, and morning trials strongly suggested he was limited in stamina. But the filly placed over a mile in the Guineas and ran fourth in the Coronation. Dropped back down to sprinting, she recaptured her brilliance and resumed her winning ways.

"So, without beating around the proverbial bush any longer, because I don't want my Turkey ala King to lose any more of its comforting warmth, I must tell you that the move to stretch out your horse is one that is fraught with danger.

"Speed in and of itself is something to be cherished, revered and applauded. The American condemnation of referring to a fast horse as merely a sprinter is comical and demeaning.

"Billy, you have the fastest horse I've seen since The Tetrarch and Mumtaz Mahal. Enjoy it but be careful about asking the lad to do something beyond his capabilities, because it very well could break him. You, my friend, have an obligation to the Turf not to muck this up."

It was bad enough that I had to endure having my cage rattled by a nonagenarian, but I had to pay for the privilege.

My bank manager Brian Dougherty was out of the office, so I drove The Limey back to Arcadia.

"I have to admire your faith in the gelding," he said on the ride back. "You are giving him every chance to etch his name in the history of the Turf. I don't need to tell you that both Charlie's Wonder Horse from The Pampas and Zane's animal will undoubtedly use the race this weekend to prep for the Sherwood.

"So, Knight Errant not only will have to face formidable opposition but two horses that will be primed by two of the game's most brilliant tacticians. And he will, of course, face them without ever having been around two turns."

The only thing The Limey failed to accomplish before I left him off was to shovel the last bits of dirt across my casket. Thanks, pal!

In the walking ring for the Sherwood prep race 3 weeks out from the big race itself, both protagonists looked the part. El Bestia del Bosque had a flawless bay coat with black points on his legs. Redeemed lacked the stature and quality of the Whittingham trainee, but his coat was vibrant and he pranced around the ring in a collected fashion that indicated he was a bomb getting ready to explode.

I decided to stay away from the press box because I had tired of the nasty looks and low-level teasing, besides which I had no standing to be up there, unless I was working on a piece. When Knight Errant won the Bing Crosby I took a hiatus from reporting on California racing for the *Thoroughbred Record* as I considered it to be a conflict of interest. So I climbed the stairs and took the catwalk to the Cupola, where I watched the race.

The Candy Spots Stakes, named after the Preakness winner bred in California by Swaps' breeder Rex C. Ellsworth, was a sixteenth of a mile shorter than the Sherwood.

The Zane horse tracked, then pressed the pace in second, before taking over at the top of the lane, opening up 2 ½ lengths a sixteenth of a mile from the wire, and holding on without being harassed by three-quarters of a length from the fast-closing Whittingham steed.

Neither horse had a hard race. Had I written it up for the *Thoroughbred Record* I would have characterized it as the ideal prep in advance of the Chester Sherwood Stakes 3 weeks later.

My *DRF* replacement Freddy Glickman joined me on the last part of my catwalk journey. "Scouting the competition Billy?" he said. "So what'd you think?"

"Freddy, at this point I think it would behoove me to keep my mouth shut on the subject," I said. "But later in the month I would be more than happy to talk to you about it. Right now I'd just like to process what I saw, if that's okay with you."

Later that evening, as I sat on a picnic table eating a bean tostada at Ceila's El Loco Taco, I inadvertently let slide onto the ground more than half of my first tostada. I had been so damn preoccupied in thought, going over and over all of the input I had recently received from Whittingham, Broadhurst and everybody else with their combination of admonitions and fear-talking that I let some of my meal cascade to the asphalt.

Anytime I would allow half a tostada to fall off of its shell told me that the impending race and all its attendant hoopla was starting to get to me.

"Shit" I thought to myself, "at this rate I am going to beat The Limey to the old fogies home."

Chapter 22

Two weeks out from the Chester Sherwood Stakes the gelding took to the track for his big work. Before the groom had finished walking the gelding around the ring for 30 minutes or so and Tad joined the horse alongside, the trainer closed the tack room door for a pow wow with me and Doc Church.

"Guys, this is it, the final big work before the stretch out," he said, somewhat solemnly. "This a move fraught with danger, because I plan to have Quintana let him roll today.

"This move will not be unlike what a power lifter does in the gym. Like a weightlifter, this breeze today will break down some muscle tissue, but I think he needs it because he will have to be at his best facing seasoned stock over a route of ground. The move will break down and damage some fibers, but like the day after a lifting session these fibers will repair and come back stronger.

"I admit to being pretty scared asking the gelding for the first time since I've had him, and I will be the first to admit that one reason I plan to ask him is that I am apprehensive. Scared not about how much talent he's got, but whether I have done enough with him so we don't let him down."

Doc and I, both having been athletes in running events and participating in weight training, knew exactly what Tad was talking about. My own feeling was that the proposed fast work was more for Tad's fragile self-confidence than about conditioning the animal.

Doc said "Again, boys, we are in uncharted waters. We know they are deep and unforgiving, but like Tad said we know we've got the vessel to withstand any storms. This should be very interesting this morning. This is as exciting as a race as far as I am concerned."

Doc and I followed behind Knight Errant as he walked from the stable to the gap. Many eyes were on our group as we walked paralleling the horse from the gap along the apron.

It was a weekend, so the apron had more folks than during the week. As we passed the outdoor area where beverages and pastries could be had at Clocker's Corner, an announcer said "There goes the Knight Errant team of trainer Tad Smithwick and Turf Writer turned owner Billy Richards down to watch their horse work. He is pointing for the Chester Sherwood two weeks from today."

I did not recall a time when so many fans peopled the apron. And I would know, because I used to have that announcer's job when I worked briefly for Santa Anita.

As we approached the finishing post, I saw Zane and Whittingham in their usual spots. With the top two contenders in the Chester Sherwood 2 weeks hence, they would be watching our boy closely this morning.

"Doc, follow me," I said and walked at a fast pace towards the elevator. It was too early to be manned, so Doc and I had a hassle-free passage to the sixth floor, where we got off and took the catwalk to the Cupola.

"Can you get the final clocking from this angle Billy?" Doc said.

I told him that I had been doing it so many times up there that I had learned to adjust. Besides, I told him, every watch on the grounds would be on our boy so we would not lack for back-up.

After getting in his usual warm up of a once-around jog and a quarter-mile gallop to the three-quarter pole Knight Errant once again eased into his work so smoothly it was hard to tell if the breeze had commenced.

"Billy, is he working from the five-eighths pole and going out the extra furlong down the lane?" Doc asked.

I smiled. "Nope. What you see is what you get with this fella," I said. "This is him. He has already started working. With him, it is impossible to tell visually. Only the watch knows the truth."

With Rafael Quintana's butt facing the heavens and the gelding advancing on a tight rein, Knight Errant hit the first furlong in 12 seconds. He went from the five-eighths pole shortly after turning onto the backside to the half-mile pole in the middle of the backstretch in :11 2/5. So :23 2/5 for the opening quarter. I called out the times for Doc's benefit.

The gelding still looked for all outward appearances to be well in hand and moving in a measured manner. He reached the three-eighths marker after another :11 2/5 furlong in a sprightly :34 4/5.

Around the turn the gelding began to take flight, as Quintana's butt lowered and his back was level with that of his mount. Anybody could tell he was rolling now. It was obvious that his turnover had increased in tempo. The watch confirmed it. The furlong from the end of the backside to the quarter pole at the top of the lane was accomplished in an eye-popping 10 seconds flat. Unheard of. I had to check my watch twice to verify it.

"Ten flat for the last furlong" I said with a catch in my throat. "Ten seconds flat. Are you freaking kidding me? What the fuck," I said. "Do we need to contact the Air Traffic Control Tower or what?"

So, the half-mile was done in :44 4/5. Even with a freak, this normally would have signaled the end of the workout, as a horse after a move like that around the turn would start getting rubber legged. And if the horse did not slow down there is every chance a trainer would start yelling and waving his arms for the rider to slow down.

But riding to explicit instructions, Quintana instead threw the reins at Knight Errant, who responded with a burst of speed down the lane that gave me goose bumps. Yes, that's right, frigging goose bumps.

I caught the gelding hitting the eighth pole in :55 2/5. He flew by us in full stride with Quintana well balanced above him. I stopped my watch after a full three-quarters of a mile in 1:07 4/5.

The clockers stand was quite aways away, but the whooping and hollering from the press box the instant Knight Errant hit the line was audible in the Cupola, as was the hoopla below us near the wire. I could not hear what the announcer way down on the other side of the eighth pole said, but whatever it was, the crowd reacted with a crescendo of oohs and aahs, followed by applause.

The bay horse galloped out another furlong in :12 4/5. Normal time is about 14 seconds. So he finished up seven-eighths in 1:20 3/5. For years El Drag was the only horse in history to shade 1:20 until Triple Bend broke it in 1972. He pulled up after a mile in 1:33 3/5. For years the world record for a 2-turn mile was Swaps' 1:33 1/5.

"Holy moly Billy, holy frigging moly," Doc said hugging me and grinning like a schoolboy that had been given a new toy. "This sucker makes Swaps look like a plater. This is what the Forty-Niners must have felt like when they discovered gold."

I said "Can you even imagine what Charlie must be thinking right now. I know he thinks he has the Sherwood in the bag. But the bottom just fell out of that container Doc."

I told Doc he could return downstairs if he chose to, but as for me I would like to just sit a while, cogitate on what I had just witnessed, then talk to the clockers to verify my splits. "You can stay or go, but I really don't want to have to endure a bunch of people staring at me or talking to me right now," I said.

He was halfway out the door before I had finished my explanation.

Cheers went up immediately upon my appearance in the clockers' stand, with ex-jocks turned a. m. stopwatch clickers slapping me on the back, shaking my hand and making guttural and high-pitched sounds to welcome me.

The head clocker, though, sat on his tall bar stool and could only shake his head. Once we had made eye contact he said, and in a serious tone and manner, "What in the fuck kind of rocket fuel is that society vet of yours putting in this gelding's tank? Does he know somebody at Jet Propulsion Lab?" Then he broke out in full laughing mode, came over, patted me on the head, as if to say "good boy" to a dog.

This time I walked all the way to the opposite end of the grandstand and took an auxiliary stairway at the end of the catwalk, so I could avoid staring eyes. I wound up taking the walkway past the receiving barn, past the Association Gate and started walking towards Tad's barn. On the way Whittingham saw me and could only stare. The Bald Eagle had his game face on. And it was still a couple of weeks from the race. I sensed our little group had just entered a new climate of high competitiveness on the backstretch.

Tad asked if I got the splits. I told him. He listened carefully, absorbing each fraction and nodding in the affirmative.

"Daggers my boy, daggers," Tad said. "That's all I saw walking back. The knives are out now boy. Game on."

I asked Tad if he expected anything remotely like that and he said "sort of but not really. Who in the history of the game ever saw anything remotely like this. When I walked by The Shoe at the gap he chirped to me like he would a horse, rolled his eyes and then shook a hand like he had touched something too hot. 'You got one there you ole hacker,' he said smiling.

I said "The guy in the hut at the gap that identifies workers for the clockers on his headset asked if the breeze was for real, as he said he had never heard the clockers in the booth carrying on like this."

Tad said the gelding cooled as he usually does. Quintana said he was strictly a passenger, but did say the horse really loved running around the turns.

"Now we just blow him out next week and a week later we go hunting for bear," said Tad. "Oh, by the way, speaking of Bear, his farm manager told me that The Bear is thinking about coming out for the stake."

When he said this he stared right into my eyes. The unsaid message was "I'd like to be a fly on the wall when you two meet to see how shriveled up your balls get."

The next day Tad did not show up at the barn. The groom had not heard from him, but he knew the routine and just walked the gelding for an hour. The next day no Tad again. I tried calling him at home but his wife said he had not been there in a couple of days and she had no idea where he might be.

On the third morning of his disappearance I went into stealth detective mode. First port of call was the Yellow Cab hub in Eagle Rock. I drove a hack for a few weeks at one point after returning to L. A. from the Bluegrass and I knew the dispatcher. He told me to check a bar on North Lake Avenue just south of the Altadena city line. He told me to speak with a guy named Willie.

It was still early, 6:30 in the morning, but the bar had been open for half an hour. I will never forget my first fare as a taxi driver. It was to pick up a fare at a bar. I had no idea guys drank that early in the day or that bars were even open at that hour. First guy I picked up told me to come back and get him at 1:45 p. m. I told him that I was getting off my shift fifteen minutes later. He said "Yeah, I know pal. I drive a hack too. Need to get a lift back to work!"

Willie was a big Black dude the size of an NFL tackle. We exchanged a few words, then he told me he would be right back. When he returned in a couple of minutes, he led me down a hall and into a secluded room behind the bar proper. There, shit-faced as could be, sat Tad Fucking Smithwick in all his inebriated glory.

He had not shaved. He probably had worn the same clothes for days. And he reeked of booze and body odor.

"Tad, do you even know what fucking day this is?" I asked.

"Yes," he said with a slur. "Today. Yeah, it is today…def-def-definitely today."

I asked if he was able to stand.

"Stand? Stand you say. Of course I can stand," he said with plenty of incredulity in his tired voice. But when he tried to stand he fell right back in the chair. Tad stood every bit of 6 feet 2 inches and there was no way I was going to be able to get him upright, so I recruited Willie to help me get Tad in the front seat of my car.

I asked Willie if Tad had run up a tab, he said that it was about $650, as he was very generous buying rounds for other customers, especially the ladies. He said Tad was such a good customer and so entertaining he would settle it for $500. I paid him, got back in the car and drove Tad to my place.

By the time we had arrived at my cottage, Tad had come around some, thanks to rolling down all the windows in the car. I led him into my room, situated him to be able to plop on the bed and sat watching him for a few minutes until he was snoring and asleep.

I went to Rod's for breakfast, then stopped by the barn to make sure all was well, which it was, and then I came back to my pad. I couldn't write because the sound of my Olivetti would probably have awakened Tad. So I did some reading.

Lunchtime and Tad was still out like a light, so I went to Celia's for lunch. When I returned to my place Tad was still asleep. Finally, just before 4 p. m. he awoke with a startle. When he sat up on the edge of the bed, rubbed his eyes, ran his fingers through his unkempt blonde hair and coughed a couple of times, he turned to me and said "Time is it? Oh 4. We've got to get to the barn to see how the horse got through his feed tub. Less go pal."

I told Tad that he could not possibly be seen in his current condition. He walked over to the bathroom mirror, took a studied look at himself and returned to the edge of the bed.

"Once again Billy, you are correct, sir," he said delivering Ed McMahon's retort he had made famous on Johnny Carson's *The Tonight Show.* He had his humor back and was sounding much more awake and like his usual self. "I look like shit."

Tad was beginning to become embarrassed and would no longer look me in the eye.

"You know," I began, "when Doc pushed me into giving the horse to you, I told him that I was fearful that our relationship would reach this pass. And now here we are.

"What the fuck is wrong with you, man," I said. "You've got what every trainer since time immemorial has longed for, prayed for and dreamt about. You've got the Big Fucking Horse. So why do you trash yourself like this when you are on the verge of success? What am I missing."

Tad actually looked tearful, as his eyes reddened and he dropped his head between his shoulders. Then he started sobbing, at first lightly, then he sobbed and at last he got a hold of himself and became more composed. He raised his head and stared me in the eye.

"Billy, I am going to let you in on a little secret," he said. "The thing about trainers…and I am talking about all trainers with the rare exception of a Charlie or a Woody or the Jones boys…all of them, all of us are afraid of one day being found out."

I said "Found out? What's that mean found out?"

Tad said "Lacking. Not having the skills to get the job done. They…we…every one of us except the Alpha Dog horsemen lack confidence. Here is something that you will absolutely not believe, but it is true as can be.

"While we all bitch and moan about not being given a top prospect, once we get it we are scared shitless, because deep down none of us think we will be able to do justice to the animal and will be found out as posers. And that's the God's honest truth.

"And while I'm at it I'll tell you one other thing, since you are so fascinated about trainers that cheat. Why do you think they hop their horses? I'll tellya. It is because they know that as a trainer there is nothing they can do to make a horse run as fast as when they are hopped. No skills can trump juice.

"After that horse did what he did on Sunday I began to doubt myself. So I decided to have one little drink. Then one more. Then I was a goner. Billy, what day is it anyway?"

Tad asked me to take him home. His wife would know how to get him back on the beam.

On the drive back I told Tad that I felt for him and that I understood. I also told him that he had done a great job training and understanding the gelding. And I said that I would give him one more chance as the trainer of Knight Errant.

Then, as a ploy to scare him straight, so to speak, I told him that I had lined up The Rabbi as the back-up trainer and that the Hebrew Horseman had agreed to wait in the wings.

"Tad, I am not kidding," I told him. "So don't fuck up this free lunch again."

Chapter 23

When I returned to my room on Huntington Drive I received a phone call from Hank Shuman.

"Connie has made what he terms excellent progress on our matter and he has called for a meeting," Hank said. He sounded excited. "Can you make it down here for lunch tomorrow?"

It was an easy drive down to Del Mar now that the summer tourist and racing season had come and gone. There is something quite serene and wonderful about Del Mar after the season. No crowds, no noise, no drunks, but sadly fewer bikini-clad young women and girls.

When I used to spend the season at Del Mar writing my column for *DRF*, it was always difficult for me to return up North. One season was particularly hard and, with no racing assignments during the Fair Circuit, I hung around for an extra couple of weeks.

I would eat breakfast at Fidele's, jog along the beach between breakfast and lunch, have fish tacos downtown or taquitos at Robert's for my midday meal, park myself on the beach and read. I would have trouble staying awake as the gentle sea breeze and the salty air lulled me to sleep. It was heaven on Earth.

Anyway, I digress...Alice let me in the front door. As usual she had made a terrific lunch. This time it was a tuna and egg salad sandwich on sourdough bread sliced thinly enough to easily fit into one's mouth. She put a layer of mustard on the bread which really punched up the flavor. Hank was one lucky s. o. b. I thought to myself.

Connie had beat me down to the beach house and was already halfway through one half of his sandwich when I sat down on the sofa overlooking the propped-up Hank Shuman.

When he finished his first half of the sandwich, Connie wiped his lips with a napkin and began informing us about his progress.

"As I told Hank here, I believe we've made excellent progress," Connie said, as usual without any discernable emotion on view. "I have to hand it to the subject, this Zane character. He has covered all his bases. Like many con men—and make no mistake this guy is a first-class confidence man—he is a charmer.

"From sources I had already enlisted on the backstretch and a couple of new players I brought in from previous investigations, we were able to learn a few important wrinkles.

Before getting into details, Connie apologized for not knowing about where Zane stashed his substances, as he admitted never thinking of tailing the trainer in the middle of the night.

"So, yes, the early morning barn visits by Zane are real" he said. "They don't occur every night, but they do coincide with race dates in my estimation. I think he shows up on consecutive days in advance of a race he has targeted.

"And like most cheaters, he doesn't jack up every animal and he doesn't juice them for each race. He is very careful and quite a clever rascal. When he drives to the track, he always uses the gate off of Baldwin Avenue adjacent to the Arboretum. He never uses the Association Gate.

"This told me that he had put the guard at the Baldwin Gate on his payroll. I noticed that when a car other than the one driven by Zane approached, the guard made them stop. He chatted with them, sometimes asking to see a license or some such credential. But when Zane approached, the gate went up well in advance of the car reaching the gate.

"At the barn only one employee was visible. It is the foreman. I never noticed his young assistant. You know the best and most careful cheaters are usually loners, guys that have few or no friends. I have always felt that this was by design. Also, the fewer bodies involved, the less chance there is to get caught, because as the saying went during the War…loose lips sink ships."

"Another thing of interest to report is that Santa Anita has no security on foot, on golf carts or in cars patrolling the barn area at night.

"After we were able to figure out Zane's schedule, we began tailing him from his home to the track. His routine included a stop at a nearby public storage facility. He would park his car on the street, enter by foot at the small walk-in gate, be absent for perhaps 2 minutes, return to his car and then drive to Santa Anita.

"So obviously the storage facility is where he stashes his substances. FYI, never once did he have anybody with him in his car. Just him.

"Once Zane arrived at the barn he would go into the tack room, immediately exit with his foreman and the foreman would lead Zane to the correct stall. Once inside the stall, their business took less than a minute.

"Zane exited the stall with nothing in his hands. I think he put the items he used for the juicing in his jacket packet and discarded it somewhere later."

Connie also said that one thing an investigator in his troop commented on was the lack of horse identification on the stalls. The horses had no name tags, unlike most trainers.

Connie said "in and out, total elapsed time about 3 minutes." He said that Zane lived about 7 minutes from the track. He never put his car in the garage, probably so as not to wake his wife. He always parked in the driveway.

Hank piped up and said "Great work Connie, great work. Do you pick up any useful clues about where the drugs were sourced and how they wound up in the storage unit?"

Connie said that he did not, mostly because once he learned of the site where the illicit juice was housed, he figured that when a raid took place at some point in time, this feature would easily come to light. He wanted to focus on the deed itself and the routine."

I asked Connie if he thought that we now had enough information to reach out to any authorities.

"I do…I really do," he said. "And I've also continued to think a lot about the right person and the right timing. I still very much like the of the idea of using the inside man, the Director of Racing, Buddy Hillenbrand.

"I've done a bit of research on him and, as you accurately pointed out Billy, he is a man of extreme power, influence and integrity. That is quite a formidable package for one man to possess. He's definitely our key guy.

"Question for you Billy. When do you think this horse of his is scheduled to make his next start, because I think it makes sense to launch this raid at least 5 days before the race so that the horse does not receive his candy at all during the week of the race?"

I gave Connie the name of the horse and the name and date of the race.

"So in an ideal world, Tuesday or Wednesday would be the best days," Connie said. "That gives us pretty much a week to nail down the short strokes of this operation."

I asked Connie if he thought Mr. Hillenbrand would want to bring in law enforcement or anybody from a governmental agency right away. Connie said "Until you or we speak to him, we won't know that, as he is sure to have his own thoughts on the matter and they will be dictated by what he would like the outcome of this operation to be.

"Let's face it, there are a few ways he could elect to go. He could ask the FBI to get involved if he wanted to go for the whole enchilada. He could go to the local District Attorney if he wanted to make something happen faster. He could simply walk across street to the local Arcadia police and have them conduct the operation. And a few others that I could see being implemented. But, as I say, the ball will be in Hillenbrand's court and it will be his call. Don't forget, Santa Anita is private property and they do have their own security."

I finished my two sandwich halves, thought about what I wanted to do next, then spoke. "If it's all right with you guys, I'd like to bring in my vet Dr. James Church on this operation.

"First of all, he and I share a passion for cleaning up illicit drug use in our sport. He is a mentor and supporter of mine. Secondly, he and his wife are very tight with Buddy Hillenbrand and his wife.

"Depending on how Mr. Hillenbrand chooses to have this operation go down, he may feel comfortable having a vet on hand when we do the raid."

Connie and Hank looked at each other, Hank nodded affirmatively and Connie said "Sounds like he will strengthen our team and our attack."

When we stopped talking about the impending action I said "You know I had lunch with your neighbor during Del Mar."

Hank said "Who, Fat Barry?"

I responded with a head nod.

Hank laughed. "I am surprised he would deplete his grub reserves on you, given his impressive physical largeness."

I said "He tried to buy my horse Knight Errant."

Hank said "I bet that went over like a lead balloon, right?"

Again I nodded in the affirmative. Then I said that if things went the way we hoped it was going to prove to be a massive downer for Fat Barry, as Zane was his main trainer.

"The irony is so rich in this vein I can barely stand it" I said. "The Fat Man detests cheating. Not on the usual ethical or moral grounds. But in terms of how it mucks up his gambling moves.

"The use of drugs brings an element of chance into his figures as they skew everything. He told me during lunch that he would never knowingly employ a cheater to train for him. This is going to blow his socks off."

Connie asked me how rampant I thought cheating was on

the backstretch in Southern California. I told him that I thought it was happening but it was not prevalent. In my opinion, I said there would always be so-called enlightened trainers, guys that considered themselves to be the sharpies out there, and their bent in life was to be able to take advantage of squares. I thought the so-called chumps outnumbered the sharpies by at least 25 to 1. But it is those bad eggs that wind up winning way more than their share and taking money out of the pockets of their victims at substantial and alarming rates.

I told Connie and Hank that I had engaged in some of the most frustrating and, frankly, most unbelievable conversations with big shots in the industry. Because I am a Track and Field buff, I am well versed on the rules for banned substances. Certain drugs are classified differently in track versus horse racing.

Lasix, for example, is banned because it is classified as a masking agent. Most involved in Thoroughbred racing did not know that, but the cheaters sure do and they use it to their great advantage, as its diuretic properties not only mask illicit drugs but they flush properties out of the system in quick order.

Clenbuterol, which most racetrack vets will prescribe to clean up a respiratory issue, is not banned in athletics solely for its effectiveness as a bronchodilator, but as an agent with steroidal impact. It buffs up the physique of a horse.

"So one morning I was chatting over a coffee with two prominent California breeders," I said. "I won't name them, but one guy is a rancher and the other a produce farmer. I was trying to get the rancher, as head of the racing board, to authorize purchase of a $35,000 machine that could immediately determine if a horse had been milk-shaked.

"Rather than focus on what I was trying to tell them, they instead told me that I was barking up the wrong tree, that there was no cheating taking place and proof of this was that no underlings had turned in their employers. So preposterous.

"Then I changed subjects to talk about the illegal benefits and dangers to the horses from overuse of Clenbuterol. I asked the rancher if he used the drug on his cattle. He sheepishly shied away from answering. But he damn well knew exactly what I was talking about. This is the sort of crap that has been going on for decades.

"And this is why I am so looking forward to catching someone red-handed right in the act of juicing a horse."

Connie asked me what I thought the agent was that Zane was using. I explained that Doc Church and I had speculated about this recently and we both suspected EPO, possibly in a newly engineered synthetic form that was developed without an accompanying test.

"Drug companies by law don't have to provide a test," I explained. "Some companies that are more ethical than others do provide a test, which is extremely helpful."

I explained what EPO was, how it impacted the performance of a racehorse or human runner and how difficult it was to detect as in the purest form it was produced in the body of a horse or human being. A synthetic EPO, if one really existed and was available, would be impossible to detect without a test being provided.

Before I left the Shumans I asked to use their phone to call my vet. When Doc answered the phone I asked him if I could pop over in a couple of hours for a quick but vitally important chat. He told me that he would leave my name at the gate.

On the drive back to the San Gabriel Valley I could not help but be excited. For years I had been in the industry's face about the unfair and dangerous use of PEDs in the game and virtually nobody outside of Dr. Church believed me. Some were downright hostile. Others talked behind my back, called me a troublemaker. I heard it from friends of mine.

The thought of finally being proven correct had made me so jazzed that I was hardly thinking about Knight Errant at that moment.

When I entered the Bradbury Estates it was nearly 5:30 p. m. As usual Doc was standing in the driveway, waiting to hear my news. I asked Doc to get in the passenger seat.

It took almost half an hour to bring Doc up to speed. I went through the whole interaction with Jilly, the blonde girl, Zane, Hank Shuman and his investigator Connie Squires. It took a lot of explaining.

I could tell that Doc was both fascinated and wondering exactly why I was taking so long and going into such detail with him. Finally, at the end of my update, I said "And you are wondering where you fit in, am I right?"

"Egg zackly" he said, stretching out each word.

So I told him that I wanted to speak to Buddy Hillenbrand. I wanted to make certain that he took this information with the seriousness that it deserved. "I am asking you to come with me when I meet Buddy," I said.

"Son," Doc Church said "I will do better than that. I will invite him and his wife up here for dinner. While the women are off gabbing about who is doing whom and getting or not getting found out, you, Buddy and I can have a powwow in a private setting with no prying eyes or big ears. How's that sound?"

In exactly nothing flat, we left the car, went into the ranch office and Doc was on the phone with Buddy. They were yukking it up pretty good, then Doc sprung the invitation on the chief executive of racing and Mr. Hillenbrand asked "Jim" to hang on while he checked their availability with his wife.

"How about tomorrow evening if that suits?" Doc said it did and he would see them at the ranch about 5:30 for cocktails.

Doc then added "And we'll have Billy Richards up here with us as well."

Buddy Hillenbrand, before hanging up, said "Fine, fine. I've been meaning to catch up with the young man since that gelding of his scorched the track at Del Mar. Should be entertaining if nothing else. Tomorrow then. Bye bye."

Doc walked me to my BMW. He put his arm across the frame of the driver's side window, leaned in and said "Tad told me what happened Billy. That was awfully white of you to go out and find his sorry ass, sober him up and give him a second chance.

"I know that you never really wanted him to train the gelding and that you only did it because you placed your trust in me. I do feel largely to blame and I apologize to you for this mess.

"I never would have guessed the pressure would get to him in this way. He's such an easy-going guy. But in looking back, I guess that's because other than his putter and his wedge he really placed no pressure on himself. Hey, it happens to the best of us. Even me or you. One never knows until one is in the heat of battle."

I swallowed hard when Doc uttered his "white" comment and once again had to trot out my separate peace initiative to retain the best thoughts possible of Dr. James Church.

I drove down to Celia's, where in line I ran into Karen Blincoe, an exercise rider for Whittingham. I got to know her a little when I lived with Jilly. We shared a table, chatting away while digging into our Mexican food.

"Damn this food is good here," I said, turning my head sideways and tearing into a green burrito.

"Yes," she agreed. "It's very nearly as good as great sex."

I about lost it, blurting out a laugh and not knowing if I could still swallow my burrito bite or if I should abort the chunk in my mouth.

She smiled.

When I was finished with my taco de carnitas and Karen had polished off her soft tostada, she asked if we should go to my cottage.

She followed me in her sports car.

It's like Hemingway wrote, maybe in "A Moveable Feast." Paraphrasing it he said that when you really needed a fuck one would pop out of the woodwork. I really needed one, I really needed the diversion and I really needed some activity after driving back and forth to Del Mar the same day. Ole Hem really knew his shit.

CHAPTER 24

As is the country club set's wont both Doc and Buddy were attired for a cocktail party, the vet wearing a charcoal-colored light tweed jacket and Buddy wearing a cocoa-colored linen sports coat. Knowing how these older guys invariably dress up a bit when booze is involved, I brought along a blue blazer so, just in case, I would not feel out of place. That was a rare smart apparel move on my part.

The meal was a treat, as the Churche's Latina housekeeper/cook always made memorial fare. This time she had prepared Camarones al Mojo de Ajo—sauteed shrimp, which she served over rice.

During the meal Buddy Hillenbrand was effusive in his praise of my talents, both in writing and as a racetracker. Even as an athlete I was always overly modest about my accomplishments, finding it uncomfortable to accept compliments and shying away from attention. I jumped and hurdled for the feeling I got from these endeavors, not for the glory or the medals.

I was getting the same feeling from my brief ownership of Knight Errant. I was not interested in the kudos, the attention or the glory, but for the thrills I got from watching the horse train, race, walk around the paddock and walk around the ring outside of his stall.

When that sucker came barreling down the lane in his first win at Del Mar, the rush of excitement made all my races and jumps pale in comparison to that feeling of watching a horse I was involved in performing at its best.

And the money was nice.

Interestingly, I had not made a single bet since the gelding won his first race. It had not even occurred to me in the past few weeks to make a bet. I realized that I probably had been betting as a form of self-validation—to prove that my opinions were valid, that they were correct. That I was right.

I had figured out a while ago that the real reason most gamblers were addicted to racing was to have the opportunity at the end of the race to be proven right. And to be able to verbalize it.

How many times have these words been uttered after a successful bet—was I right? Did I tell you? I knew that horse would win and I was right hot damn it!

So while Buddy and Doc praised me to the skies, my thoughts drifted to what we would talk about next, after the meal and all the back-patting had run its course.

As predicted, the wives moved to the outside patio. The men ambled a couple of rooms over in the sprawling ranch-style house to a den. Doc closed the door. We all sat within earshot out of an abundance of caution and habit.

Buddy leaned back in his big over-stuffed leather chair, crossed his legs, drew in a deep breath and said "So now, what's this all about. I knew when I spoke with Jim last night there was something important on your minds. Spill it."

Doc began, but I cut him off, jumping in to seize the

initiative, because I felt I knew the details and could tell the story better. Doc was relieved based on his expression, which made me feel less rude for interrupting him.

"Mr. Hillenbrand, you've known me long enough and read enough of my pieces to know that I am not a disgruntled loser that wants to blame others for his own shortcomings," I began.

"And, even though I have been a bettor since my early youth, I have never been one to point a finger at trainers that I suspect of unscrupulous behavior unless I think I have cause to believe any accusations.

"So what I am about to unfold here now is based on solid evidence, anecdotes from people that have first-hand knowledge and evidentiary reports from professionals in criminal investigations."

Buddy Hillenbrand had probably heard one crazy, unfounded, preposterous story after another in his more than 5 decades in the game, so it would have been understandable that he would look at me with a bit of skepticism. Yet he seemed genuinely interested in hearing me out.

I was not nervous talking to Buddy Hillenbrand, but I was starting to get some indigestion from the garlicky shrimp. My dad had been allergic to garlic. My mom loved it, would sneak it into a meal. When my dad woke up in the middle of the night with indigestion there was hell to pay. They rarely fought, but when she surreptitiously adulterated my father's food with that spice she was in danger of feeling the full thrust of his wrath. I remember once that she hid in a closet until he went back to sleep.

So I asked for a club soda, which I sipped during the rest of my presentation.

I recounted the entire saga. I told him about Hank Shuman and his investigation. I told him about our meeting with Connie Squires. I told him about Jilly Grant and her meeting with the blonde girl. I brought him up to speed on Connie's newfound information.

Buddy sat there, absorbing all the news. Doc occasionally looked at Buddy, nodding his head, raising his eyebrows and occasionally winking. When I completed my updates, Buddy sat there, thumping the fingers on one hand against his thigh, making "umhum" noises and finally coming out of his deep thinking to smile at me.

"Utterly fascinating," he said. "And plausible, Billy, both of us being writers, we understand that without plausibility no reader will take our stories with more than a grain of salt. In your story you have a veritable mountain of salt."

"Mr. Hillenbrand, I'm grateful to you for listening to what I have to say," I said. "The reason we—that is me, Mr. Shuman and the investigator—wanted you to hear our story is that Mr. Squires thinks you may have the best idea of how to handle this issue to bring it to fruition.

"Mr. Squires laid out numerous possible scenarios. But in the end, because these misdeeds are taking place on your property, you might have the best idea how to move forward."

Buddy was listening, but it was obvious from previous conversations I had had with him that the wheels in his skull were churning a mile a minute. He took out a tobacco pouch from the side pocket of his coat, as well as a pipe. He carefully filled the pipe bowl with what turned out to be a cherry tobacco blend that smelled wonderful but no doubt tasted like shit.

"Young man, you have no idea how much I deeply appreciate

you giving the Los Angeles Turf Club this opportunity to figure out the best manner in which to deal with this revelation," he said.

Doc could keep his yap shut no longer and he piped up, saying "Buddy, even though we have not yet come into possession of the substance being used, it seems pretty clear, based on how it has been described, how it is being delivered into the bloodstream, when it is being done and how Zane's horses never seem to get tired down the stretch that we are talking about some form—whether pure or synthetic—of EPO. Now I don't know if a synthetic version has been developed yet, but I know scientists are working on it."

Buddy nodded his head. He lit a match, held it over the bowl of his brown wooden pipe, then drew in a few times to get the thing going. Then after a while he spoke again. "Billy, this is your show. You did the groundwork, you know the players, you have the team. So I am wondering what you would like to see happen.

So I said that I would like to see Zane caught in the act, arrested and charged by some law enforcement entity, then ruled off the Turf for life after he was released from prison.

Buddy listened, his eyebrows going up and down, a faint smile starting and then retreating. He drew in a mouthful of smoke, leaned back and let it waft above him towards the ceiling.

"Jim, what about you?" Buddy asked

Doc said that first of all he would like to get his hands on the substance and share it with a chemist he knew at UCLA. Secondly, he said he did not particularly care what happened with Zane, but whatever it was should be severe enough to act as a deterrent to would-be cheaters in the future.

Buddy took in everything that Doc and I had to say.

After a while Buddy Hillenbrand said "I am going to sleep on this. Don't think I am going to sweep this under the rug by any means. I consider this to be both a shock and an opportunity.

"A shock because for the first time since I've been here at Santa Anita we have a chance to catch somebody in the act after all the rumors and innuendo. And an opportunity because it will allow us to rid the game of a very bad element.

"But this needs to be done with a high degree of sensitivity because there are a lot of ripples in the fabric of our game this can impact. A scandal like this can help and hurt the game and the thousands of people who work in the industry. It must be handled correctly.

"Any time something like this is tried, all the steps must be done with precision so as not to jeopardize any possible legal proceedings that follow. So some thought needs to be brought to bear on any enterprise that we decide to undertake."

Two days later after I came back from the track I had a message on my answering machine from Buddy Hillenbrand's private secretary asking me to attend a lunch meeting that very afternoon at The Derby Restaurant on Huntington Drive at the east end of Arcadia.

The Derby was an old-fashioned steakhouse, dark inside because the lights were purposely kept low. Legendary jockey George Woolf bought it in 1938, the year he famously rode Seabiscuit to beat War Admiral in a match race at Pimlico.

This time around I missed being able to view all The Iceman's memorabilia displayed on the walls and in cases throughout the dining rooms because I was advised to park on the street and enter through the rear, where I was led into a private dining room that I never knew of.

Buddy Hillenbrand introduced me to Edward Smallwood, the district attorney for the country of San Gabriel, Sergeant Frisco Canarsie of the Arcadia police department and Ruddy O'Brien of Santa Anita's security squad. I knew Buddy's director of racetrack operations Ray Cassidy and I shook his hand last.

Before getting down to business, we were asked to order. Naturally I ordered a steak, as this was the specialty of the house. I went for a bone-in ribeye, mashed potatoes and spinach. Normally I would have ordered a baked potato, because they knew how to cook them properly and a waitress wearing a short skirt would prepare the toppings from a cart right in front of you. But I correctly sized up the situation and realized that no young women would be infiltrating this boys' club meeting of great import and no little secrecy.

Buddy opened the floor to all of those in attendance and invited them to ask me any questions. Each professional there asked me at least three or four questions. They were pointed and all relevant.

Then Buddy laid out his goals of any operation that might be undertaken. He said that first and foremost was protecting the integrity of the game. Second was dealing strictly with the alleged perpetrator, Russell Zane. And third was to safeguard the sport going forward so as not to jeopardize the investments of the Los Angeles Turf Club, the jobs of its employees, everyone that earned their livelihoods in racing and breeding and the investment of the owners and trainers in horseflesh, land and equipment. He said that the tax base that contributed to the functioning of governments from the City of Arcadia to the State of California also needed to be considered.

Mr. Hillenbrand said "The biggest dilemma we face is how to deal with the crooked trainer. Is the goal to punish him as severely as possible to create a deterrent that would discourage his peers from engaging in such activities. Or is saving the game by not sullying its reputation more important?

"Billy, besides making you available to answer questions, the main reason I wanted you here was to deliver some news that you will undoubtedly find quite sobering and disappointing," he said.

"We are going to launch an operation next week, the week of the Chester Sherwood Stakes, to catch Mr. Zane in the act of administering an illegal substance to a horse.

"However, we do not plan to prosecute him. Instead, after he is brought down to the offices of the district attorney, he is going to be given a choice. He can choose to fight any action the DA has at his disposal to use against him, or he can accept a deal to walk away from the game. A lifetime ban. He will be given just a few hours to announce his retirement.

"I will confront Mr. Zane and promise to use our publicity department to craft a news story explaining that he has decided to walk away from the game. We can cite his desire to spend more time with his family and to delve even more deeply into his religious beliefs."

Mr. Hillenbrand looked at me as he spoke and I am certain that he saw the grave look of disappointment I wore on my face. But he never took his eyes off me.

"As for a deterrent," he said "you and I both know that everyone with half a brain will know that he would never leave the game unless forced out. So, in a way, a deterrent will be established, the game can move forward all the better for eliminating a cheater and a test will be made of the illicit drugs.

"The police will remove all of the drugs and paraphernalia from the storage unit. We will turn over all of it to the FBI so they can use their domestic and international resources to find out exactly who the suppliers of the drugs are or have been.

"Finally, I think a lot of good will come of this sordid affair. Santa Anita will beef up backstretch security. The FBI will have some new folks on their radar. Horsemen will think twice about what they consider putting into the bodies of their horses. And veterinarians will be put on notice to be extra careful in how and when they treat their animals.

"What say you young man?"

If I had been dealing with anybody other than Mr. Hillenbrand, I probably would have walked right out of the room then and there. But given the enormous respect I had for the man, his career and his intelligence, I forced myself to deal with the facts as they were presented and offered.

"Well," I said, with a catch in my throat. I swallowed a gulp of water. "Well, this is not what I or my associates in this little venture had envisioned. Certainly not ideal, that's for sure.

"Mr. Hillenbrand I am going to be dead honest with you, as this is the only way I know how to act. First let me admit and inform all of you here in the room that I have had an issue with authority from the time I could talk.

"Let me refine that. I have an issue with authority that uses its powers in unethical ways. So I am always skeptical of one's motives. Sir, if not for you, I would have walked out just now.

"But I admire you. I am going to trust your judgment and

follow your lead. Now I cannot speak for my friend Hank Shuman, who is really the guy that started this whole ball rolling. He put up more than a hundred grand to seek a resolution that would clean up and improve our game.

"What Hank will say when he is presented with the facts is something I cannot predict. But as for me, I am a team player. You can count on me."

Buddy asked if Hank Shuman had the ability to be transported to Santa Anita. I said that I thought it was likely. Buddy then said that he would offer to include Hank in on the bust. This way he would feel that he really had gotten some bang for his buck. "And I can offer him a clubhouse box until he no longer wishes to use it," Buddy said. "And we can give him a lifetime, complimentary membership in the Turf Club. If you thought it was necessary we could also create and present him with a plaque to hang on his wall from the Los Angeles Turf Club for meritorious service to the Sport of Kings."

The Director of Racing told me to confer with Hank as soon as possible. He said that the bust was scheduled for Tuesday morning. The police and district attorney would coordinate with Santa Anita security. Also, he wanted to bring Connie Squires in on this as soon as possible and asked me to contact him after the meeting.

"Billy, you can leave now and get to work on Mr. Shuman and Mr. Squires," he said. "You have quite a busy agenda coming next week, but rest assured that on this front everything will be done with the utmost professionalism. And when we make the bust, I want you, Doc and Hank right there by our side."

Once again I had to drive down to San Diego County to

meet with Hank and Connie to fill them in on what had transpired. They refused to talk on telephones. I was really getting tired of having to motor all the way down there. If traffic cooperated, it took 2 hours. If not it could be 3 to 3 ½ hours. No fun for sure.

I stayed overnight at the Winners' Circle Lodge. At 11 o'clock the next morning I met with Hank and Connie, as Alice stood behind the sofa and listened intently.

Hank at first was tremendously disappointed. Connie understood the underpinnings of the decision at once. He was 100 percent instrumental in bringing Hank across the finish line to support the operation.

"I guess my payoff will come when I stand next to that rat-bastard Zane when he is cuffed and walked off," Hank said. "If that doesn't wipe the shit-eating grin off that prick's face I don't know what would."

CHAPTER 25

One week out from the Chester Sherwood Stakes trainer Tad Smithwick decided not to give Knight Errant's a traditional blow out in his final piece of work.

In the tack room, with the door shut against prying eyes and open ears, Tad explained to me and Doc that the last thing he wanted to do was put more speed into the gelding.

"Blowing him out 3 furlongs would be like pouring kerosene on a fire" he said. "He's retained all his speed. I honestly don't think anything I could do would blunt it. It's always there, just under the surface, ready when needed.

"My idea is to produce a relaxed animal on the day, not one jazzed up or on his toes too much. I want to bring a horse over there that is composed, collected and poised to pounce. Not interested in bringing a tightly-wound horse with his eyes popping out of the sockets and all oiled up like one of those Russell Zane productions."

Once again, with all the hoopla and publicity Santa Anita's publicity department and advertising crews could generate, the gap to the track was crowded and the apron looked to be loaded with onlookers, all there to get a glimpse of all 3 major contenders for the Sherwood.

"Doc, since there's not going to be any fireworks this time, I am going to watch the move from the apron near the finish line where Charlie hangs out," I said to Dr. James Church.

"I am afraid there are going to be some mighty disappointed fans out here this morning, because there will not be a fast workout by our steed."

A crescendo of murmurs gradually increased as the announcer intoned "There he is folks, the equine rocket ship himself, the incredibly fast speedster Knight Errant. Trainer Tad Smithwick told the clockers that he plans to breeze him an easy half-mile, but for this horse easy could mean anything with his speed."

As was Charlie Whittingham's modus operandi, his horses hit the gap first and the very first worker after the renovation break was El Bestia del Bosque. Charlie did not give the Argentine Wonder Horse a great deal of warm up.

The Beast jogged to the three-quarter pole, galloped around the clubhouse turn and broke off at the 5-furlong marker on the backstretch. Employing long strides as opposed to quicker ones, he went evenly down the backside, picked it up a bit around the turn, and moved steadily down the lane, getting a tap on the shoulder as a reminder that Charlie wanted him to work out an additional furlong past the wire so that The Bald Eagle would be able to get a fuller look at him as he went past him.

Charlie turned to Doc and said "Just what the doctor ordered. Not you, of course." Then he winked and walked off.

A clocker called out "one eleven and two Charlie, last

quarter in :23 3/5." Whittingham looked up at the top deck of the grandstand to the clockers' booth and gave a thumbs up.

"That was a terrific work," I said to Doc. "For him to go that fast and finish up as strongly as he did bodes very well for him next week. He looks strong and, as they say, is a credit to his trainer. He is going to be very hard to beat."

Doc gave me a puzzled look. "You're not actually worried about him beating our horse are you Billy?"

I said "I will never be worried about another horse unless the next Secretariat or Dr. Fager jumps out of the woodwork. But I would be foolish to discount the chances of any rival that works as well as The Beast just did. And getting the better of Charlie Whittingham in a major race over a distance of ground with an older seasoned horse is never going to be a piece of cake. I am just giving credit where credit is due."

Knight Errant was still jogging the wrong way around the track on the outside rail for his warm-up when Redeemed came by us and headed around the turn to begin his final work for the Sherwood.

When he went by us his neck was sweaty, and not just where the reins rubbed against the neck, but between his legs, with thick gobs of sweat running down his hind legs and down his hocks.

Redeemed pulled hard all the way down the backside as he fought for his head. When the rider turned him loose just before the 3-furlong pole, he jumped into the work with a fervor that was frightening. This sucker had some kind of speed. He flew around the turn, cut the corner sharply at the quarter pole while hugging the rail and he barreled down the lane with no let up.

The crowd on hand clapped lightly as he finished off his move by galloping out around the turn. Plenty of wows were heard from those gathered for this free morning entertainment.

"Wonder what the hell else he is putting in this one's gas tank," Doc whispered to me. "I am going to get closer to the track and check for skid marks." Then he laughed and moved closer to the rail for a better look at the impending work of Knight Errant.

"Russell," a clocker called out from the rooftop perch. "Thirty-two and four my man. Unbelievable. Shivers...shivers is all I can say. See if you can keep his feet on the ground for a week."

Russell Zane beamed with that big, toothy grin of his. If he smiled any wider the corner of his mouth would start to bleed. If this asshole only had an inkling of what was in store for him that smile would be long gone. He literally strutted towards the stairs down towards the paddock. Enroute a few people came up to him, patting him on the back, wishing him good luck and extolling the virtues of his speedy animal.

Knight Errant, with the crowd not thinning out in the slightest, came by us at the wire. He was galloping now and at what appeared to be more of a 2-minute lick than a normal gallop.

The gelding maintained that pace steadily until approaching the half-mile pole, where he gradually increased the tempo. Rafael Quintana was in the irons. I never saw him let out a notch of rein at any point during the work. The gelding took the turn smoothly, switched leads so effortlessly at the top of the lane it was hard to notice and he came steadily past us in what looked for all outward appearances like a common gallop.

"Tad," a clocker called out. "Twenty-three and twenty-three. Forty-six flat. Out in :57 4/5."

Right in front of a large assemblage on onlookers, the clocker temporarily forgot where he was and blurted out "Jesus Christ this horse just ain't human!"

Laughter followed from many in the crowd and a large amount of applause followed the spits and final time.

I turned to Tad and said 'Well, so much for that theory of not letting him use his speed today."

He looked me square in the eyes and said "Billy believe me when I tell you that he was not showing his real speed today. You have no fucking idea of what lies under that sucker's hood. If we really want to cash in and score big we van him over after he cools out to Edwards Airforce Base and sell him to the government, because they ain't got the rocket fuel this guy has."

Doc looked at him and his expression said that he believed every syllable of Tad's preposterous analogy.

I owned the horse, I thought I had as much admiration for him as anybody, but my two partners in this venture were outwardly more bullish than me. It was weird.

When we turned around and started to take the apron shortcut to follow the horse exiting the racetrack, walking through the paddock, past the receiving barn and clear to the Association Gate at the entrance to the stable area, Buddy Hillenbrand came up behind us.

"That was some show was it not?" he said. "I've always said that I would rather be out here in the morning than in my office. This is where the fun is and the fireworks erupt.

"You know in all the years I've been here we've never had this many folks out to see public workouts. These three animals we have pointing for the Sherwood have really ignited an enormous amount of fan and community support. It is so gratifying to see."

Doc agreed. "Whodda thunk it, right? But a good horse stirs the imagination. Proof positive is we three gentlemen right here. That's what brought *us* all here."

I said "I cannot imagine what next weekend's going to be like. The crowd could rival Big 'Cap Day itself. S'gonna be a great week of anticipation."

Buddy said early estimates of the crowd size indicated that upwards of 66,000 very well could be in the offing and the weather looks like cooperating.

"Billy, meet me in the Cupola today between the fifth and sixth races," Buddy said to me. "It will be brief."

Knight Errant, based on his physical appearance on the walk back to Tad's stable, had taken the fast move in stride. He was not breathing particularly hard, he was prancing a bit when he walked around the ring before heading back to the barn and he seemed to be happy with himself.

Buddy said "I sure hope he can route. I must admit to having my doubts. Not based on pedigree of course. But anytime a horse has this much pure speed I have a difficult time believing they can stretch it over ground.

"Take that work today, him coming down the lane that last furlong in less than 12 seconds, that was the move of a sprinter. That's the way the old timers trained their sprinters. The best ones always gave you that eleven and change furlong on demand and without apparent effort."

Then he dropped a bombshell.

"I guess we'll find out what his breeder thinks in terms

of any stamina he might have hidden deep in the recesses of his pedigree, because Bear Harwood will be staying at my place when he arrives at the end of the week," Buddy said. "Never heard him so excited about one horse before and I've known him a good many years. We'll have dinner on Saturday night after the races and, of course, you will be expected to join us."

Doc looked at me to gauge my expression and gave me the old side eye, which if spoken aloud would have said "Oh boy."

Back at the barn Quintana was cleaning his tack. His English was not very good and I wanted to talk to him about a few things, just for my own curiosity, so I asked Hoppy, our groom, if he could help interpret.

Hoppy, whose English was not out of the top drawer either, was actually named Javier Soto. His nickname among the Latino community on the backside was Hovvie. The first trainer he worked for when he emigrated from Sud of de Border was a redneck old cowboy who thought he heard Hoppy instead of Hovvie. Everyone knew Hoppy, the nickname for Hopalong Cassidy, the hero of radio and TV programs. "Close enough," the redneck proclaimed. So Hoppy it was.

"Hoppy, please ask Quintana if I can ask him a few questions," I said. "Tell him not to worry about his English, as you will interpret as best as you can. Tell him this is not for the media, just for me, okay?"

Twenty-something Quintana was respectful of 50-something Hoppy, so he said "bueno." I replied "belly goo" which was backstretch for "very good" and everybody knew it. First few times I had heard "belly goo" used I flashed on some nastiness sticking to a belly button after sex.

"Quintana, what does it feel like to ride a horse like Knight Errant?" I asked.

When he shot back after Hoppy asked the question in Spanish with the obligatory "belly goo" I said "Yeah, yeah, yeah belly goo, right. Look, Quintana, I want you to think about this and tell me exactly what you feel when you are on an 'especial caballo' like this. Entiendes? Capiche?"

Shit, I had inadvertently tossed in an Italian word. My mistake. The only foreign language I knew a bit was Yiddish from my upbringing and Italian. I took Italian for a year at LACC. This jock probably thought I was nuts dropping in capiche, but such were my limitations.

Quintana smiled when capiche came out of Hoppy's yap.

Quintana was seated on a chair in the tack room. "Si si Bee-Lee," he said. "Ho-kay."

Leaning forward in his chair, crouching like he was astride a horse, with both arms placed in front of him, he started to explain something. He talked in such a rapid-fire manner I wondered if Hoppy would even be able to follow him. But my fear was groundless.

Quintana told Hoppy that riding the gelding was like riding no other horse he had ever been on. First, he is grateful for Tad telling him to just be a passenger, because aboard Knight Errant, all that was required was to get into his rhythm.

The special thing about Knight Errant, to hear Hoppy tell it, was the rhythm the horse was able to get into and how smoothly he went through his gears. Quintana had never ridden in a fancy car like a Rolls Royce but he imagined that must be close to what the feeling is he gets from riding Knight Errant.

The other thing he would say is that it is impossible to tell while astride the horse at what speed he was traveling. He says he had no idea. Each time he dismounts and is told the fractions he is completely surprised. He says that at times he thinks that Tad is pulling his leg.

One other thing that he thinks makes Knight Errant so different is that he does not seem to raise his feet very high off the ground. There is very little up and down, it is all forward with him. He is so light on his feet he barely feels the ground beneath him."

What Quintana and Hoppy said reminded me a lot of the way Jesse Owens looked when he ran. Asked what his secret was. Jesse would reply "spend as little time on the ground as possible." Jesse ran in an ultra-composed manner and his feet looked as though they were avoiding running over hot coals instead of soft cinders. So I guess the same could be said of Knight Errant.

Quintana also he would ride Knight Errant for free if it ever came to that. As he is young and has dreamt about being a jockey ever since he can remember, he worries that Knight Errant is so special that he will spoil him for life and wonders if he will lose interest sooner rather than later in being a jockey, as he knows he is unlikely to ever have a chance to ride another horse like him. Every night before he goes to bed he prays to God to take special care of Knight Errant, Meester Tad and Bee-Lee.

Quintana then started talking again, slowing down this time, as I imagined, for Hoppy to fully understand him. I heard the words "The Chew" and "Chewmaker." He was talking about Bill Shoemaker, arguably the greatest modern-day jockey.

Hoppy was told by Quintina that it was very interesting that I had asked him the same questions as "The Chew." Hoppy went on to tell me that Bill Shomaker had cornered Quintana in the jocks' room after the gelding's last win and asked him questions just like yours. Shoemaker said that he had ridden nearly all the greatest horses in America and even the world the last 25 years or so and had never seen one like Knight Errant, so he wanted to know what made him so special and what it felt like to ride him.

Hoppy then says that Quintana was asked by "Chewmaker" if he thought that Tad might allow him to breeze the horse one morning so that he could feel what it was like for himself.

I thanked both of them. I slipped two Benjamins in Hoppy's hand before I left the barn.

On the way back to my car I thought about Swaps, which until Knight Errant had been my favorite horse of all time. Swaps had a very unique action, but it was different from that of our gelding.

Swaps broke a bunch of world records two decades earlier when the tracks in California were manicured and honed for speed, so Easterners by and large never took his feats seriously, even though he took his record-breaking act on the road to establish new track records in Florida and Chicago. And even though he beat Nashua in the 1955 Kentucky Derby.

Key to Swaps success was the mechanical nature of his stride. It was like he had a built-in metronome that guided him. All of the action took place with his front feet flicking along in a machine-like manner.

Knight Errant, on the other hand, had a more supple and athletic way of going. There was none of the mechanical look to his stride. It was more like he floated, like a dancer, than a machine. He was more akin to a ballet artist like Baryshnikov.

Chapter 26

I met Buddy Hillenbrand in the Cupola later that Sunday afternoon, one week out from the Chester Sherwood Stakes. He was seated and motioned for me to sit down next to him.

"I know this is your retreat Billy," he said. "As you might well imagine I have ways of finding out who goes where around here. Although it is a cavernous plant with lots of nooks and crannies, we have excellent security within the confines of the plant. I don't mind, I just want you to know in case you ever have a notion to use the Cupola for any extracurricular activities a healthy young man such as yourself might consider becoming engaged in."

I laughed out loud and so did Buddy.

"Okay then," he began. "So tomorrow's the big day. Or more accurately the big night. I just wanted to touch base with you one last time before we gather for our operation.

"The plan is for all of those involved to meet at my home in San Marino. We will meet for dinner, then go over the fine strokes point by point. We will do this two or three times to make sure we are all on the same page and that everybody knows their role.

"Hank and Connie will be at my home tomorrow and they will be involved in the bust. You and Doc are coming and, obviously, are both going to be involved.

"The team consists of the following participants. Me, you, Doc, Hank, Connie, the Chief of Police in Arcadia, the District Attorney of San Gabriel Valley, Ray Cassidy and Santa Anita's head of security.

"Have you had any further thoughts about any of this you wish to share with me. If you do this would be the time to lodge them Billy."

I told Buddy Hillenbrand that as far as I am concerned I was ready to roll and looked forward to being on hand with the others.

Buddy stood, shook my hand and clasped the upper part of my hand with his other hand. My interpretation of this gesture was a show of gratitude for my bringing together all the elements that led to tomorrow's bust.

Promptly at 6 p.m. on Monday I knocked on the front door of Mr. Hillenbrand's stately home in San Marino. On the drive over I reflected on how things had improved for the lives of Jews in the pricey enclave, as it was not that many years ago that the City of San Marino had covenants barring members of the Tribe to purchase houses. And yet, here I was, about to be welcomed at a seat of power helping to improve our mutual lot in life. My dad hated racing, but he would have been proud to learn of my involvement in this operation that began this evening in, of all places, San Marino.

There would be no cocktails before the meal and no wine served with dinner on this day. As we all stood or sat around the large living room of the home, I sensed there was no fear or apprehension in the air. The general mood was one of excitement and anticipation, not unlike the mood before a major race. Buoyancy filled the air.

Hank Shuman surprised me. He was moving around like a new man. He told me that his back had improved dramatically, both because of the many months he had spent on the floor and the prospect of seeing something he basically funded come to fruition. Alice was there with him. She would not participate in the operation. She would remain with Mrs. Hillenbrand at the San Marino residence and wait for the members of the equine version of the Navy Seals to return to base in the wee hours of the morning.

The meal was not elaborate; it was light, befitting one for troops about to go into battle. This contingent would not, as Napoleon Bonaparte said, be traveling on its stomach. It was more of a cerebral maneuver, peopled by mature citizens of the realm of horse racing.

One interesting reflection, as offered by Buddy during the planning stages back in the living room after dinner, was that the enlisting of the guard at the Baldwin Gate answered a question the Director of Racing at Santa Anita had long wondered about, which explained why Zane's horses always seemed to race more effectively at Santa Anita as compared to Hollywood Park and Del Mar.

Hillenbrand said the piecing off of the guard allowed for unfettered access to the stable area with the fillip of security. The guard was a permanent employee of Santa Anita and did not work at the other two tracks. Also the unique configuration of the Santa Anita backstretch allowed for this flaw in security to be exploited.

As requested by the Chief of Police, everybody was clad in dark-colored clothing. Being in Southern California and still early enough in the fall, the climate was still a bit summery, so no heavy coats or sweaters were required.

The Chief of Police had stationed plainclothes detectives outside of Zane's Arcadia home, at the neighboring Los Angeles County Arboretum directly across from the Baldwin Gate and across the street from the storage facility. No police band radios were used in this operation so as not to tip anyone off.

Three unmarked black vehicles lined up in the circular driveway in front of the Hillenbrands' house at midnight. Everybody climbed in the cars and we caravaned toward Santa Anita Park, using Huntington Drive, going right past my cottage on the left, driving past Baldwin Avenue, past the Police Department and, after making a loop, turned back towards the racetrack.

The Chief decided to use the usually barricaded parking lot off Colorado Place to make the caravans entry, to avoid both the Baldwin and Association Gates where the operation might be observed.

Santa Anita's security detail had the Colorado Place barricades and the entrance to the Clubhouse manned to clear the way for the cars. When we all piled out of the vehicles we were led on a circuitous route through the bowels of the plant that led us to the executive offices. It being a dark day there were no clean-up, janitorial or security staff about to detect our presence.

"I miss the morning aroma of the donuts being prepared," Buddy said and it elicited some gentle laughter among the contingent. We waited in the tunnel on folding chairs provided by Ray Cassidy's team.

Once the Chief received word from the cop surveilling the Zane home in Arcadia, the plan called for our foot soldiers to walk past the executive offices, down the pathway between the stable area and the track to a small rarely used gate that would allow us to gain access to the backstretch without detection.

Once situated near the stable area we were a short walk of perhaps 2 minutes from Zane's barn.

At precisely 2:05 a. m. on the Tuesday before the Chester Sherwood Stakes the chief got the alert that Zane had left his house.

"Let's roll" commanded the Chief. Mr. Cassidy led the single-file line on the appointed route. Once we had all cleared the gate that was large enough to provide entry of one person at a time, we waited in a line with our backs facing the chain link fence. We were standing on the pathway that the horses used when walking to and from the racetrack at the gap.

All was still except for the occasional whinny of a horse. It was pitch black outside. About 4 minutes later the Chief's phone buzzed. It was game on. He raised an arm, motioned for us to follow him and we walked in a single file line. We all waited outside the back of the barn that was situated one barn behind Zane's.

Three minutes later the Chief's phone buzzed once again, signaling that Zane had arrived at the Baldwin Gate. The Chief, no dummy when it came to operations of this sort, had left one wrinkle out of his plan as disseminated to the members of the contingent.

Working with Santa Anita's head of security he had stationed one more detective in a barn with full-view access to Zane's barn. When he saw Zane enter a stall, he alerted the Chief, whose phone buzzed. The Chief waved his hand vigorously and motioned for all of us to move our asses as fast as possible without making a commotion.

The fourth detective on this detail was standing in the shedrow and when he saw the Chief he pointed to the stall in which Zane and his foreman had entered. In a flash the head of security breached the stall by unhooking the webbing from its screw eye.

Single file we all followed one another into the stall, lining the sides of the walls. Second in line was none other than Buddy Hillenbrand. "Well good morning Mr. Zane," he said in a most pleasant manner. "Fancy meeting you here at this hour. And what is that you have in your hand there, sir, a syringe. A little early in the morning to be giving your animal there his vitamin B shot, hey?"

The contorted look on Zane's face will live with me until the day that I die. The shock of this law enforcement intervention caused a look of horror to take over his features. If a face could explode, it would look like this I thought.

The needle was still in the jugular vein when we walked in, as Zane was frozen in place from the shock of the intrusion. His foreman just stood still and stared at the yellow straw bedding on the floor of the stall.

The Chief took a few photographs to document the raid.

Doc, who had slipped on a pair of rubber surgical gloves, piped up, saying "Russell, please remove the syringe right now just as it is and hand it to me." Once in receipt of the partially spent syringe Doc put it in a medical container and handed it to the Chief. In another bag Doc collected the remainder of items used in preparing the horse for the injection and handed that one to the Chief as well.

Buddy then painstakingly introduced each member of the contingent, explaining each participant's role in the operation, but being careful not to reveal methods and sources, such as the blonde girl.

Mr. Hillenbrand acted as prosecutor making his final argument to a jury. He was complete where he needed to be and unflinchingly blunt where that was called for.

"Russell, you are a very lucky young man," Buddy said. He tried to look Zane in the eyes, but at this point the cheater could not bring himself to do it and only looked at the ground.

"The team here has discussed how we want to handle this mess and in order to safeguard the game for all of those hard-working men and woman who have devoted their adult lives to Thoroughbred racing we are not going to send you to jail.

"Instead you are never going to be able to train a horse again anywhere in North America. You are never going to be allowed onto the frontside or backside of any track in North America.

"You will never be allowed to work in this industry again. You will not be allowed to advise anybody, you will not be allowed to breed horses and you will not be allowed to sell horses.

"As far as this industry goes, it has washed it hands of you. You are done.

"My Director of Publicity at Santa Anita will meet with you before lunch today and help craft your statement of retirement from training horses. You can say you want to spend more time with your family. Or that God has called you to a higher purpose. Frankly I don't give a damn what bullshit you want to foist upon the public. That's your call. But this announcement will be released later today.

"You have that assistant trainer of yours be in my office before noon today. When you leave here you will be taken to the offices of the District Attorney of San Gabriel Valley. He will have a plea for you to sign, admitting among other things that you have for years been engaged in practices that are illegal and detrimental to the game.

"The DA will hang on to that plea and it will never see the light of day unless you break the rules that you will agree to, all of which I have outlined right here this morning.

"Now get your sorry ass out of this stall, out of this barn, out of my stable area and take a long look on the way out, because in your entire life you will never see it again you selfish, disgusting, uncaring little piece of merd."

With that Russell Zane walked out of the stall, was met by 4 policemen who handcuffed him and led him to an unmarked patrol car that headed out of the Baldwin Gate.

A trio of other officers walked to the Baldwin Gate hut, handcuffed the guard and put him in another unmarked car. The security chief already had his replacement on site.

The foreman met with the security chief. Mr. Hillenbrand had told the chief to have the foreman stay put, take care of the barn until early in the afternoon, when Zane's assistant would let him know what to do next. The foreman was strongly advised not to try to flee, as he was being watched. The foreman handed over the keys to his car. He was advised to keep his mouth shut.

By the time Buddy, me, Doc, Hank, Connie and Ray arrived back at The Hillenbrand home it was nearly 4 in the morning. Buddy had called ahead so that when we arrived the dining room table was filled with an array of pastries, eggs, oatmeal, cookies, bacon, sausages and a fruit bowl.

We sat around the table, where Alice joined us along with Buddy's wife. We felt like conquering heroes returning from a battle. I was completely worn out, as the anxiety of the bust and the lateness of the hour had sapped my energy. I was having trouble staying awake. But the occasion demanded that I try my best to pay attention.

Buddy said to nobody in particular, "So now that we have been through this battle, we have captured the enemy of racing and we have restored order to the realm, how are we feeling right about now?"

Hank broke the silence that followed Buddy's question.

"Well, speaking strictly for myself and hopefully my patient wife who indulged me in funding part of this project, I feel a lot better than I thought I might," he said "because, frankly, I wanted to see the book thrown at Russell Zane. I worried when I heard the plan as set out before me that I would feel hollow afterwards.

"But thanks to Mr. Hillenbrand allowing me to face the devil and watch him squirm and knowing we will never have to deal with him again, I feel all right. Better than I thought I would."

Connie said "I am relieved to hear you say this Hank because we have worked long and hard for a good outcome and this has been a difficult compromise for you to swallow.

"But, I have been involved in many a contretemps like this one, and most of them work out along similar lines. One never gets everything one wants. On the whole I for one am quite satisfied with the outcome. And not bringing in the FBI allowed us to tidy things up in a very speedy manner."

Doc said "I for one cannot wait to see what's in that syringe."

Ray said "And I cannot wait to see what the police find when they get the contraband out of the storage unit."

Then everybody stared at me.

"Well," I began, "one thing is for sure and that is I am happy as hell not to have to write about what just happened before going to bed."

Laughter followed but everybody still looked at me.

"Ok, ok, I know you are all concerned that I am bitterly disappointed to see Zane get off the hook with a light sentence. I understand that the most meaningful thing in his existence has been removed.

"Like all of us here now with the exception of Connie, a civilian when it comes to racing, we would die if not allowed to be able to participate in this game, so I know how important it is that we have taken this away from him.

"Retribution against him was never my goal, as maybe it was for Hank. But the lack of a known deterrent concerns me the most. I get not alarming the public, the betting public in particular. But how will we know what rank and file horsemen think about this whole thing and will it in any way change the culture of cheating in racing. That's what banging around my brain right now."

After eating everybody went their separate ways. We all shook hands and went to our waiting vehicles. I drove very slowly back to my place. For the sake of interest I took Colorado Place down to Baldwin Avenue, hung a right turn and drove slowly past the Baldwin gate. As it was nearly 7 o'clock there was quite a bit of activity in the parking lot where the trainers, exercise riders and grooms parked their cars. But otherwise things appeared as usual and, importantly, there were no signs of cops or security.

Back at my place I took off my shoes, lay my head on my pillow and fell asleep above the covers with my clothes on.

CHAPTER 27

Tuesday before the Chester Sherwood Stakes I awakened, fully clothed except for my shoes, just before 3 p. m. So if I was lucky I may have gotten about 5 hours sleep. Not horrible, but not great either.

Sitting on the edge of the bed I had that dazed sensation I always get when I don't get enough shuteye. I function best on 8-plus hours but have learned I can get by fine on 6; however, 5 hours just doesn't cut it for me.

I was hungry, so without even changing my clothes I drove up the street on Michillinda Avenue to Tops, got in the drive-through line and ordered a bacon and egg sandwich with fries. I pulled over, parked the car and proceeded to indulge myself in the totally unhealthy but delicious sandwich. Such was my irresponsibility that I even had them make it with mayonnaise slathered on white bread for chrissake. If The Rabbi only knew!

As I methodically bit into the soft bread, chewed and swallowed the bites of Tops' fare, I recounted the events of the early morning operation, which had taken place just half a mile down the road at Santa Anita.

By this time, I reckoned, Santa Anita's Director of Publicity

Sally Goldfarb and Ray Cassidy had sat down with Russell Zane, gone through the points that the Los Angeles Turf Club and the San Gabriel Valley District Attorney wanted to incorporate in a news release and had churned out something that would appear in less than 2 hours in *Daily Racing Form.*

The fact that my phone never rang once from the time I fell asleep to the time I woke up told me that no news had yet been leaked, because as much as I had railed against Zane, surely if the news had been on the streets, so to speak, somebody would have contacted me if for no other reason than to tell me that my suspicions had been confirmed.

When I got back to my cottage I was still a bit groggy from lack of sleep and still a bit edgy over having to be involved in such a tense operation in the middle of the night.

So I sat on the only comfortable chair in my pad. Next thing I knew it was 6:30 in the evening. I had unknowingly fallen asleep while sitting on the chair.

I decided to take a shower, which I figured would get my juices flowing and wake me up, as it always did in the morning. After I got dressed, I got in the car and drove down Huntington Drive to the drive-in liquor store on the corner of Santa Anita Avenue, across the street from the iconic windmill-topped Van de Kamps restaurant.

That windmill always made me giggle a bit internally as it reminded me of the response in print of some English novelists that swarmed Hollywood after WW2 to earn big bucks writing crap screen plays. They never got over making fun of L. A.'s homes that were built to resemble chateaus, chalets and the like. You know, the kitsch that symbolized the New World's lack of sophistication and make-believe in Tinsel

Town. Evelyn Waugh brilliantly satirized the phenomenon in his novel "The Loved One." As far away as little old Arcadia was from Hollywood, we had our very own representation of this fun architectural feature in that Van de Kamp's windmill.

When I was not at the track and I was home in Arcadia, I always got my *Form* at the drive-in liquor store. Rather than wait to get home, which was a drive of 5 minutes, I pulled around the back, stopped my car in the alley near the smelly trash cans of the local bar and began to read what I suspected would be some prize fiction writing from Miss Goldfarb. I was not disappointed.

Daily Racing Form, because the release had been churned out on a dark day at the track and very late in the afternoon when all its staff had left Santa Anita, simply printed word for word the entire release as sent by the publicity department.

Here is the news release, word for bloody word, as sent out by Sally. *DRF* did not even bother to change the suggested headline:

Zane Retires from Training

Russell Zane today surprised the racing world by announcing his retirement from horse racing. The shock revelation was made this afternoon at Santa Anita, where the 56-year-old horseman personally told Director of Racing W. R. (Buddy) Hillenbrand of his decision.

"My entire life has revolved around horse racing," he said. "I have been at the track since I was a kid, helping out my father, then working for Farrel Jones and eventually going out on my own.

"There's an entire world out there I know little about, but I want to know more. And I want to spend more time with my family, so we can explore it together and I can support them in a way I have not been able to given the all-consuming nature of horse racing.

"As many people by now know, I am a very spiritual person and credit The Lord Jesus Christ with getting me and keeping me on the straight and narrow. I had a 'Come to Jesus' moment this week. Jesus came to me and we both felt that there was more for me outside of this sport. The church can expect to see a lot more of me going forward.

"My wife and family totally support my decision, as they know how hard I work and how many hours I spend away from them. Because I have shorted them by being unavailable, I have made the further refinement to my decision by planning to completely abandon my involvement in any aspect of the game and its demanding lifestyle.

"Naturally I will miss all my friends in racing. I will especially miss my clients. However in my young but well-tutored assistant Steve Di Carlo, I know they will be in good hands."

One of Di Carlo's first starts as a trainer will come in Sunday's Chester Sherwood Stakes, for which the 29-year-old college graduate will saddle one of the favorites in Redeemed.

"Russell surprised us all, didn't he?" said young Di Carlo, who first came to the backstretch half a dozen years ago after attending the races with his family since childhood. Zane has often commented that Di Carlo's biggest strength is his handicapping ability and his expertise in placing horses for maximum effectiveness.

Hillenbrand said "Racing's loss is the Zane family's gain. It is always difficult for the sport to lose someone of Russell Zane's stature. He will be missed. But there are a lot of fine young horsemen in the wings ready for their opportunity to shine and Steve Di Carlo is one of them. Such is the natural progression in the training ranks."

When I got back to my digs, the phone started ringing. The calls did not stop until about 10:30 in the evening.

Gossip-monger Murray Stronzo was the first batter at the plate.

"You were right Billy Boy," he said. "You nailed it pal. From the first day I started following you around the Del Mar backstretch you said it. You must feel gratified knowing he got the boot."

I asked him how he had come to that conclusion from reading the news release.

"Uh, because unlike the Scarecrow in *The Wizard of Oz* I have a brain" he quipped.

I suggested that he was not an atypical New Yorker that saw the rotten side of everything and was always willing to go there first without any facts.

"Oh c'mon Billy," he said in a softer tone than normal. "I figured you would be celebrating this news. What's the back story here, anyway?"

I told Murray that the whole thing was news to me and that I had been preoccupied with my own life at the present time and had lost touch with all the backstretch gossip since I stopped writing for the *Form*.

Next batter was Will Christiansen of *The Mirror*. "Some wild speculation out there Billy," he said, sounding more like Walter Winchell than the old boy himself. All he was missing were the sounds Walter Winchell made by tapping telegraph keys.

I countered with "Out there? Out there. What does that

mean anyway?" I said, "Where exactly is out there? Ah, I'll bet that's where *they* live. You know that gigantic amorphous body of unidentified individuals that drop a horse's odds at the last second. The group that knows the identity of a winner before a race is even run. The ones who know precisely who shot JFK and the identity of the Unknown Soldier. You know: *they*. *They* are out there. What's on your mind Will?"

Will was caught off guard by that little burst of pent-up angst from me.

"Wow, got a bee in your bonnet tonight do we?" he said. "I just thought I'd check in with you to find out anything you can tell me about Zane's decision to quit the track

"You've got your ear to the ground out there. Fuck I cannot fucking believe I said out there again. Woe is fucking me. I need to be more cognizant of this phrase and find an alternative. Anyway, whatcha hear, you know, round and about?

Basically I repeated the same line that I had given to Murray.

Will said the rumors circulating included a mysterious side piece of ass, the sudden disappearance of Zane's longtime foreman and an inordinate amount of silence from Santa Anita's racing and management staff.

Fat Barry was next in the batting order.

"Billy this whole thing with Zane is wild," he said. "As you well know I have been giving him more and more horses. He wins a lot of races, so naturally I had always wondered about him. But with all that Jesus stuff I figured he must have been on the up and up.

"Now I am hearing a lot of stuff from my contacts and none of it is good. What can you tell me Billy? I have not heard a single word from him or his assistant."

After I assured The Fat Man that I knew nothing, he said his sources—guys he employed to work the crowd on Pick Six carryover days to find live tickets—have heard grumblings about that car dealer he trains for, you know, Dick Hamilton. That guy wins an awful lot of races, many times with some suspect animals. They say he may be involved in some way, possibly as a supplier of hop for Zane's horses."

I told Fat Barry—or as some of us that were raised in a Jewish household would call him Fat Barra-La—that this was news to me, but that if I heard anything interesting I would keep him informed.

I was beginning to enjoy the shit out of this fall out. As I had told Mr. Hillenbrand, I was very concerned that his muted approach to exposing and punishing Zane would let his enablers and partners in crime to be shielded from the entire incident.

Mr. Hillenbrand, with a knowing expression on his face as well as a half-raised eyebrow, assured me that this would in fact not be the case. "Billy, as much as we will take every precaution necessary to shield everyone involved in this operation, I will not be totally successful.

"After all, we are not the CIA. We are just a sporting venue with minimal security staff. It will be impossible to contain any leaks. Word will get out. I advise you to be ready for it and to concoct the story that best addresses your sensibilities on the subject.

"As little credence as I know you gave this operation in creating a deterrent, may I humbly suggest to you that this is an incorrect assumption of what is almost certain to transpire.

"The merd is definitely going to hit the fan. And as it unfolds it should prove to be highly entertaining to those of us who have been involved. You will see Bill. You will learn that I am right."

Doug Denton, administrative head of the Horsemen's Benevolent and Protective Association, called out of the blue. As a journalist I often found myself at loggerheads with this self-appointed dispenser of good news that invariably placed the actions of horsemen in a most favorable light, whether deserved or not.

"Hi there Billy, long time no see," he began. "Good luck this weekend with your horse. I am so happy for you, you have no idea. Hey, I know you no longer write for the *Form* but I was wondering if you could steer some of your pals there and in the press box to generate some positive stories about this Zane thing."

I responded "Zane thing? Zane thing you say. What exactly is this thing?"

He tried, but failed, to adequately explain that while the publicity department's release was all "fine and dandy" that there were so many negative rumors flying around the backstretch, that he was concerned some of these preposterous tales might leak over to the general populace and hurt the reputation of all horsemen.

"Doug, listen to me," I said. "I have no fucking idea about any rumors. But, as I have been warning you for years, if rank-and-file trainers don't stop clamming up and begin to share their knowledge of unscrupulous goings on in the stable area, a pickle like this would never come about.

"You and I both know why trainers practice omerta. They are worried that if one trainer is caught or outed that it paints them all with the same brush. This is unhelpful in creating a clean game and level playing field.

"So I am completely without sympathy for you or your members that see a trainer or a vet juice or milkshake a horse, say nothing, then look for cover when the truth comes out. You are barking up the wrong tree with me Doug."

Undeterred by my lashing, Doug came right back at me, saying "You know Billy, for somebody so deeply entrenched in the game and so fortunate you have quite a jaundiced take on this matter."

I interrupted, saying "Doug what a shame you were not born a little sooner and in Germany, because Hitler could have used a good apologist like you." I hung up the phone.

As it turned out Doug Denton had little to worry about, as the pathetic racing press took up his side of the argument with little need for prompting. The thing about Turf Writers, which is why I have so little use for too many of them, is they are less interested in doing their job for a readership that deserves better and instead put their energy into buddying-up to a horseman based on the misguided notion that this close relationship will inure to their benefit in some way. They are some of the worst ass kissers in all of sports. Can anyone imagine a boxing writer or a baseball writer taking up the side of an athlete that hung the public out to dry? No. But in racing it happens day in and day out.

In publications both local and national, stories surfaced extoling the virtues both as a horseman and as a human being of Russell Zane. He may have lost his profession and his livelihood, but he seemed assured of a place in Heaven.

Zane, of course, was unavailable for comment, having packed his wife and luggage in the car and driven off to some unknown location to escape the heat. His two kids were adults and on their own. Nobody, it seemed, knew where the Zanes went or how to get a hold of them.

But if you think this stopped the press from churning out one puff piece after another you would be dead wrong.

Will Christensen, as was his wont, trotted out comments and quotes from his vast morgue of previous pieces and knocked out a glowing tribute to the man in question.

Jeff Dayton obtained quotes from several trainers on the backstretch which he incorporated into a nicely done puff piece on Zane's standing among his peers. Trainers who had gotten their butts fried by juiced Zane rivals stepped up to the plate and knocked home run after home run out of the park in praising the horsemanship and humanity of a guy that took food off their table and depleted their bank balances.

These gutless wonders, trainers who would undoubtedly have stuck a shiv in the belly of Zane if they knew they could get away with it, tripped over themselves to praise the man, probably in hopes of getting some of his clients, as not everybody was certain to leave horses in the care of a green kid whose biggest calling card was that he knew how to read the *Racing Form.*

I phoned Doc Church even though it was starting to get late. I just had to vent to somebody. He was up, sounded wide awake and listened to me rag on about the phone calls.

"Doc, one question I have that keeps nagging at me," I said. "This Di Carlo character. Do you think he was in on the play?"

Doc said "Good question for sure. It is, in fact, *the* question. As we've seen before, the most successful cheaters of our time are loners, guys who never share their secrets for fear of getting caught.

"We know that he brought his foreman in on the caper. But there is, as far as I can tell, no evidence that he involved his assistant. I guess it is entirely possible that he brought him up to speed at one point and purposely kept him in the background to shield him until he needed to bring him in.

"But our operation struck so fast and so out of the blue that there was no time to bring Di Carlo up to speed at the inflection point of our bust. So right now it is a mystery. For the sake of the game I hope that he is clueless. But this may be totally naïve thinking."

Shit, fuck, piss I thought to myself. Wouldn't this be a total pisser if it turned out that we had done all of this for nothing.

CHAPTER 28

Chester Sherwood Stakes going a mile and a furlong on the main dirt track highlighted the Sunday card. In fact it anchored the entire fall race meeting at Santa Anita

The evening before the race, Director of Racing at W. R. (Buddy) Hillenbrand hosted a small gathering that featured some of the prominent connections with horses in the race. Because only 5 entered the contest, the numbers that had to be catered to by the Hillenbrands was smaller than would have been anticipated.

So there was plenty of room for the visiting Bear Harwood. Dr. and Mrs. Church, dear friends of The Bear, naturally were invited.

Mr. Harwood, a house guest of the Hillenbrands, was as his nickname suggests a physically imposing man. Standing more than 6 feet 3 inches, he was well into his 60s yet still possessed the straight shoulders that characterized his career as a WW2 major in the Army. When he spoke in his deep commanding baritone voice it only served to strengthen the impression he gave as the unquestioned leader in the entire Thoroughbred breeding industry.

When he shook my hand in the Hillenbrands' deep

cherry-wood paneled bar and I felt his strength and looked up at him into his rich brown eyes, I said to myself "and this is who I told to take a hike when I was asked if he could have his name join mine on the ownership line of Knight Errant? What the fuck was I thinking." Anyway, what was done was done. Moving right along now!

The Bear could not have been more gracious or kind in his comments to me and I will never forget the class he showed when he did not have to.

"I wouldn't be standing here tonight if not for you my young friend and for that I will be eternally grateful," he said. "Thank you, sir, for what you have allowed to occur with the many families of horses at Ellerslie whose lineage has been greatly enhanced by the exploits on the track of Knight Errant. And let's hope tomorrow adds yet another glorious chapter to this unusual saga."

The Bear motioned me aside and I followed him out into the patio that was void of people since it was cocktail hour. "Billy I don't want you to feel badly because you wound up with Knight Errant," he said. "I can only imagine how difficult it must be for you to face me today, having taken an Ellerslie reject and grabbed the brass ring.

"And I don't want you to walk around thinking that I harbor ill will towards you in any way. Between us two, I have been in your position. What you did is part and parcel of the game.

"Today, as an elder stateman in racing, I appear as an important, well-entrenched owner. But in reality, I am nothing but a simple farmer that raises some horses. If not for the truly important men of great wealth and sporting instincts I would be nothing.

"So, we are both a couple of working stiffs trying to do the best we can and take our shots when and where they might arise. Just know that I am indebted to you for your insight, your instincts and your cleverness.

"When all the dust settles in the coming days and weeks, keep me in mind. I am sure there are things we can do together and, if not, I surely would like to have a hand in guiding you in the right direction to achieve any goals you might have."

He shook my hand again. This time I was so overwhelmed with emotion that I did not know if his grip was strong or not. I was numb.

Charlie Whittingham caught sight of Bear Harwood talking with me. He came outside to join us.

"You mean you are still willing to talk to this punk after he ripped off the best horse you've bred in a decade?" Whittingham teased. Bear was having a difficult time suppressing a smile, but eventually he lost the battle, embraced The Bald Eagle and they laughed.

Charlie said "He's a good kid, Bear. I've known him for a while. But I could never train for him. Every time these Jews lose a race the first thing they want to do is go to the wailing wall. Not for me," he said, then gave me a slap on the back. "No Bear, this one's all right."

Back in my room after the party, I noticed that much was written and uttered in advance of the Chester Sherwood Stakes, but the bottom line was that it was on paper a 3-horse race bringing together for the first time Charlie Whittingham's Argentine Wonder Horse El Bestia del Bosque, Shifty Stable's claimer of the decade Redeemed and my very own Knight Errant.

Bernie Bokun most likely fretted over his morning line,

because there was much emotion that played into which horses folks would bet.

"The Beast" was trained by the most successful and popular horseman in the modern era and had been meticulously prepared for the Sherwood.

Redeemed had won the hearts and minds of local horseplayers and fans by climbing out of the lower claiming ranks and scaling the heights for trainer Russell Zane. He still carried any conditioning put into him by his former trainer and he still retained his regular jockey.

Knight Errant was the mystery horse. Yes, he had his supporters, but their loyalty was being rocked by those favoring the other pair, which pointed out that no matter how speedy the gelding might be he lacked the foundation and experience to rise this quickly in class and distance.

Detractors of Knight Errant also pointed out that his rider was more suited to plying his trade at a Third World track like Agua Caliente and his trainer was more interested in hitting the links than the backstretch.

Interestingly, but not shockingly as I was to learn firsthand, not one of the many Turf Writers bothered to reach out to me or write about me. If not for Sally Goldfarb nary a mention of my name would have surfaced, and as it was, it only appeared in the mimeographed publicity department handouts located in a rarely trafficked bin in the press box.

Sally wrote that Knight Errant was the first horse owned by ex-*DRF* columnist William (Billy) Richards. She also wrote that Tad Smithwick would be looking for the third stakes win of his career, having taken a minor event at Latonia before he won the Bing Crosby..

Bokun put "The Beast" as the 8 to 5 favorite, Redeemed at 7 to 2, Knight Errant at 12 to 1 and a pair of long shots at 25 to 1 and 30 to 1.

Walking into the track the next afternoon on the pathway that led from the receiving barn towards the paddock, a writer for a small Orange Country newspaper came toward me and said "Good luck, pal. And you'll need it. I don't follow your thinking here fella," he said shaking his head. "Just don't get it."

As an owner of a horse in the feature race on a weekend I was entitled to have lunch in the Directors' Room overlooking the Turf Club, so I went up there, checked in with Nancy Wallen at the entrance and was shown to a seat. I checked out the buffet. It looked pretty damn impressive. Everything Santa Anita did in terms of presentation was always first class.

I approached the bar, ordered a pineapple juice with no ice. I stood there for a bit, then eventually moved toward my seat. Chester Sherwood, for whom the race had not-so-oddly been named, saw me and nodded.

There were some owners up there that I had interviewed multiple times. And there was Mr. Sherwood. Not a single one of them bothered to give me anything but a cursory glance. Based on my experience at Del Mar and now at Santa Anita I was learning that when I posed no threat and was capable of giving them publicity, owners were all too happy to receive or engage me. But now that I was a rival I suddenly had contracted a terminal case of the cooties.

Without taking so much as a potato chip or cracker, and walking past a bowl of some of the best-looking cocktail shrimp I had ever seen, I beat a hasty retreat from the Directors' Room and made my way to the elevator for a ride to what I hoped would be more friendly ground in the press box.

Jake Janikowski's absurd mug greeted me when the doors parted. He treated me to that goofy-ass nervous laugh of his. "Sally told me I could have lunch in the Press Box today if I wanted to," I told him.

He reached for the phone and said "let me check" while watching me for any change in expression. He stopped short of lifting the receiver and said "just kidding! Just kidding! Bill, think you got any shot at all today with that horse of yours? Tell me: what do you know that none of the rest of us do? Or are you just taking a shot, taking a shot?"

I winked at Jake and said that I was just trying to get lucky like everybody else.

Pat Smith saw me through his unoccupied mutuel window, stuck his hand out for a shake and told me how much he had missed seeing me. He wished me good luck and told me that he would be rooting for me.

Sally saw me walk by, came out to engage me, walked me over to the food dispensing area and informed Jimmy that I was Santa Anita's guest today. "Billy have a seat when you are ready," she said. "Bon chance today. Win, lose or draw, this has got to be some day for you. Best of luck Billy and I mean it."

Well, those initial greetings—all coming from people employed by the racing association—would represent the sum total of any positive comments I would garner from my visit to the press box.

I took a quick glance at the writers situated behind the glass that separated them from their workspaces and the outside world. They were inside their inner sanctum. The rest of the world, as the saying goes, was out there. And rarely will the two worlds collide, especially if the writers have anything to say about it.

The place was fully packed with writers from up and down the West Coast, as well as reporters from UPI and Associated Press, *Sports Illustrated*, the major L. A. dailies and with a few obligatory hangers-on, motion picture actors, ex-star athletes… you name it, they were there.

In the approximately 3 minutes that I stood there waiting for someone to reach out to me, I never garnered a look. So I went to the food counter, and asked for a rare cut of prime rib, some mashed potatoes and gravy, with sauteed green beans. The food was always great as Santa Anita's culinary department served the same fare they offered to Turf Club patrons.

When he handed me my plate, Jimmy said "Enjoy it Billy. Because the rest of the day is going to be strictly uphill for you I'm afraid. Just try not to shit yourself while you're up here in the press box toilet willya."

I sat down, basically ate by myself as I had arrived after the second race on the 9-race card and the regular press box denizens had long since eaten as much as their gullets could handle.

Allesandro Cambi, a short, squat balding out-of-town handicapper from the *Desert Dispatch* in Barstow, leaned over across my plate and said "Buh buh Billy any chuh chuh chance that throw away horse of yours cah cah can run with these today?" When he spoke, because of his speech impediment, white sticky scuz formed in the corners of his mouth and some of this orally generated moisture found its way onto the dining room table. I don't know if any got on my plate, but I was in no mood to find out.

As I rose from my chair to bus my own plate, I said to Cambi "Hey, let me ask you a simple question, ok?"

He nodded.

"If Charlie Fucking Whittingham was seated here instead of me, would you ask him that same question in the exact same way?"

He donned a puzzled expressed, thought about it and said "Yeah yeah but you're no Chuh Chuh Charlie Whittingham, so fuh fuh fuck you buddy."

I walked down to the far left of the press box, which served as the domain of *Daily Racing Form*. Well, I thought to myself, apparently this was a special day, because standing right there was Fred Sandman, who served as the publisher of the *DRF*. A rare occurrence to say the very least.

As I approached and he saw me coming he put his hand out and engaged me in a vigorous handshake as though we were long-lost old pals. I had known for a long time that Mr. Sandman had a healthy respect for my talents as a scrivener, which was the only reason he put up with my aggressive and trouble-making ways.

"Hey gotta go right now, but good luck today Billy and I look forward to chatting again real soon," he said as he reclaimed his right paw and moved away as though he had 5 seconds left to get a bet down even though post time for the next race was not for at least 15 minutes. Sure, he gave me the bum's rush, but at least he had the class and style not to be rude about it.

None of the *DRF* regulars bothered to look at me for more than a second or two except good old Jasper Ward, the teletype operator. He was a big guy. He put his arm around me, offered a warm smile and said "You go out there and kick some serious butt today Billy and know that I will be rooting for you and betting on your horse. My fingers will be crossed for you."

While he was imparting his well wishes, two of the *DRF* staff stole a glance, pursed their lips and shook their heads in a manner to suggest that Jasper was either patronizing me or he had lost his mind.

I sensed I was not wanted in the press box anymore. Who knows. maybe these guys thought that my head had somehow instantly swelled and I considered myself to be above having to deal with their likes anymore.

As I made my way toward the exit Will Christensen chased after me. "Billy, hey Billy, hold up wouldya please," he said. "Thank you, thanks for waiting." He accompanied me past the two mutuel windows out onto the catwalk.

He caught his breath and then haltingly said "Zane... Russell uh Zane...so you heard any more scuttlebutt?"

It would be more difficult for me to answer him face to face, as I was a pathetic liar.

"Look Will, I wish I had something to tell you," I said, crafting my answer as best as I could to avoid a real answer.

He looked at me. He was a seasoned reporter. He had covered murder trials, he had covered the nation's biggest sporting events in New York and New Jersey. He knew damn well when somebody was bullshitting him.

A slight smile crossed his lips. "Well now,' he said. "Now we are starting to get somewhere, aren't we Mr. Billy Bo Billy?."

I said "Will—look—as you can well imagine this is a big day for me and as much as I'd like to talk to you, can it just wait until next week? I am trying to stay composed right now. I have out-of-town visitors and family here today. Can it wait?"

He softened his facial expression. "Yes, it sure as shit can wait," he said. "What in the hell am I thinking anyway. You can expect a call from me next week and we can have a nice long chat, because I am pretty sure you can help me out. And, hey, sincerely—good luck today and I mean it.

"None of these geniuses up here give your horse a chance in hell today, but I am not one of them. These pricks are so jealous of you and riled up about one of us making good as an owner they are beside themselves. Bring home the bacon, or whatever it is you Yiddles bring home. The corned beef? I don't know. Just go get 'em Billy."

I used the staircase downstairs to avoid Jake and whomever else might be on the elevator. As I descended the clubhouse steps I could see Doc and his wife heading toward their box. I called out to him. They waited until I reached them.

"Thanks Doc. Hello Mrs. Doc or however I am supposed to address you" I said with a nervous laugh. She smiled. "I will gladly accept Mrs. Doc from you Billy any day of the week."

I asked Doc if we could chat somewhere semi-private for just a minute or two. His wife got the message at once, excused herself and headed toward their box on the main lower level.

Doc and I turned around and took the escalator down to the ground level, walked towards the gift store and set up shop out of sight and ear shot behind the small building.

"What's troubling you kid?" Doc asked me.

I said "Nothing I'd care to talk about right now. But I have one question. Do you think that Redeemed is going to compete on the level today or does he have enough of that drug in him to tilt the playing field."

Doc could tell that I was nervous about the race. "Billy,

Billy, Billy don't worry your head about it. First of all, if he does there isn't a goddamned thing we can do about it today. If that sucker does pop up and win I have arranged for samples of his blood to be taken and held for a while. If need be we can have them frozen.

"My sense is that, yes, he does have the stuff in his system, but he has not been topped off, so he will not be at the same full strength as he would have been had Zane gotten to him later in the week."

I thanked Doc.

As we headed back up the escalator towards the box seat section he whispered in my ear from behind me on the stairs "Billy: that ex-claimer couldn't beat our boy with a full dose, a wind sail and a firecracker crammed up his butt hole. So relax."

CHAPTER 29

Before my visage was plastered on the back page of the *Form* each day, my favorite thing to do before each race at Santa Anita was to assume a position along the paddock railing that afforded me a view of the horses walking straight toward me as they each entered the walking ring. From this vantage point I was able to see how the front end of each animal was conformed and I would get at least two looks at each animal as they passed by.

But once my *DRF* picture outed me and made me a target for unwanted fan chitchat and any number of complaints about one thing and another, I moved my act to that patch of ground where the horses front-limb conformation could be seen as they headed towards the paddock after leaving the receiving barn. It provided a shorter time frame, but nobody else occupied that area.

Once I had seen what I wanted from that angle, I would enter the paddock proper and wait for the animals to arrive, after which I had an opportunity to size up the horses from the side and interview or chat with the human participants in the race.

So on the day of the Chester Sherwood Stakes, I duly

assumed my spot on the grassy area where I could watch the horses as they headed to the saddling enclosure.

The first two to come past me were the long shot runners that had no business being in a race like the Sherwood. One was quite narrow in front and looked more like a young filly than a colt. Then came a knock-kneed old gelding with a wide chest that served only to worsen his prospects on the track.

Third horse to pass me was Charlie's Argentine Wonder Horse. He was very nearly perfectly conformed in front. He was tall, elegant yet masculine, with a well-proportioned chest. His groom had plaited his mane as had been done in The Pampas and he was a picture of health. His fine, velvety bay coat exuded well-being and his black points set off his coat in a beautiful fashion. "Wow" I said to myself. "This is some prized animal. Just the kind that Charlie could do justice to."

Knight Errant followed in post position order. He would break from stall number 4 in the gate. As he approached, I marveled again at his movement. His front limbs were correct and normal. Everything about him was in proportion and nothing really stood out from a conformational perspective. But when he walked he was so light on his feet that they gave the impression of never touching the ground. "So smooth," I thought to myself.

All Thoroughbreds are bred to be athletes, so to say he moved in an athletic manner sounds trite, but that is the only way I could think of to describe what separated Knight Errant from the crowd. He was simply athletic. End of story.

Last horse to come past me was Redeemed. He typified many of the horses I had come to know that were bred in State of California. His front limbs had excellent bone. The left leg was well conformed, but the right leg rotated out a bit from the knee and more severely from the ankle. He was a medium-sized horse. He looked eager and on edge.

The thing about California is that what it lacks in the bloodlines of its Kentucky counterparts, it can occasionally make up for in environment. Everyone knows about the soil and grass that is enriched by the limestone deposits in the Bluegrass, but California has some of the most varied and fertile farmland in the entire world and the animals bred there benefit mightily from it. So a marginally bred animal can exceed expectations from time to time. Redeemed was a typical Cal-bred over-achiever.

He was bred by media giant Ben Ridder. The Knight-Ridder Chairman of the Board had enough money to buy and breed to any horse he so desired, but the point of the game that Ben played in California was to try to compete with the big boys by relying on what he referred to as "recessive genes."

As he explained to me one afternoon in the press box while carefully spooning his daily cup of vanilla ice cream into his pie hole, stallions in California may not have raced well, but their sires or grandsires did. And while it may take several matings to produce what he was hoping for, the recessive gene from a generation or two back would kick in and provide him with a Champion that would justify his investment and support his dreams. It took longer and required more matings, but this worked well for Mr. Ridder, who raced more than his share of top Cal-bred stars.

When the horses made their way into the saddling area, which at Santa Anita is recessed below the ground level of the paddock, I stayed on the concrete steps outside of the saddling area with the horseplayers and fans instead of joining some of the other connections down below or in the walking ring.

"Looks fine today Mr. Richards," a middle-aged graying woman said to me.

"Mr. Richards was my father. Call me Billy. And thank you," I said. "Yes, he looks a picture."

A wise acre cracked from behind me cracked "Is this a Max Gluck play Billy?" It was a snide remark, made to question whether my steed belonged in this company. Former Ambassador Gluck ran a very large outfit of home-breds raised in Kentucky at his historic Elmendorf Farm. He raced many Champions, but in Southern California towards the end of his career he was better known for entering long shots ostensibly so he could be invited to lunch in the Directors' Room.

Knight Errant behaved like the gentleman he was, only kicking out once during the saddling process when he probably felt a bit cinchy behind as his girth was tightened by Tad Smithwick.

Once the saddle was in place and the horse began circling the saddling area, I slipped out of the throng and made my way past those fans lining the pathway to the paddock.

The paddock was jammed as it usually is for the weekend feature, but more so for this race as it was the *piece des resistance* of the fall meeting at Santa Anita. Only time the paddock would be more crowded was for the Santa Anita Derby or perhaps the Santa Anita Handicap.

First person to invade my space was the over-the-top Murray Stronzo, who made a show of loudly calling my name, vigorously shaking my hand and putting his arm around my shoulder, so nobody could possibly miss the fact that Stronzo knew me. A star fucker of the first magnitude, that was Murray.

"We gonna win today?" Murray asked, with the same old girlfriend still in tow. She must have been a glutton for punishment to still be hanging out with this creep.

"We?" I said, feigning surprise. "Have you bought into this horse behind my back you old rascal.

Murray laughed. "Hey, I just chatted with Grace out back. You two no longer an item?"

I did not respond. He apparently got the message. He moved a couple of steps farther away as he herded me with him, away from his girlfriend. "So okay if I ask her to lunch?" he said.

I could only stare at him in an intense fashion. I did not realize that Murray was capable of embarrassment, but I found out right then and there that he was. He made a silly face, shook my hand again and wished me good luck. Then he receded into the crush of connections and hangers-on in the tightly-packed paddock.

Hoppy and Tad led Knight Errant into the walking ring, one on either side, with Hoppy on the shank and Tad there for support. After one turn Tad went to the spot where he would chat with me and Rafael Quintana.

Tad said nothing to the stoic looking Mexican rider. He merely winked at him. When he gave the jock a leg up, he patted Knight Errant on the neck and said "It's your day boys… go get em."

When Tad came back he said "Where's Bear? Not seen him out here this afternoon."

I told him that earlier in the morning Bear said he would see me before the race.

I left the paddock last and right at the exit of the walking ring, true to his word, stood he Bear in all of his grandeur, dressed tastefully in a black and white tweed sports coat and wearing his signature grey felt hat.

"The horse looks the part Billy," he said. "Just as you explained. Physically nothing stands out. Temperament is serene. He is a man and nothing fazes him. Knowing his sire and his broodmare sire and having stood a great many from this bloodline, I am at a loss to tell you which one of the clan he most closely resembles. He is, in this regard, unique.

"And as you say, it is his movement that is the key. Good luck out there today Billy. You know that I'll be rooting for the both of us." He smiled, turned around and disappeared into the crowd.

"A rare bird indeed for a man of his stature," I thought. "Most people in his position would have been attached to me at the hip so as not to miss a single second of the limelight. But not this fellow. He was all class."

I wondered what the chances were of me being able to make it to Doc Church's box without one more shit-bag comment from somebody. I had glanced at the tote board while waiting for the horses to enter the paddock.

Knight Errant had been bet down from 12 to 1 to 4 to 1. "Holy cow" I thought to myself. So while none of my former peers or racetrack wise guys gave Knight Errant a shot in hell, the gamblers and the fans had bought into the fantasy that this speedy sprinter could stretch his brilliance over a route of ground and while up significantly in class. That stunned me, I have to tell you. They drank the Kool-Aid.

To avoid the crowd when walking to Doc's box, I ducked into the clubhouse section where the roast beef sandwiches were sold and started to parallel the track towards the eighth pole exit.

Just then Mickey Cheraldi, the ex-jock who ran bets for Charlie Whittingham, tapped me on the shoulder. "Kid, what do you make of the action on your horse. Surprised?" he said.

I told him that I was stunned, to be perfectly honest.

"You faded or you buying this bunk?" he asked. He was looking for some inside info. That was part of his job. He wanted to know if I would be betting against my own horse because I knew better and wasn't swayed by the emotion behind the gamble or if I planned to wager on my own steed.

I told Mickey that, surprisingly, ever since the gelding broke his maiden first time out that I had not made another bet on him or any other race. He looked at me as though he had come face to face with an insane asylum escapee, exhaled while shaking his head and began to walk off. He turned back and softly said "Just so you know, The Man makes his horse a mortal lock."

I reached the box with 3 minutes to go before post time. It was just me, Doc and Mrs. Doc seated in the 6-seat box, located between the sixteenth pole and the finish line. A close finish always posed a problem in determining the winner from this angle.

As the runners entered the gate, the tote board flashed for a final time. The Beast held firm as the 6 to 5 favorite, but Knight Errant had been hammered down to 3 to 1 and Redeemed softened to 6 to 1. With Russell Zane gone those that normally would have backed him obviously went elsewhere.

As the start was less than a furlong from my vantage point, it was easy to tell that both no-hopers were urged from the gate and they led the field in front of the packed apron, grandstand, clubhouse and Turf Club, with the 60 to 1 chance showing the way along the rail by 1 ½ lengths followed by his fellow outsider. Redeemed was third about 3 lengths off the leader. Before he started rounding the turn the pacesetter had run his opening quarter-mile in a rapid :22 2/5.

Knight Errant was fourth, 1 ½ lengths behind Redeemed and 1 ½ lengths ahead of the favorite. It was a parade, as the single file procession raced around the clubhouse turn with each runner saving ground along the rail.

The 60 to 1 chance turned on to the backstretch, reaching the five-eighths pole in with an initial half-mile in :45 2/5. Fast but not insanely so. The other long shot had been passed on the outside by the progressive moving Redeemed.

The long shot was in front now by less than a length. Redeemed moving along the outside and poised to pounce was half a length ahead of the fading long shot. Knight Errant was now 2 ½ lengths off the pace, staying put along the rail. The Beast tracked the gelding by a length, drafting off of him in typically heady Bill Shoemaker fashion.

Redeemed built up a head of steam down the backstretch, reaching the end at the 3-furlong marker in a blisteringly fast 1:08. The California-bred was every bit of 2 ½ lengths ahead of Knight Errant and 3 ½ ahead of The Beast. While Redeemed looked to be running at very close to top speed, both Knight Errant and The Beast seemed to be under control.

When Knight Errant reached the start of the turn, Quintana coyly eased the gelding off the rail. Once Knight Errant saw daylight he was gone. He passed Redeemed before the middle of the turn and reached the quarter pole 2 lengths to the good. The Beast tried to cover the move but lost some ground to the leader while continuing to look viable turning in for the stretch run.

From the quarter pole to the eighth pole, Knight Errant was back on cruise control, while The Shoe had El Bestia del Bosque flat to the boards. At the furlong marker The Beast had reached the gelding's flank. He had given everything he had and was inching closer to the girth of Knight Errant.

Quintina was ice itself, maintaining his balance, not reaching for his stick. He turned his head to the right, smiled at Bill Shoemaker, turned back to look straight down the stretch and threw the reins at his mount.

The mile had been reached in an unheard of 1:30 4/5. Completely off the charts. Neither horse deserved to lose. And The Beast had shown himself to be special in his own right. But when Knight Errant was given his head he did something horses that are in front at that point in American racing are not supposed to do. He kept on going.

Knight Errant had stopped The Beast's powerful stretch challenge dead in its tracks and found another gear when given his head. By the time Knight Errant reached the wire he had put 4 ½ lengths on his rival and won with the reins safely back in full possession of his rider. He hit the finishing post in an astonishing 1:42 2/5, which obliterated every record in the books.

He accelerated instead of decelerating down the lane, recording an utterly amazing final furlong in 11 seconds flat. Now, if a horse in Europe ran an 11-flat final furlong, nobody would bat an eye. They do this every day of the week, because their races are run so slowly in the first part the horses retain enough energy to produce a negative split at the end.

But in America, where the pace is flip-flopped and all of the speed is used early, something like this has never ever been seen. Not even close. Especially on dirt, which places more demand on the animal than grass.

When Knight Errant hit the line I was standing and cheering. After the race I started to walk toward the steps that lead down to the winners' circle in front of the grandstand. I turned around and motioned The Churches to join me.

"We'll see you down there," Doc said. "You lead the way. Let these people see you. This is your moment Billy. You go ahead."

As I traversed my way down the aisle that separated one side of the box seats from another row, I started to notice that some owners that I had interviewed for years just stared at me. No smiles. Nada. When a few of them made eye contact, they turned their heads away. One guy cranked his head and pursed his lips as if to say "Son of a gun, I'll be damned."

When I arrived at the so-called "hallowed enclosure" Chester Sherwood himself was there to greet me. He wore a big smile and seemed genuinely happy to see me. But I figured this was strictly for show. I imagined that he had envisioned himself standing there being presented the trophy for a race named after himself. I joked with myself, thinking that if Chester could make the weight, he probably would have tried to ride Knight Errant as well. For some people, they just don't make enough trophies to satisfy their appetites for success, glory and newspaper ink.

Doc, Mrs. Doc, The Bear, Tad, Hoppy and Quintana all beamed for the winners' circle photo. When the race caller announced the winning result, a loud roar erupted from the stands. And why shouldn't it have—in the end Knight Errant had been bet down to the 5 to 2 second choice.

And when the announcer said "Ladies and gentlemen,

may I have your attention please. In winning today's Chester Sherwood Stakes, Knight Errant has broken not only the stakes, the track and the American record, but the world record as well with a time of one minute forty-two and two-fifths seconds while remaining unbeaten in his three racetrack appearances."

Doc whispered in my ear "Did you notice where Redeemed finished?" He was third, but he was beaten more than 15 lengths. Completely ran out of gas."

CHAPTER 30

Sally Goldfarb and Freddy Glickman approached me right after the winners' circle photos were snapped. "Billy can you and Tad please come up stairs to answer some questions from the press before you head off for your champagne toast with Mr. Sherwood in the Directors' Room?"

She grabbed Tad by the arm and led him away from some of the more enterprising Turf Writers that had scaled the stairs to get some fresh quotes before the protagonists were escorted to the press box.

Jake slapped me on the back so hard that I thought he might have winded me. "Billy! You duh man. I have always told these other writers that you were the smartest of the bunch. Am I right or what?"

Everybody on the elevator laughed.

Before we reached the sixth floor Glickman said "Billy when did you know you had it won?"

The query was met with silence.

"Freddy, Freddy, Freddy…did you actually ask that question and say it out loud?" I said.

Again uproarious laughter from the elevator gang.

Pat Smith shook my hand as I passed by his mutuel window, Will Christensen also slapped me on the back. I was beginning to wonder if my back was some sort of magnet for slaps.

Tad and I sat at the head of the long oblong dining table, with writers sitting around us and others standing behind them. It was the type of throng only seen in the press box following the Derby or the Big 'Cap.

Literally all of the questions, until Sally tossed me one, were directed at Tad. He was, after all, the trainer. He was very patient, very calm in answering questions both insightful and absurdly lame. He acted as though he had done it all his life.

Sally, trying to get the writers to engage me, said "So what's it like to be asked instead of asking the questions Billy?"

I looked down at the table, then at Tad, and I said something innocuous like I thought it was something I could get used to.

Then the questions continued to be asked of Tad. When it looked like the session was about to wind down and a few writers drifted back to their typewriters, Tad began to look frustrated.

"Excuse me gentlemen" he said. "No questions for Billy? If you think that Knight Errant is a one-man show you've got it wrong. None of the members of our team would be here if not for Billy."

He waited. No questions. No response.

Tad pushed himself back from the table, as if he were getting ready to leave, then caught himself in mid-move and returned to his seat.

"What is it jealousy, is that the issue?" he asked in a sincere tone. "So when one of you inmates finally breaks free from this asylum and makes a name for himself with a horse that can actually run, you just cannot stand to see it happen? Is that it?

"One would have thought after decades and decades of you wanna-bees acting like you invented the game, but never getting as far as first base, that you might want to celebrate one of your minions finally achieving something. But I guess it's just too much for you sorry bastards to bear."

Then he stood up and said "C'mon Billy. These jerkoffs are not worth our time."

Will Christensen cornered me near the mutuel windows before I could make my way behind Tad to the catwalk.

"Billy that was quite the soliloquy from Tad there," he said. "Wish I had a friend like that. Now don't forget I will be calling you this week. And Billy, I cannot speak for anyone else up here, but out there and for my money you are something special. I could not be prouder or happier for you. Congrats pal."

By the time Tad and I had reached the Director's Room, the place had basically cleared out, save for Chester Sherwood and Buddy Hillenbrand. Buddy had invited The Churches for the Champagne toast, as well as Bear Harwood.

Toasts were made all around, everyone drank (or in my case sipped) the bubbly and eventually three bottles had been popped open and consumed.

Chester shook The Bear's hand and said "You know, I tried to get Billy to sell me all or part of the horse a while back, but the young man wisely refused my overture."

The Bear could only smile. "Yes, he is a young man of great conviction and insight. I can attest to that myself."

As is invariably the case after any horse performs up to expectations, talk upstairs in the Room turned to what was next for the gelding.

Doc immediately spoke up.

"Well this evening the principals—those being me, Bear, Tad and Billy—we be discussing that in great detail after dinner at my place. Normally Buddy would be invited, but there may be some conflicts of interest that will arise, so we will spare him having to weigh them with equanimity," said Doc.

Concern beat back a potentially warm smile as Buddy said "Well now that sounds ominous. You fellas are not thinking of taking this show on the road are you with all of the money you've just taken from us and planning on racing elsewhere are you?"

Doc came right back at him and said "All will be revealed soon enough Buddy."

The dinner and the powwow were news to me. We all went back to the barn, watched the gelding being walked and then headed up to Bradbury Estates.

Since everybody was still jazzed from the day's race, dinner was not planned to be served until about half-past 8 p. m.

In Doc's den Tad, me and The Bear sat on leather chairs.

I sensed Doc had something on his mind.

"Men" he began. Now I knew I knew something was up. Normally Doc would have said boys. "What I am about to reveal is very likely going to shock you. Before I tell you what I have to say, let me warn you right now that I have made up my mind after considerable thought on the matter and I will not be swayed or made to change my mind."

To lighten the mood in the room I piped up.

"I knew it, I knew it Doc. I am so happy. You have finally decided to convert to Judaism! Hot dog, we need a good vet."

It worked. Everyone laughed. I thought Tad was going to fall down on the floor.

Doc said "Thanks for that. The temperature in the room needed to be lowered. It's just that I dread having to say what I am about to say."

He drew a deep breath and said "Knight Errant has run his last race." He then waited for reactions. I for one thought he was following up my joke with one of his own. Bear was not laughing. Tad looked at Doc hard trying to figure out what was going on.

"As you all know I have a deal with both The Bear and with Billy that if and when I thought it was advisable for any reason to pull the plug on the gelding's career, that it was up to me. It was my call."

Tad said "What am I missing here Doc? There's nothing wrong with the horse. If there was I'd know it. So what gives?"

I was absolutely blown away by this line of chatter and so was Tad. But The Bear seemed to be taking it in stride.

Doc continued. "As we all know I have been supremely successful in diagnosing and treating the metabolic disorder that had prevented the horse from being able to gain enough nutrients from his grub. Maybe too successful.

"In this current climate, where the FBI could blow the roof off the game when it gets down to brass tacks with the haul from Zane's storage unit, I don't want to face scrutiny over what I have been doing."

Tad said "FBI, Zane, storage unit? I feel that I just walked in the middle of a movie."

Doc said "Shit, I'm sorry Tad. I have been so wrapped up in my own little world I forget that you were not involved. Strictly on a mum's the word basis, Billy, Buddy and I were involved in busting Russell Zane illegally injecting a horse in the middle of the night in his barn with a substance that I reckon is some form of EPO.

"Sooner or later…and I am hoping sooner…the contents of the syringe we grabbed will be analyzed. After that the shit is going to hit the fan. And my biggest fear is somebody putting two and two together and looking into what I have been putting into the system of Knight Errant."

I said "But Doc, you've told me that what you have achieved is bringing the horse's microbiome up to normal. He is not getting anything that is making him a super horse. He is not being enhanced, he is being normalized, right?"

Doc said "Absolutely Billy. You have it right. But look, what Knight Errant has done in his three races is about as far from normal as possible. So much so in fact that I have been second guessing myself about whether it is therapy I am giving or some potent elixir that has turned a regular horse into some kind of Pegasus without the wings. Of course that is only my fear talking and I don't actually believe it. What I have told you guys from day one holds. He has not been enhanced. On that I stand firm."

Finally The Bear spoke up. "Tad. Billy. I can only imagine what it must be like to hear this decision, as this horse is at what normally would be the beginning of his career.

"But what Doc is concerned about are the consequences if what he has done comes to light and is misinterpreted. Too many folks—including all of us here in this room—could be cast in a very unfavorable light."

Doc said "The Bear's got it right men. A lot of brilliant, sincere and dedicated scientists have aided me in my quest to correct the metabolic disorder of Knight Errant. The last thing

I want to do is get any of them in trouble. The fallout could be dire not just for us, but for them and, if them, a large portion of the human race that counts on the scientists to solve their medical issues. Believe me when I tell you that I am not exaggerating my concerns."

Tad asked "if what Doc has done did come to light, could not some form of damage control be used to explain it?"

Doc said that he had considered that, but in all the time he had been a vet, the members of the racing community—and even some equine practitioners—were unable or unwilling to differentiate between legitimate therapeutic and illegal banned substances that enhanced performance.

"Billy and I have talked about this off and on for the last few years as it relates to Track and Field," Doc said. "Billy, surely this is understandable based on what you've seen, heard and read about. Someday maybe people will listen, but right now, I just don't see it playing well in Altoona as they used to say."

The Bear spoke up next. "Gentlemen, even though Knight Errant ran but three times, he accomplished more in those 3 contests than practically any horse that ever looked through a bridle.

"We received more than we all were entitled to. Doc proved his theory was correct with the fastest lab rat in the history of chemistry. Tad had the chance to train what may very well go down as the fleetest horse that ever lived. Billy had an opportunity to show what he could do if given half a chance. And Ellerslie Stud bred one of the swiftest horses ever to come out of a Bluegrass paddock and race in California. We have each been blessed. There is no need to gild the lily."

Tad said "Well, in the final analysis, it's just not my call.

Damn how I wish it were. It's been a hoot, will never happen again in my lifetime and, frankly, although the ride has been sweeter than life itself, I can see myself moving on. I never wanted a big stable, especially a big public stable."

The Bear, as if waiting for his cue, said "Tad you have no idea how long both your dad and I have waited to hear those words from you. I spoke to your father today because I want to make you a proposition and I wanted his take on it. Tad, how would you feel about moving back to the Bluegrass and take charge of breaking and training at Ellerslie. To sweeten the deal, if you so desired, you could have some stalls at Keeneland and train a few for us."

Tad said "That would be the dream of a lifetime for me Bear. I accept, even without asking my wife. I think that getting off the track out here would give me a leg up on trying to quit alcohol. Hey, who knows, anything's possible."

I asked exactly how in the hell we were going to explain our move to the public, to Buddy Hillenbrand, to the press.

Doc said "As far as I am concerned that is the key consideration and, frankly, even though I've thought about it, I confess I have no idea."

I cracked "Well, one thing's for sure, we cannot say that Knight Errant wants to spend more time with his family."

The laughter that followed lightened the mood.

Then, on a serious note, I said "You know what, this looks like a good time for me to get out of Dodge as well. Maybe I'll head back to the Bluegrass too. Be good to get as far away from this place as I can for a while."

Doc said "Well you have a tidy little bank account at this

point, you have no wife or, as far as I can see, no significant other. This might be a good time to explore your future.

"This may sound like sacrilege, but you may want to consider making racing your hobby instead of an industry to work in. Billy, you are a gifted writer, you have good instincts, a nose for news and you are a good person. This could be a good time to take some time off and reassess."

I told Doc that he very well could be right, because it was going to take a lot of time to get my head around how corporate America treated a scumbag like Russell Zane.

I said "Maybe I saw too many double features at the Saturday matinees when I was a kid, but I did not like one bit the way the Zane thing went down. He is a bad guy. He took advantage of regular everyday Americans. And he gets off Scot free so that these fleeced citizens won't get discouraged and will continue to support Santa Anita Park. That is, in my opinion, an unacceptable trade off. What's the message: preserve the flock at all costs? Shouldn't the message embrace integrity and fairness even at the expense of corporate dividends?

"I grew up in a household that believed in being honest and fair. We embraced merit and fair play on the field. My family did not own stocks. We inherited no bonds to clip.

"We belonged to no country clubs. We lived in normal everyday neighborhoods. We were Cub Scouts and Boy Scouts. We played Little League and Pony League.

"My dad and my brother and I all jumped and ran track in high school and college.

"We grew up with a notion that if somebody cheated or stole or was corrupt, they would be tried, adjudicated and thrown in the clink if found guilty.

"Yet this miscreant Russell Fucking Zane completely tilts the playing field, robs from the rich and poor alike, is never scrutinized for his abhorrent behavior that has been patently obvious to anybody with half a brain, becomes wealthy and is lionized by the press and his peers, all of whom know goddamned well that he is a cheating slimeball.

"So yeah, I need to take some time off to think about this."

I sure as hell was in no mood to eat again.

Told Doc I was just going to go home, sit and read for a bit before heading to slumber land. I was whooped.

"Chances are I will be climbing in my car tomorrow and heading back to Kentucky," I said to Doc. "Do me a favor and keep track of any invoices that need to be paid, take care of them and reimburse yourself for whatever you wind up paying. I have some cash, so I am good. If anything changes, you can count on hearing from me."

I thanked everybody for everything, shook hands with Doc, Tad and The Bear, kissed Mrs. Doc on the cheek, patted their black lab Captain on the head, said goodbye to the brilliant housekeeping cook and walked out the front door.

Stopped at the Bradbury Estates gate until the arm went up, I was thinking about what a wild ride it had been, from cashing bets on the My Swallow offspring and Knight Errant, getting Keiran O'Boyle pissed off at me for no reason at all, winding up owning one of the truly fastest horses of all time for a mere $1, forming meaningful bonds with Doc, Tad, The Bear, Buddy, Hoppy and Quintana.

Driving down the canyon road I thought that I was one lucky son of a gun. The only thing missing from the entire equation was having some girl that I loved to share it with.

Without someone to be part of things it sort of hollows out and one feels empty. It's sort of a form of ego or professional masturbation. Without a relationship it's just not as fun, relevant or meaningful.

Back down on Huntington Drive, passing the Derby Restaurant, the drive-in liquor store where I buy the *Form*, Van de Kamp's iconic windmill, then the East gate to Santa Anita and headed towards my cottage on the West side of Santa Anita, I thought about my favorite author J. D. Salinger's epigraph to his *Nine Stories* published by Salinger two years after *The Catcher in the Rye*. You know the one about "What is the sound of one hand clapping."

It is a Zen koan whose meaning and relevance to the brilliant pieces have been debated for some 20 years. Most of the interpretations were too esoteric for me to follow, but my own take on it had more to do with loneliness than mysticism.

In that moment in time I was longing for the sound of another hand clapping instead of just mine.

I parked the BMW in the garage, walked around the front of the complex to check on my mail and then headed up the dimly lit walkway to my pad. As I drew near to my front door I could make out in the dark a silhouette of a girl leaning against my front door with her back facing me and her legs crossed.

I know that ass, I said to myself.

www.ingramcontent.com/pod-product-compliance
Lightning Source LLC
LaVergne TN
LVHW090554110826
845146LV00001B/116

* 9 7 9 8 2 3 4 0 9 3 0 1 1 *